Also by Jim Gullo:

Just Let Me Play: The Story of Charlie Sifford

Seattle & Portland for Dummies

The Insider's Guide to Seattle & Portland

The Importance of Hilary Rodham Clinton

A Traveler's Guide to the Plantation South

Trading Manny (April 2012)

FOUNTAIN OF YOUTH

a novel

by Jim Gullo

Yam Hill Publishing
McMinnville, Oregon

Fountain of Youth. Copyright © 2010 by Jim Gullo. All rights reserved.

Yam Hill Publishing, P.O. Box 1702, McMinnville, Oregon, 97128

ISBN-13: 978-1456316754
ISBN -10: 1456316753

for Kristine Irene,

with all my love…

got that right

[1]

PROLOGUE

I stood on the private balcony of my cruise ship cabin, and in spite of everything I had to admit that it was the kind of day that practically made one believe that there was a God...made you believe in me, in other words. The sky was bright blue, the air warm and the water that spread out, eleven decks below me and as far as I could see was the kind of cobalt blue that suggests teeming life, wonder of nature, and a swelling-of-the-spirit happiness. Off to starboard were bright green, jagged hills – Tahiti, I think – and the sounds were of tinkling glasses, a five-piece combo playing dance music, happy conversations and the deep shush of the water against the hull.

So forgive me, dear reader, for standing against the railing of my balcony, my weight straining even that polished, immutable teak, and shouting against the wake that the screws churned up from the ship, as loud as I could, "I'm a lousy God!"

And, "You think God knows everything? I don't know jack shit!"

And, "If this is what you call divine, you can have it."

I was a little out of control, admittedly. I was drunk with the sea air; I hadn't been outside in several months, and was frankly surprised that I could still fit through the sliding-glass door that led from my penthouse-category cabin to the balcony ("The largest in our fleet!" cried the brochures. "Luxurious and private!"). I owed this sudden freedom, once again and for always, to Costas, who had ingeniously sewn together the two complimentary bathrobes from my cabin to make one giant swath of cloth that barely closed around my girth. Costas was a good butler, but no Yves St. Laurent: His skills with the needle and thread were rudimentary, and my new garment had a sleeve emerging from the middle of my back to go with the two on the flanks. Cleverly, I think, he had sewn the two extra sleeves together to make one, so I had what appeared to be an elephant's trunk emerging from between my shoulder blades.

I didn't care. I don't get out much. "I can't save anybody!" I shouted to the sea. "Why do you give me such power when I'm powerless to use it?"

I looked up and behind me and caught the couple above staring from their own penthouse balcony. They had probably just boarded that day, and were also drunk with the ship and the beauty of the colors and the allure of going *to sea, not to mention from the champagne that filled the flutes they were waving around. The pictures in the brochures that had convinced them to take this voyage depicted sensible, attractive, wealthy and well-heeled passengers and used words like "discriminating" and "exclusive" to strongly suggest that there were no people like me allowed on the ship.*

Tough break for them.

I waved; they tentatively waved back. They wanted to believe in the instant community of people thrust together on a voyage. They wanted to ignore what their eyes told them and believe that I belonged in their exclusive company. I could tell from a glance that he had about five years left; his heart wasn't so good, thanks to two arteries racing to see which could plug up first. She had maybe fifteen or twenty years of life remaining...something about dementia, but I couldn't get the whole thing. That's how crappy a God I am.

"Five years, tops," I shouted to him. "Enjoy it while you can."

The puzzled look on his face suggested that he didn't hear me. (Some God, I repeat; I should know what they were thinking and sensing before they thought or sensed it. I should make myself be heard. Some omnipotence.)

So I pointed at him with a fat finger and then held up my whole hand – five years, buddy. And then I pointed to her and flashed the hand three times – fifteen for you.

They frowned and then her eyes grew round and big and I thought for a moment, holy cow she understands. I'm finally reaching someone. But then I realized that she wasn't receiving God's wisdom at all. The robe had flapped open and I wasn't wearing anything underneath, and they had both just received a vision of God's privates and immense, swollen belly. The two soft, cotton cinch belts that Costas had sewn together were barely adequate to the task and had given up the ghost, so to speak; the divine wind had done its deed on my flimsy garment.

Her hand flew to her mouth, and he clutched her arm and pulled her away from the balcony and they disappeared from my view. "You're still going to die," I shouted after them, a trifle petulantly.

I turned back to face the sea. "Nobody would believe me anyway," I shouted to the thrilling blue water. "What good is it to be God if nobody ever believes you?"

I turned and waddled back into my stateroom, slid the door shut and bolted it, drew the curtains against the light and beauty.

Costas wasn't there, but the narrative group had begun to assemble in the sitting area. They looked restless and eager to get on with the task of creating a story – creating lives on the spot, as it were, which is what we Gods do – and were waiting for me.

On shore, I was given the power of a God, and it practically gave me hives. On the ship, I'm a deity of a different sort. I'm creating this story, so I'm the God of this book. I decide what goes in, I decide what comes out. Who lives, who dies, who gets second chances.

It occurs to me as I step back into my cabin that I don't have a clue how one does this.

"Well?" said Floyd Little, the cardboard football player.

"Well what?"

"Well, where do we start?"

"I don't know." Seized with an upwelling of despair, I re-opened the curtains and slid open the balcony door and shouted to the sea, "I don't even know where to start! I'm a terrible, terrible God."

Floyd sighed and figuratively shook his big head (which can't actually shake, because he's made of cardboard). "Start wif breakfas' and that day y'all went to the cemetery," he offered.

Nods of agreement from the other three members of the narrative group. "Just write SOMETHING," one of them whines.

This is my – check that, OUR – story.

Chapter One
The TOWN of MORONGO in upstate NEW YORK Scrambled and fried at BUCKY'S DINER; a COTTAGE by the lake; trolling the HIGH SCHOOL

This was about three years ago.

Ray Jensen was forced into Bucky's Homeslyte Diner when, like an 18th-century clipper ship whose rats carried plague, like a destroyer on the horizon with guns loaded, his ex-wife Janice turned onto Water Street and jogged towards him. She was farther down the block, by the Western Union, and Ray calculated his odds at approximately four-to-one that she hadn't yet seen him. That was a wager that he was willing to accept, so he turned sharply left into Bucky's, jingling the ancient bells on the door, which made Bucky startle awake at his customary place on a stool by the cash register. He regarded Ray dimly through thick reading glasses, puzzled, because Ray wasn't a regular.

Ray nodded to Bucky and moved briskly to the side of the dining room where Janice couldn't see him from the sidewalk, but his plan began to fall apart when he saw that the corner table was occupied by a pair of grizzled, old farmers who looked like they had had to make a choice with their last dollar-twenty-nine between a shave or eggs, and eggs had won. There was no place left to hide, and if she glanced sideways during her jog, Janice would see him. Ray had little choice but to hide under a table, which he did calmly and with as little movement of furniture as possible. There was lots of room; Bucky's was not a very popular place to eat breakfast in Morongo.

Janice had left two messages to call her on Ray's machine at home that morning, and now he was struck with the thought that she was literally going to run him down, crash into him like bad news, or plain out tackle him in the open field of Morongo's business district, which was euphemistically referred to as downtown. They had been divorced for thirteen years, but were held together umbilically by their son Daniel, who was fifteen and a sophomore at Morongo Academy. For that reason, neither of them had left Morongo, the community in upstate New York alongside Morongo Lake, and alternately blamed and praised the arrangement. Morongo was a poor village in the state of New York's most economically depressed county, but was pleasant enough if you could afford a cottage on the lake, which Ray had. It was a good rule of thumb that everything in Morongo grew more depressing by half again every mile you were distanced from the lake.

Ray is 47 years old, pudgy around the middle but not unattractive. Dark hair graying at the temples. Maybe five-eleven, medium height and build. Brow: Unfurrowed. Attitude: Generally oblivious to the small stuff, worries about the big.

People who really know him, though, will pull you aside and confide in hushed tones, because this is a small town and word gets around, that lately, Ray has been thinking too much about his father. His father died suddenly of a heart attack many years ago; they're coming up not only on the thirtieth anniversary of the event, but Ray is approaching the same age that Dr. Farrell Jensen Sr. was when he went to The Great Beyond. "Ray should just forget about it," they'll tell you. "The way he acts, he might as well be the only person in the world who found his father dead twice, on two different floors in two different parts of Morongo."

It did not escape Ray's attention that Bucky's occupied the same corner of Morongo where he and Janice had once quite literally crashed into each other, in separate cars traveling at cross purposes, and that collision had simultaneously landed Ray in the hospital and the family court in Geneva for a divorce proceeding. Respectively, his ribs were bandaged and mended and his heart was broken when the court ordered custody of Daniel to Janice, conferring on Ray the awkward status of being a father whose offspring was, in the court's opinion, more of a visitor than a son. He saw his son every other weekend, on Tuesdays, and on the nights when Janice bowled and didn't want to pay for a sitter.

Crouched under the table, Ray tried to accomplish the difficult feat of craning his neck sideways to watch the window and Bucky's door, with fervent hopes that Janice would not linger in either, and keeping his hands and knees off the dirty floor. He had a busy day ahead of work and visiting the cemetery with his brother and mother – an annual obligation on the anniversary of his father's death. Ray did not have time to return home to change clothes. This gymnastic exercise under the table may have been easier to do ten years earlier, but Ray's joints seemed to have exhausted some essential lubricant in recent years, and hiding from Janice in this fashion would bring him two days' worth of sore knees and hamstrings.

"You want coffee?" asked the kid who waited tables. From his vantage point, Ray could only see the baggy black jeans flopping to the floor and partially covering worn tennis shoes that were on temporary leave from the Good Samaritans thrift store in Naples. Ray craned his neck upwards to see a tousle of brown hair covering two sleepy eyes. The boy did not seem to be the least bit surprised to find a customer under the table, as if it were a customary dining choice for Bucky's regulars.

"No, thanks, I won't be staying," said Ray. The boy shuffled away without a word.

As he watched the window, Ray felt a familiar electric vibration begin in his chest that frequently accompanied interactions with Janice. Years of experience in co-raising Daniel had revealed that theirs was a treaty that might be amended or abrogated outright with almost no warning. The anxiety that he felt began with the sensation of a single nerve thrumming and then seemed to well up inside him and fill his chest cavity with a palpable anxiety that made his heart race, his hands shake slightly and his breath shorten. Ray likened it to a heart attack without the pain, the collapse or the imminent death.

One such attack had in fact made him pass out, seven years before on Ray's fortieth birthday. His birthday party was interrupted that day by the odd sound of a nearby hammering, and when Ray went to his back door to check, he found Janice (who had not been invited for coffee and cake) nailing an invoice to his wall in a Lutheran manner. She said it was for dental bills that she had incurred for Daniel that Ray had ignored. After two written reminders! Ray, who had cake on his face, said something vague about piles of bills that had to be paid. The ensuing argument (Ray focused on style, Janice on substance) ended only when Ray began to hyperventilate, clutched his chest and collapsed theatrically on the porch. He had felt his heart pause, gather itself, surge with an intense "catch-up" beat, rinse and repeat. The ambulance was summoned; the party was over. It took the doctors in Rochester a week to figure out that Ray had developed an arrhythmia that was more annoying than perilous. He had been on a daily dose of digoxin ever since.

  He wondered, as his head bumped the underside of the table and the anxiety crept into his chest, if he had taken his medicine that morning, and then remembered that Donna, his girlfriend, had left the bottle out with a note to remind him to take it before she had left that morning for her class in Syracuse. He relaxed and waited.

  Ray was in luck. Janice sailed by the window with the comically determined, out-of-my-way-I'm-exercising pace of the middle-aged jogger. He caught a glimpse of her brown hair bouncing in a ponytail, and a battleship-gray sweatsuit that was not long removed from the racks of the Geneva Pennys. As with most things Janice, the exercise routine had been undertaken wholeheartedly and passionately, and would last for approximately four days until her attention was diverted to another cause. Rising weed levels in Morongo Lake, perhaps, or global warming. Ray waited three minutes and then beat it out of Bucky's in the other direction.

Bucky's Homeslyte Diner was one of three breakfast options in downtown Morongo. Across the street was The Wagonwheel, which doubled as a nightclub and bar at night. In the morning the whole place seemed to be stale and stiff, barely cleaned up from the previous night's excesses and wishing for a few more hours rest. The room had dark wooden tables and chairs and beige walls; the lighting was low and not particularly effective, and everything appeared to have a yellow cast about it. The waitresses who worked the room, the daughters and sisters-in-law of the owners, wore tight jeans and short, stretchy tops that revealed a bicycle-tube-like roll of pale-white belly and back; their hair was frosted, mulleted, page-boyed. Besides the farmers and local merchants who came for breakfast, the Wagonwheel hosted a cast of characters who seemed like they too had either never left the place from the previous night's beer drinking, or were arriving early in order to secure a good spot. Counting heads, you might get the idea that the four turning-thirty waitresses were somehow related to the nine grizzled young men who wore dirty denim jackets, greasy hair under tractor caps and moustaches that flowed into the stubble of six-day unshaven whiskers, or you might have thought that all thirteen of them were or had once been married, and you wouldn't be far from wrong.

Bucky's, with its hastily misspelled sign that had become something of a source of misplaced local pride, was the cheapest place in town. Breakfast cost only eight-nine cents, not including coffee, but Bucky's could be a soul-withering experience. The plastic tablecloths on the cheap, folding tables were designed for a picnic in the early-'60s and had long since frayed at the edges and faded into pastel streaks. The placemats in the shape of New York State with a map of the Finger Lakes region added little cheer; the chairs had been patched by duct tape. Bucky, who was in his seventies and in ill health, himself did the cooking when he could get up from the stool where he perched all day. The toast and eggs were served by his wife Cora, an emaciated old woman with thick glasses, or by a sullen fourteen-year old grandson, who was pressed into service day after day like a full-time temp without benefits. Delivering thin pancakes and plastic tubs of imitation maple syrup would make him late once again for first-period English at Morongo Academy, which through a snowballing chain of events caused him to fail sixth-period science. His young face was just beginning to register the dull shock of having entered a life-long cycle of always being an hour behind and a few dollars short.

When he wasn't hiding from Janice, Ray avoided Bucky's. His eatery of choice was the Morongo Diner, which had been built in the mid-sixties to resemble a sleek, stainless-steel Airstream trailer. That is, the façade was curved and painted to resemble stainless steel, but big chunks of the paint had flaked off to reveal plywood primed in dull green, which diminished the futuristic illusion considerably. Tables and booths inside were laminate topped and edged by chrome that had dulled to a pewter finish over the years of scrubbing and wiping. The floor needed replacing; the tiles had permanent black marks that looked like grease accumulation but were un-cleanable marks left from generations of heavy work boots dragging across the floor, the residue of weary farmers and road crews. Despite all this, the food was plentiful and inexpensive and Ray could usually find a friend or two lingering in the booths.

He would have gone there, but pictured Janice jogging in place in the parking lot, waiting for him. Instead, Ray decided to swing by the high school, two blocks away, to look for Daniel. High school kids always cheered him up. Unlike Ray, they knew everything that was going on in their worlds: Who was about to be suspended, and who was dating whom, and which boys would be fighting under the football bleachers, and with which weapons. With the flimsiest of supporting evidence, they could put themselves at the center of the universe and believe that nearly everyone else, especially the adults, were idiots. Their faith in this was practically religious. Most of all, they could make themselves believe that Morongo was an important, blessed place, a town favored by the Gods and the envy of the poor fools whom nature had capriciously banished to the laughably inferior towns of Waterloo, Naples and Himrod, the away games on the Morongo sports calendar.

Ray had a keen eye out for a certain physical type, a tall, thin boyish figure who would be wearing jeans halfway down his ass and a long hooded sweatshirt – preferably in a dark, solid color – with the hood completely covering the head and tied tight, like a skinny boxer awaiting a pummeling. He moved slowly past the athletic field and then the main entrance to the school, guarded and fortified by a line of big yellow buses against the curb. There were plenty of sweatshirts and low-riding jeans walking about, but none was quite the right one. Ray turned the corner onto Taylor Street and felt a pang of disappointment, but just then he spotted a clump of boys lingering farther down the street. He made out Daniel, his son, his sophomore, with hands in the pockets of the navy-blue hooded sweatshirt. The other boys were unfamiliar to Ray, and he wondered how it was that he did not know his son's friends, that there were whole worlds that Daniel inhabited of which Ray had only the vaguest clues.

Daniel saw the car coming and turned away quickly, but not quickly enough that Ray did not see the cigarette glowing in his mouth. When Daniel turned back, the cigarette was gone. He did not wave to his father or approach the car, but he did not ignore it either, just nodded as Ray slowed down, waving his awkward wave.

Ray moved past the clump of boys a discreet distance, pulled over to the curb and waited. In his rearview mirror he saw Daniel glance back, hesitate, and then separate himself from the group. He walked slowly to the car, conserving his energy, and Ray rolled down the window on the passenger side.

"Good morning," said Ray.

"Hey." Daniel's face was in shadow from the hood drawn around his head, and his hands were still in the pockets of the sweatshirt. He looked thin and cold, and Ray wondered if he had been eating.

"You're coming over this afternoon, right?" Ray asked Daniel on the sidewalk. It was a Tuesday, his visitation day, thanks to Janice's bowling schedule. "It's Tuesday," he added.

"Yeah, I think so."

"What was that in your mouth that I saw a minute ago?"

A small smile appeared at the corner of Daniel's mouth. A rueful smile with the barest hint of a smirk; an acknowledgement that there were in fact secrets that he kept that would not soon be shared with parents, and they had better get used to it. The senile fools. The well-intentioned, doddering boobs. How could they possibly understand that a guy occasionally likes to have the taste of tobacco on his tongue in order to get through first period algebra? It wasn't like he was hooked on it, or like he was going to die from it. "Gum," he lied. "But I spit it out."

Ray hesitated, formed a lecture in his mind about the evils of tobacco, but decided to save it for another day. "That kind of gum can kill you if you don't watch it," he said. "Hey, do you want to come to the cemetery today with me and Grandma?"

Daniel smirked again. "Is somebody getting buried?"

"No, somebody already was. It's that time of year again. The day your grandfather died. Thirty years ago today."

"That sounds really exciting, Dad, but I've got tons of stuff to do. But tell Grandma I said hello, okay? Grandpa, too, for that matter."

"Very funny," said Ray. "Okay. I'll see you for dinner."

Daniel nodded and jogged back to the group of boys. In the stiff way that Daniel's shoulders moved, his hands cemented inside the pockets of the hooded sweatshirt, Ray wondered if his collar hurt where it was injured as a child. He wondered if he should discuss the cigarette incident with Janice, a thought that made Ray's own shoulders shiver. He put the car into gear and headed back downtown, with thoughts of stuffed French toast at the Morongo Diner filling his entire being. The coast should be clear; even Janice couldn't jog in place that long.

Chapter Two
Also in MORONGO
On eyebrows, the CEMETERY, a PORCH overlooking the LAKE

An hour later, and stuffed with stuffed French Toast, Ray arrived at work at Truman County Social Services and found his brother, Farrell Jensen Jr., parked in his pick-up truck in the agency's lot. Farrell was smoking a cigarette and listening to WBBF from Rochester on the radio. He sat back in the driver's seat, his head resting on the headrest, his eyes closed. Smoking in his sleep, Ray thought.

Ray had an impulse to call out, "Dad!" and in this case he was only half-joking. Farrell Junior looked an awful lot like Farrell Senior had in the last year of his life, the way Ray remembered his father. Bushy eyebrows that were now just as white as they were black. A lean, handsome face and neatly cut dark brown hair. Broad shoulders and slim arms and wrists belying a big belly that had bulged out in middle age. At forty-nine years and ten months old, Farrell Jr. was fast approaching Zero Day, the name that Ray had assigned to the age of fifty years old, two months and four days that was all that Farrell Sr. had remained among the living. It was as good a mark as any for predicting the day that Ray or Farrell Jr. might drop over dead, or begin to appreciate a longer life than their father had enjoyed.

"You don't look so good," Ray said by way of greeting.

Farrell Jr. ignored him, and didn't open his eyes. "Call your wife," he said.

"I'm not married," Ray replied. This was a standard conversation between the brothers, and one that Ray never particularly enjoyed.

"Then tell her to quit calling me," said Farrell. Janice was never content to leave messages for Ray, perhaps because she was unwilling to believe that he would ever return her call. She tracked him down stealthily, leaving messages all over town with his relatives and friends.

"You tell her for me," Ray said. "She always had a soft spot for you."

"Shit," Farrell said, drawing out the word and accompanying it with a long exhalation of smoke. The truth was that Janice could never bear Farrell, and it was a sore spot early in the marriage that she would never go to the house that he shared with his wife Bump and the ten little wildpersons, as practically everyone referred to their children.

"You know," Ray said, "I just saw my kid with a fag hanging out of his mouth down by the high school. He must be taking after you. Why don't you have a favorite uncle talk with him and tell him how sad you are that you got hooked on that crap as a teenager, and how you'd give anything to not have started?"

"Because it wouldn't be true," Farrell said. "He wouldn't believe me. He's too smart to buy that kind of bullshit. Best friends I've ever had, these things. He'd be a fool to turn his back on such good company."

"Super," said Ray. "Remind me to put a carton or two in the ground with you."

"Wouldn't bother me if you did," said Farrell, sitting up. "Throw in some matches while you're at it."

"Are you coming to the cemetery today?" Ray asked.

Farrell frowned. He snapped the cigarette past Ray and into a puddle on the ground. "That's today, is it?"

"Same as every year."

"God, I hate going to that fucking cemetery."

"Hey, maybe this time it will be fun," said Ray. "We'll tell a few jokes, have a few laughs and watch Mom wipe the headstone with her face like she does every year."

"Oh, Christ. As if the old man would have ever thought twice about visiting her in the grave."

Farrell opened the door of the truck and stepped out, pushing roughly past Ray. He stopped to light another cigarette. In profile, Farrell was even rounder and heavier than Ray remembered. An unwelcome thought flashed into Ray's mind: Heart attack. Just like Dad. Could be any day now. Also just like Dad. "What time are you going?"

"I'm picking Mom up at two-thirty."

"I'll be out here waiting for you," said Farrell. "I've got nothing better to do today."

"You should take better care of yourself, Mom would say," said Ray. "You're just about the old man's age, right?"

"Eat me, Ray. You don't look so good yourself. In fact, you look like you've already got one foot in the grave."

Farrell moved heavily away from Ray and towards the lobby of the building. It occurred to Ray that his brother had come to apply, yet again, for unemployment benefits or to search for jobs.

"Bureaucrat," Farrell said as a final insult.

"Bureaucrat with benefits," Ray called after him, but Farrell Jr. was gone inside the building. Ray went inside, too, but turned in the other direction and headed for his office.

Weeping on the headstone every April 15th was something of a sport for Caroline Jensen, Ray and Farrell Jr.'s mother. She threw herself on the smooth, violet stone with remarkable vigor for a woman her age. She may not have been as strong as in previous visits to the cemetery with her sons, but like a crafty veteran, she made up for diminishing physical skills with some advanced grieving techniques that she'd been cultivating. She wailed incomprehensible things. She dug her fingers into the black, etched letters of her husband's name, and then brought them to her lips and kissed them. She caterwauled and beat her brow. She fell to her knees and dug at the grass growing against the headstone like a dog digging up a bone. She straightened up and dug into the pockets of her long, cashmere coat for the inevitable wads of tissue paper, dabbed at her cheeks with them, thrust them back into the pockets and then flung herself again at the rock like a linebacker in a tackling drill.

"Oh for fuck sakes," muttered Farrell Jr.

Ray just stood silently, his hands crossed in front of him and his head bowed, trying to look pious for his mother. He was thinking that heart attack victims have a way of passing along the bad news to their offspring. They're rather blunt with the message. "Heart of my heart," they slyly announce, "this is my genetic legacy to you. Your heart will break, and probably without warning. This I bequeath to you! Have a nice life!"

"Thanks a lot, Dad," Ray muttered. He wondered again if he'd taken his heart medicine that morning, and then remembered for the fourth time that day that he had.

"What did you say, honey?" asked his mother. She could somehow make out the smallest of whispers, even while she was bellowing.

"I was just thanking dad for everything," said Ray.

Dr. Farrell Jensen Sr. had worked his life out rather well by the spring of 1972. He published a volume of short stories that received a favorable review in the Rochester Democrat & Chronicle; he was awarded tenure as an English professor at Morongo College; and he bought a house on Morongo Lake that faced the college, with a boat that he intended to use to go to work when the weather warmed up. He imagined living the rest of his life in the house and watching his boys grow up there, but he was only partially right. He was only fifty years old on that spring day, a Sunday, and presumably had few doubts that he would make it to fifty-one. But on God's post-it note for Professor Farrell Jensen Sr. that day was this things-2-do list: Breakfast of bagel with cream cheese, coffee; read New York Times and compose letter to Book Reviews Editor to beg for a review; admire lake from the comfortable chair on the porch; expire shortly after noon of a blown-up heart. My-oh-my-oh-myocardial infarction. He had a massive heart attack and he was gone.

Farrell Jr. was away at college when it happened. He returned for the funeral, of course, but Ray barely remembered his brother's presence during the months that followed. After the initial shock wore off, and the burial details were thrown together and his father was laid to rest in Morongo Cemetery, there was a long period of time when Caroline never left the house and rarely left her room. Ray recalled that he was alone much of the time when he wasn't in school, and that he entered a period of reciting to himself a litany of people who had died: Anne Frank and Captain James Cook and Civil War soldiers blown to bits on both sides and the Lindbergh baby and grandmas in the newspaper who passed away and were remembered by photographs from the '30s when they were in their primes. And Jim Thorpe, Lenin, Fatty Arbuckle, FDR and Babe Ruth. And so on. It wasn't the least bit comforting to be reminded that everybody died, but his mind insisted on the exercise until it exhausted itself. It occurred to Ray now that Farrell Sr.'s death was the most significant thing to have ever happened to the Jensen family – right up there with the births of Daniel and Farrell's kids – and in thirty years time they had barely come to understand its impact.

There is one more detail about Farrell Sr.'s death that bears mentioning. Ray was the first person to find his father's prone body on the porch that day. He rushed to him and felt for the first time that rising panic that he would later get from some of his encounters with Janice. His father was lifeless and slumped in his chair, but when Ray reached him and shouted his name, Farrell Sr. stirred. His eyes fluttered open, and in a last-ditch attempt at mortality and fatherly advice-giving, he gathered himself from his mortal pain, smiled weakly, and offered his son the view from astraddle the living and dying worlds. With the last energy in his body, he tapped his chest weakly over his heart, nodded to his son and croaked out his dying words: "You're next."

Let us repeat as one on Ray's behalf: Thanks a lot, Dad!

"What did you say, honey?" asked Caroline with a dramatic sniffle.

"I was just thanking Dad again," said Ray.

"He loved you both very much," she said, and latched onto her boys' strong arms and allowed them to lead her away from the cemetery for another year. "He was a good man, and good men shouldn't be taken so young. It wasn't fair to you boys that you should lose your father so young."

"Since when is life fair?" said Farrell, Jr.

"Since when did I raise a philosopher?"

Ray giggled at that.

When they were driving past Knapp & Schlappi Hardware and almost to Caroline's cottage, she said, "Raymond, call Janice. She's been trying to find you. She called me twice today."

"I'm right here," said Ray. "It's not like I'm hiding from her."

A word about the NARRATORS of this story

"We have a saying in my native Portugal," Costas was telling me. "The saying is that it is the just man who eats the desserts."

At the time of that particular pearl of Portuguese wisdom, Costas was in fact serving me a delightfully creamy coconut rice pudding that I had persuaded him to filch from the tropical buffet upstairs in the Lido Lounge.

I planned it beautifully. I called him to my cabin when I knew that they would just be opening the tropical lunch buffet and the huge pan of coconut rice pudding would be at its freshest, with an unbroken custard membrane stained walnut-brown by cinnamon on top. The earlybirds who came to lunch would, by habit, be loading their plates with mahi-mahi in a mango salsa, hearts of palm salad, Jamaican jerked chicken skewers and coconut prawns. They might admire the dessert buffet but – the fools – they would never consider making a pre-emptive strike on the coconut rice pudding. But I, with my butler as my reconnaissance drone, would swoop in there and get it all for myself.

"Take this bowl," I had told him, offering a very large salad bowl that I had found with the dishes in my bathroom sink and hastily rinsed, "and take your largest spoon, and don't stop with the coconut rice pudding until the bowl is very heavy."

"We have some very nice desserts on the room service menu," he had offered in mild rebuke. "I could bring you the menu."

"I've seen the room service menu," I said. "I've seen it for a year, and nowhere does it say, 'Huge overflowing salad bowl full of coconut rice pudding.' And that's what I want."

"Or you could go up to the buffet," he said lightly. "I could help you. They have very lovely desserts besides the coconut rice pudding." (He pronounced it poo-ding.) "A whole table full of lovely desserts." (He said loaf-ly.)

I laughed. He genuinely amused me sometimes. "Nice try, Costas," I said admiringly. He knew as well as I did that if I stepped one foot out of my cabin, I would be seized and thrown off the ship.

"Of course, Sir," Costas said.

"Thank you, Costas."

It is the just man who eats the desserts. Honestly. There was a time when I found Costas to be charming and amusing, before I realized that even though he was a very good butler, he was a bit of an idiot. He used to linger in my cabin to tell me things about Portuguese history, of which he was proud, or report on amusing things that he had seen during his brief shore excursions. Just to cheer me up. At times, I long for those days, when the ship was still new and fresh to me, all of the staff were interesting and exotic with their European accents and manners, I could leave my cabin (Penthouse Suite number 1125), and I had some optimism remaining about my life.

Before I got so fat, in other words, and for the first time in my life, followed through on a plan that I made. We make such silly noises about the worth of following through with plans in our culture, as if sheer, mule-like resolution is the ultimate virtue, but if the plan to which we are following is ultimately, morbidly destructive, is it such a great thing to say, in the end, "Well, at least I stuck to the plan?" I'll soon find out. I'll let you know if it was worth it when I get to the end of this particular bit of self-immolation. As the part of me that is Falubio would say, practical advice is the greatest gift one can offer, and I'm full of it.

Let's sort this out, shall we? Bear with me while I think aloud. I do know that you are the reader (heretofore known as "YOU" until further notice) and I ("I", "ME") am the person who is telling this story. I picture you as a model of consistency and good sense, but I'm sorry to say that, like a good airfare, I am subject to change without notice.

There are different parts to me, different people who narrate my story. They're all stuck in the cabin of the cruise ship, but sometimes they hide and I can't find them for days, sometimes only one or two of them shows up and sometimes they all talk at once.

Writing a story – playing God, I like to call it – is harder than I imagined.

It's because of the narrative group. For starters, I am Floyd Little, the once-great running back for the Denver Broncos in the 1960s. That is, one of the voices in my head, the chairman of my narrative group as it were, is the voice that I associate with a full-sized cardboard cutout of Floyd Little the running back that somehow (don't ask how...long story) wound up in the corner of Penthouse Suite #1125. In the cut-out, Floyd is helmet-less and stiff-arming an imaginary opponent with his right hand, the ball tucked into his left elbow and his right knee raised high. I go through life in a similar way, picking up my knees high, shedding would-be tacklers and other literary critics. He was a great athlete and a great man. After his career was over, he owned car dealerships in the Denver area, and somebody I knew once bought a nice pick-up truck from him. Ran great, in other words, just like Floyd Little did with the Broncos.

Life would be so much easier if Floyd Little were all that I am. Another member of the group, however, is a topless dancer named Poodle who hails from a gentlemen's club in Windsor, Ontario. She grew up in a small town in Quebec and never finished high school. She composes her parts of the story in between lap dances and drags on a cigarette in the dancers' lounge, which smells of cheap perfume and sweat and the residue left on bare skin of diaphragm exhalations from excited men.

Because the narrative part of me that is Poodle has a bitchin' bod; she's all about structure.

The story of Ray and Janice, Farrell and Daniel is just one of many stories being composed in the dancers' lounge, but nearly all of the rest of them have to do with no good bastard boyfriends what took their tips for a week and never even said thank you, and mothers watching the-baby-who-has-a-cold that night, and what I says to that bitch Jackie so she shuts her mouth good and fast.

Sometimes my mind is a terrible place to be. The racket can be deafening. You can see why I live, mostly alone, in the cabin of a cruise ship.

It doesn't end there, in the dancer's lounge or on the football field, with my arm out stiff and my knee raised chest-high. Depending on the time of day and what I have eaten, I can also be a handsome model named Falubio who can break your heart just by looking at him. He has some peripheral connection to the Hollywood movie scene, I gather. He doesn't say much, but boy is he handsome. When you'd rather look at me than hear me, when an image of a sullen, disinterested, yet extremely attractive man is worth many hundreds of ill-chosen words, when you wish that everyone would just stop talking and something exciting might happen, that's when I am Falubio.

Finally, my story is often and quite helplessly taken over by a somewhat lumpy and unattractive Guy Named Brad. Big thinker, small talent. The Guy Named Brad part of me is frightfully withdrawn, and it's not entirely his fault. For one thing, he has a voice like a mosquito. If he had a house, he wouldn't leave it much. He wants to write great things, but is continually frustrated by blank pieces of paper. It is something of a miracle that he weaseled his way into this narrative group. The best thing I can say about him is that if Janice could meet him, she might say, "He's very bright, but he lacks people skills."

They're like the voices inside my head, these four; they're my constant companions in Penthouse #1125, and brother, believe me when I say that that cabin can feel very small very quickly. They come and go, as does my ability to control them. They're as real to me as any of the people whom you meet on a cruise who occupy your life for a week or two and then vanish. They make it more difficult to tell my story, since everyone has an opinion of how a story should be told, but they also keep me company. On a long cruise when you're confined to your cabin by certain international laws of commerce and free passage, it's nice to have some company.

Well, that's a hell of a way to tell a story, you might say. Again referring to Janice, the character in the book, she would be one of those people who shake their heads and say (with an exasperated tone of voice), "Four narrators? Four points of view? It just doesn't WORK."

We'll see about that; but first, the pudding. Costas has set the table with a white tablecloth, and laid out heavy, silver cutlery and the oversized glass of ice water that I like to have handy. He has freshened up the pot of coffee, because he knows how much I enjoy a good cup throughout the day. The salad bowl brimming with coconut rice pudding has been placed upon the table. My slippers and blanket are within easy reach, so that when I am finished with my bowl of rice pudding, I need only reach down, recline the chair, cover myself and take a nap.

The ship continues to surge forward, ingesting new passengers every week and through a unique process that one might think of as reverse digestion, excreting them a week later a little larger and fatter and poorer than when they arrived. I've come to view the ship as a worldwide fattening agent, which, if it sails long enough and processes enough people, will increase the world's caloric count by some small increment that will eventually tip a narrow natural balance. In that regard, I am their prize pupil, and I fully expect to be the subject of serious scientific study in the future, long after they haul my carcass out of Penthouse Suite 1125 (most likely in sections). In me, they will find the perfect microcosm of the society gone calorically amok, a gorgeous specimen, preserved in its own lard, of "the cruise ship syndrome," as sociologists have begun to refer to the fattening of the population.

I am something of a lab animal, I admit. I have gained 300 pounds since I boarded this ship a year ago. And I wasn't that small to begin with; I must be around 500 by now.

With the very large spoon, I take a very large dollop of rice pudding and place it squarely in the center of my mouth. Creamy. Satisfying. I take another, and then *another. And then I call the narrative group to order. We have no problem telling what happened next. What happened next is rather important, and which led me to think I was God.*

You want to disagree with that? Then show me the real God and we'll talk. And none of your metaphors about God being the water and the pudding and the clear, blue skies. I know pudding, and I know what water is. I almost drowned in it once, and believe me, there was nothing divine about it.

Now back to our story.

Chapter Three
The PICZAK SNOPS

To say that young Daniel Jensen "discovered" the secret of eternal life and its happy cohorts – how to reverse aging, arresting death, unbelievably good health, a pinkish complexion – is not being entirely accurate. He stole the fountain of youth from a basement with his ne'er-do-well girlfriend. And he thought it was booze. He wanted to get drunk and feel up his new girlfriend, but never mind the back-story. It will all come out in the paper soon enough, and if the facts aren't quite right when it does, it really won't matter. Morongans like to make up the facts as they go along.

To put it another way, if Daniel had been a character in a movie that his father Ray wrote, his actions would have taken place deep in the background, barely noticeable behind the car chases and the flying bullets and the hero clutching the heroine to his bosom and sobbing, "Just stay alive!" Only the most discerning viewer would have noticed, at the edges of the frame, two teenagers quietly and sneakily keeping the blown-up and bullet-riddled minor characters alive by offering sips from a flask. The wounded ones were revived, and even the dead ones, if they hadn't been gone too long, could be seen sitting up and rubbing their eyes.

We have two stories to tell here, and we'll try to tell them both at once. The reason that Daniel's story did not garner much local attention at first was that it was Daniel's fortune – let's leave it up to you to decide if it was good or bad – to steal the secret of everlasting life on the same night that young Timmy Marcionda decided to make his mark on the world. Timmy, a freshman at Morongo Academy, had only recently made a key decision to transform himself through sheer force of personality into an interesting, if undersized, thug who could successfully recruit dim-witted tenth and even eleventh grade boys into being his accomplices in petty crime.

Morongo had a steady and reliable pool of talent in the dimwit department. There was even a charming local term – Dickwalters – for a whole class of local dolts. Stop anyone on the street in Morongo and ask them what a dickwalter is, and if they don't point one out on the spot, they'll have an answer. The boys who steal bikes and get in fights, barely graduate from the sixth grade, are suspended from high school in the first two weeks for drinking beer on campus and are on the fast track to contribute to Morongo

Academy's seventeen percent drop-out rate? Those are dickwalters.

Whole families of greasy, dull people who live in trailers on the edge of town near the migrant-labor camps, who sit in white, molded plastic chairs from Wal-Mart as the Mexicans go off to work picking the produce of Morongo and still somehow feel superior to them? Dickwalters.

The slow ones, the ones with knit brows, who move their lips when reading or can't read at all, whose parents are on social services and Medicaid, who can't throw or kick a ball, who learn to swear as children but never swear cleverly, who learn to smoke young and call it learnt? As in, "It was my dad who learnt me how to smoke when I was eleven." Dickwalters.

They got their name from Vincent McWalter and his family of buck-toothed, stultifyingly slow and stupid white trash who live out in Dresden and seem to be raising a garden of rusting, useless cars that multiply in their yard every year. Ask anyone in Morongo what a dickwalter is and they'll tell you: A lout, a thief, a moron, a dullard of the dullest order, a McWalter.

Timmy Marcionda could have gone either way; he was on the cusp of being a dickwalter. To his credit, he somehow became formidable between the eighth and ninth grades, although he barely topped four-feet-nine. He had developed a wolfish look and red, rheumy eyes that seemed to have moved from those of a sickly child with constant colds to those of a chain-smoking man who has knocked over a gas station or two. Ray used to see him come with his mother to pick up support checks at Morongo Social Services and it was all Ray could do to not blurt out, "Timmy, how you've grown (into a con) since I saw you last."

It was on a cold April night – two days, by the way, after Ray and family visited the cemetery -- that Timmy got to work on his front-page news. Deciding with a teenager's bold assurance that there was nothing to do in Morongo on a Friday night, and succored by a quarter-cup of vodka that had somehow, miraculously, escaped his mother's notice (she was passed out on the couch and wasn't noticing much), Timmy crept out of the house at 11 p.m. with an ill-defined mayhem on his mind. He wandered down Elm Street and briefly considered throwing rocks at the stained glass windows of St. Michael's, Morongo's Catholic Church. This desecration was averted when he ran into two of his bicycle-stealing cohorts, a pair of junior boys named Tom and Bruno (not McWalter, but they were dickwalters) who were also struck in a dim way by the lack of recreational opportunities for teenagers at midnight in a small town like Morongo.

They wandered downtown and made a fire to warm themselves in a garbage can in the alley behind Long's Cards and Books, where they discussed kidnapping and killing a sophomore boy that nobody liked by dangling him by his ankles with his head in the lake until he drowned. Bruno said that he knew a good spot where they could do it, and they could take his uncle's rowboat from the boathouse and row the body to the middle of the lake opposite the college and weight it with rocks and dump it. Timmy reminded him that the lake was mostly frozen, but Bruno said that he had stepped onto the ice the day before and heard it crack, and the rowboat would be like a little ice-breaker if they all four (the three boys and the dead one) got in it to weigh it down. Timmy called him a dumb-ass because the channel of broken ice would lead directly to the murder site and the boathouse, and Bruno punched him hard on the arm, which brought tears to Timmy's red eyes. Tom said he had seen a similar murder in a movie, and they talked about the movie, movies, girls in movies, hot girls in high school and really stupid people who they'd like to kill. Timmy ran out of cigarettes and said he needed more.

That was when Tom remembered the extra pack of cigarettes that his uncle always kept on the table near the door of his cottage at Indian Pines, so they walked a half-hour, hands thrust in pockets, giggling and trying to kick each other to keep warm, to the lake and Tom's uncle's house. It was nearly one a.m. when they got there, and Tom walked right into the cottage through an unlocked door, and beside the pack of cigarettes on the end-table, he found a set of keys, which he also boosted. Laughing and enjoying the adrenaline rushes of being out late, being left alone and not, for a change, being told what to do, they unlocked the SUV parked across Indian Pines Road in an empty lot and climbed inside to get warm. They turned it on and turned the heater on, and while the car warmed up they smoked two cigarettes each in a silence that was broken only by Bruno roaring, "Somebody SAY something!"

These details, by the way, all came out in the paper over the next three weeks, and were discussed and repeated around Morongo, embellished with conjecture as to motive and antecedent, laden with opinion and personal relevance, until they comprised a sort of community fiction: A book that everyone in town was reading and simultaneously re-writing.

Timmy wanted to drive, but he was barely tall enough to see over the steering wheel, so Tom went back into his uncle's cottage and stole two couch cushions. The couch cushions allowed Timmy to see, but now he couldn't reach the pedals, so Bruno squatted down in the well and pressed the gas pedal with his hand. Bruno revved the engine and they squealed like delighted children at the engine's racing sound as Timmy only pretended to drive, because he had never driven a car before and was still two years away from driver's ed. It was Tom (who did know how to drive) who grew bored of the game first (but only after a good ten revs and laughs), and he reached over Timmy's shoulder from the back seat and yanked the gearshift lever into reverse just as Bruno revved the engine, causing the car to jump backwards ten feet, narrowly missing a tree, and stall.

The relief of teenagers after a scary moment when they realize they're safe and unharmed? Brother, there's a lot of money to be made in horror movies that deliver that particular special effect. After yet more peals of teenage braying, Timmy, who was anything but chicken, put the car into gear and, with Bruno operating under strict instructions that he was to accelerate only when told and brake without question, the SUV pulled out jerkily onto Indian Pines Road and headed past the Seneca Farms ice-cream stand to East Lake Road.

Would you mind if we cut away here (a popular device, as Ray would tell you, in any screenplay)? Shall we, for once, exclude explicit description and just do as they did in the movies of the '30s and '40s, when nobody needed to be reminded of violence? We'll insert a sound effect of squealing tires, a careening car, perhaps a flash of Timmy's excited, scared face displaying his last childhood emotion before he grew up all at once, a terrible screech and collision sound, and an image of an SUV nose down in a lake. Just for the sake of pictorial impact, we'll make the back tires continue to roll, uselessly, in the air, and then be still.

Within two days, everybody in town knew that when they hit the patch of icy pavement and caromed off the tree and plunged into the lake, Tom nearly drowned headfirst as he popped out of the window and had his large-and-still-growing feet entangled in the seatbelt, holding half of him above water, and the wrong half at that. He survived, thanks to a miracle, but his brain was deprived of oxygen for too long and he barely ever functioned after that. Bruno-in-the-footwell was broken several times in ways that would never completely heal; he wound up in a wheelchair in a Watkins Glen rehab center. Timmy was lacerated terribly, but you can get over cuts, although not quickly. His face and neck showed bright, red stripes like awful stretch marks when he appeared in court many months later to plead guilty to Grand Theft Auto and enlist in juvenile detention in Elmira, commencing a long career in law enforcement. He never could explain – either publicly or privately -- how he got himself out of the car and then, blinded by a wall of blood on his face, dove back in and managed to get a motionless Bruno out of the footwell, through the window and out of the car, and onto the shore. But as you can imagine, this became the focus of Timmy's personal narrative for many years, the story that he would always return to as a validation of his inner goodness and heroic nature. In other words, he got a lifetime of mileage out of that stalled and dripping SUV.

    The whole incident sparked a strenuous community discussion. HOW COULD THIS HAPPEN IN MORONGO?, wailed one headline. TEENS NEED MIDNIGHT OPTIONS, began one letter to the editor. COUNCIL DEBATES ORDINANCE TO KEEP ALL COTTAGE DOORS LOCKED AT NIGHT, said a news item (it didn't pass).

    Okay, that is the first story. The second one has to do with Daniel Jensen, who on the same night had a date for which he had to sneak out of not one, but two homes. Ray thought Daniel was at Janice's house; she thought he was at Ray's house. The oldest game in the divorced-family book, you say, and with a boyish blush Ray has to admit that you're right. I don't suppose that it makes any difference to you that Ray had raised his arm once and waved it vigorously and announced, vis-à-vis divorced-family games, "Not playing!" to his ex-wife and offspring. Any schoolyard lawyer (including the one whom Ray hired to represent him in family court) would clear his throat over that one and launch into an explanation of implied consents and responsibilities and community standards regarding parental involvements, and in summation, people who wave their arms and shout "Not playing!" are very much playing.

    The short answer is that Daniel was with Jodi Bullock, who was also a sophomore at Morongo Academy. She told her worried, withdrawn mother, between TV shows in the double-wide trailer, for the Bullocks were not only poor, but dickwalters, that she was going to a wrestling match at school and then downtown with her girlfriends. The mother waved wanly; the father was out long-haul trucking. Tiny and undernourished her entire childhood, this Jodi Bullock, this developing character, had apparently grown winsome between third-period Spanish and sophomore lunch, because when she had passed Daniel a note earlier that day through an intermediary and smiled her sliver eyes at him across the cafeteria, he was suddenly smitten. These were kids who used to hand over obligatory Valentines to each other in the second grade, who ignored each other for years of kickball and multiplication tables and middle school dances, who had referred to each other as "stupid" and "boring" as recently as five months previously, and now suddenly they were mating.

Daniel agreed to meet her at eight at the McDonalds on the far side of Red Jacket Park.

Jodi had cute little almond eyes, practically Asian, and with her jeans she wore a tight, stretchy top that clung to a figure that had changed from scrawny to lithe and taut as a gymnast. Over this she wore a blue parka with a fake-fur ruffle around the hood. The half-inch of belly that was revealed below the top was firm and the same chalk-white as her neck and chin, but her cheeks had a natural pink glow of pubescence. Daniel thought she looked like a model, choosing to ignore that most models were taller than five-foot-two. At Morongo Academy, you're either a model or you play field hockey. When she smiled, her eyes narrowed even more, which made her look knowing and amused. Daniel, in jeans and basketball shoes and the green hooded sweatshirt (which he felt was dressier than the gray), decided before the first box of French fries was consumed that she was cool, yet hot, and thus worthy of his attentions.

She had come to much the same conclusion about him, and as he finished the box of fries (not noticing that Jodi only pretended to eat), she popped the question. "Do you like to drink?" she asked. Her eyes were expectant, even sensual, and her mouth was framed in a challenging grin. "Because I know where we can get some schnapps."

She pronounced it snops. SHE PRONOUNCED IT SNOPS! The temptress of Ray's sweet, apple-cheeked boy, who would put sin itself to his lips and offer him a hearty endorsement to chug it, could not even name her poison.

Daniel said, "Sure."

How many cottages need to be ransacked before Morongans get the message? Put a damn lock on your door, and use it! This particular cottage, also on the south end of the lake at Indian Pines, belonged to John Piczak (pronounced the same way you would instruct your young child to urinate in the potty, not on the floor: "Pee, Zack!"), a retired chemistry professor from Morongo College whose grandchildren were babysat by Jodi. She had been in the basement to retrieve lost toys and saw the green bottles stopped with corks, and over the course of many visits she had by turns sniffed the bottles themselves, pulled a cork and sniffed the contents, returned the cork and the bottle to their places, for Jodi was a reluctant eater, and then one gray afternoon, with the children watching videos upstairs, opened a bottle and took a swig. It was a viscous liquid, devoid of color. It tasted of oranges and ashes and a deep bitterness. The very essence of schnapps, or snops, as any member of a Bavarian oompah band will tell you. An adult flavor and sensation that made her wince, but want more.

On the night that she seduced Daniel, she knew that the Piczaks wouldn't be home. She knew that the basement door was unlocked, because she had unlocked it herself earlier that week. From McDonalds, they cut across several lawns to warm up to the rich, heady thrill of trespass, leaned against each other with shoulders touching as they cased the Piczak house, and then walked in with Jodi holding Daniel's arm at the bicep. They boosted a bottle of the Piczak Snops and, giggling, beat it out of the basement. Three doors down the beach, in front of a cottage that had been deserted for the winter by Rochesterians, they uncorked the bottle and drank half of it hidden under an old rowboat that they propped up with logs on the beach to make a crude shelter.

They decided that it tasted like shit but was making them drunk, drank some more, laughed and swore and spat, and spilled half of the bottle onto the ground. They didn't know – how could they know? – that the snops they poured into the pebbly sand, if judiciously doled out, could have bought every cancer patient in New York state another five years, easy. Because the Piczak Snops was not schnapps at all, but a chemical that can keep you alive forever. It was, in fact, the fountain of youth that they stole from the basement of a cottage on Morongo Lake.

On the beach they kissed, and Jodi's almond eyes looked quizzical and pleased, and then she pushed Daniel on the chest, kissed him again fast and ran all the way home. Daniel watched until he couldn't see her any more. He carefully corked the bottle and put it in his backpack, and began to walk the long way around the park towards Ray's cottage on the lake.

He was halfway there when he came upon the disconcerting sight of the car that Timmy and company had stolen, nose down and upside-down in the water. He almost continued to walk past the scene, because although the sight of it made him pause, he did not understand what he was seeing. It was quiet, with none of the auditory cues of catastrophe (i.e. alarms, screaming, glass shattering, circling helicopters, police radios squawking), and the lake had almost stopped rippling around the still SUV. Daniel heard an unfamiliar sound and saw that two boys were sitting on the beach, their legs still in the water. One of them was crying and the other one was still, his head in the first one's lap.

"Dude, what's going on?" Daniel asked carefully. These were situations that could get out of control quickly, situations where people got beat up just for being out late and alone, and Daniel wondered if he was heading into trouble. He did not recognize the two boys in the water, and recognition is a crucial survival skill in a small town like Morongo. For all he knew, they could be toughs from Geneva who would like nothing better than to beat up a local boy and dunk him by the ankles off a dock. He took a step closer, and then all he could see was that the boy who was crying had a face covered in blood, and Daniel's heart began to race.

"Tommy. He's in the car," wailed Timmy Marcionda. "Somebody help."

Without another thought, Daniel dropped his backpack and leaped into Morongo Lake. He swam hard to the side of the car, but saw nothing. The driver's door was open underwater, and he dimly made out what appeared to be a shoe on the seat. He surfaced for air and then dove back in again, swimming over the hood and windshield of the car and coming out at the passenger side. That was when he saw the two large feet sticking out of the water in the rear passenger-side window, and realized all at once who and where Tommy was. Gasping and spitting water, he grabbed the feet and pulled hard on them. They were stuck fast in the straps, and it took him a moment to figure out in the dim light how to untangle them. When he did, the body seemed to sag down and away from him, towards the bottom of the lake, and he almost lost it entirely. He grabbed the legs again and pulled hard, and this time, Tom's lifeless body came into his arms. The face was horrible to see. The eyes were open and the mouth looked like it had been calling someone. He was quite dead.

    Daniel towed the body to the shore and tried to administer mouth-to-mouth resuscitation the way he had seen it done in the movies. Nothing happened, so he turned Tom onto his side and whacked his back hard, and water poured out of the mouth, but there was no movement. Daniel tried three more breaths on the open mouth, but the body did not respond. He was crying himself at that point and did not know what to do next. For some reason – and he would long wonder why this came to him – he thought of the green bottle in his backpack. Maybe he thought, also as suggested in the movies, that alcohol could revive a cold, unconscious person. He pulled the cork out with his teeth and splashed the liquor into Tom's open mouth. A moment passed and he splashed it in again. Within five seconds, a film seemed to withdraw from the eyes of the victim. They became clear and began to see, and then the body shook to life and began to cough and vomit what seemed like quarts of lake water.

        Daniel stood back in amazement. "Dude," he said.

        Timmy was still crying and bleeding, and it began to dawn on Daniel that he was the first one at the scene of a major accident. The third boy, who lay in Timmy's arms, was still not moving, and Timmy cried out once more for help. Daniel ran. He found a payphone at the gas station a quarter-mile down West Lake Road and called for an ambulance. When they asked who he was, he hesitated and then hung up. A moment later, he heard the sound of sirens approaching, and he watched quietly, hidden behind a tree, as the paramedics arrived and gathered up the three boys. He had the sense that he had done something terrible by saving Tom's life with liquor that he had stolen.

The kid had been dead. There was no doubt of that. When Daniel read the account in the paper two days later, and found out that Tom had survived, he did three things. He went back to the Piczak house and stole two more bottles of the green liquid. He drank more of it and didn't feel a thing. Over the course of the next two days he slipped healthy slugs of it into his father's coffee and his mother's tea. He waited to see what would happen.

On Monday at school it took him three periods to find out something that everybody else already knew: He and Jodi Bullock were going together.

The NARRATORS
A question for GOD/Falubio

    We're having a story conference, and if the truth be told, we're all feeling a little sorry for ourselves. Well, all of us except Falubio, who loves himself too much to regret anything. He has no problem with that "there is only one God" doctrine, because as far as he's concerned, that one God is himself.

    The part of me that is Poodle shyly raises her hand.

    "You know, remembering our own Dad while we write the story of Ray and Daniel and their dead father makes me helplessly sad," she says. "I loved him so much. I couldn't imagine ever living without him, and even now at my age, I hardly know how I do it. I know I have to face it every day, but I still don't like it. I wish we could bring him back."

    General nods of agreement here from the parts of me that are Floyd Little, Falubio and A Guy Named Brad. There are husky sighs and bobbings of manly Adam's Apples. Floyd Little gently taps the remaining pages of the book, the ones that are blank and as yet unwritten. "But, you know," he says gently, "we've still got a lot of work to do."

Poodle nods and smiles bravely. She reaches for a tissue and delicately blows her nose. "Oh, God, look at me, crying over a dad who has been dead to me way longer than he was alive," she says, and giggles bravely. She gestures to her running mascara and her tear-stained cheeks.

"Is there anything more pathetic," she continues, "than a weepy lap-dancer who knows full well that she has to straighten the g-string, put on a big smile and go back out there to amuse the troops? To write another chapter in some poor slob's lap-dancing history, as it were?"

Floyd Little nods his big head. "Or a running back who can no longer run?" he says from the corner of Penthouse Suite #1125. His stiff-arm waves helplessly in the air; as a cardboard cut-out of a running back, he can hardly run. "Who stands still with his danged stiff-arm out, waiting for someone fool enough to run into it? Isn't that the damndest thing you ever heard? You talk about pathetic, Miss Poodle; is there anything more pathetic than that?"

"I've got one," says A Guy Named Brad. His voice sometimes sounds just like a mosquito in your ear, the kind of mosquito that finds you when you're camping and, just *before you're about to fall asleep in your sleeping bag, screams its name in your ear. A Guy Named Brad sounds just like that. "Is there anything more pathetic than a writer who has lots to say but finds out that he has been given the voice of a mosquito? Could there be anything worse than that?"*

He looks around, hoping for sympathy. Hoping that they would all say, "God, you're right, Guy Named Brad, you have it worse than anyone." But nobody says a word to him, or even much cares about his annoying mosquito voice and utter lack of writing talent.

Your turn to share, Falubio. Go ahead, tell us what pains you the most.

Falubio?

Since we're sharing, I'll tell you that my problem, if you can call it a problem, is that I am no longer sure how long I'm supposed to live. The careless ingestion of very large amounts of the Piczak Snops can do that to a person. It is not so much that I am afraid of dying; I am now afraid of living too long. Certain events in the past suggest to me that I might live forever, and frankly, I'm not taking the news well. Sure, I could end it all with one quick dip in the drink outside of my penthouse verandah, but suicide has always seemed too arbitrary to me. To tell you the truth, I tried it once and, like dieting, the best I can say about it is that it didn't quite suit me. Nor did it work.

I also have a small problem with figuring out if I deserve to be God. I'm realizing that when you consider the qualities of the deity – omniscience, omnipotence, deep and overwhelming love – introspection is not one of them. So half the time I sit around my penthouse suite wondering why I was chosen to be God, and the other half trying to pawn the duty off on one of my narrators.

"Okay," I say, "who wants to be God today?"

No takers. I ask again. Nothing. So I make Falubio do it.

A Guy Named Brad clears his reedy throat. He is armed with a list of questions that he intends to ask God. He turns to Falubio, who looks like Michelangelo sculpted him out of marble. Strong, silent type.

"Okay," says Brad to Falubio in his high-pitched whine. "Since you are the God, I'd like to know a few things."

"Shoot," says Falubio who, characteristically, looks utterly bored.

"Here goes. Why did you claim Farrell Jensen Sr. so early in his life? I mean, he was young, he was vital, he was a good teacher and writer. You went to all of that

[59]

trouble of getting him to that stage in life…why even bother ending it then? For that matter, why are there even heart attacks? Would good does that do you, God? Awfully painful way to go, don't you think?"

It is hard to know if Falubio is even listening, what with the sunglasses. He sits stock-still in the comfortable chair and appears to be either staring at the ceiling or dozing.

Brad continues. "Don't answer all at once. There's more." He consults his notes, which turn out to be something of a scroll that unwinds onto the floor. "Wait a minute," he mutters, "I lost my place."

As he pores over it, Poodle pipes up. She is just plain likeable, is Poodle. You would have her sit on your lap for any number of reasons.

"I've got one," she says. "Here it is. I knew this guy? And he lost his arm when he was young to cancer? And then a few years went by when he was okay? And then the cancer went to his jaw and he lost that too? And I'm just wondering, God…what's up with that?"

Falubio just shrugs.

Brad clears his throat and continues, reading from his scroll. He's clumsy, and the scroll begins to unscroll faster than he can read, so he picks from a section here, a section there, all of it questions that he has prepared for

God. "Why is there Lou Gehrig's Disease?" asks Brad. "What good does that do anyone, least of all Lou Gehrig? Why on Earth do babies and little children die? What's up with cancer? If we have to die, okay, so be it. Everything dies, I suppose, but I don't really understand why. But why die prematurely? And here's a good one: Why die painfully? And don't give me that line about free will, God. You're omnipotent, so couldn't you have made free will exclusive of tremendous suffering? I mean, I can have just as free a will without feeling like my guts have been grabbed by red-hot pliers and are being pulled through my liver. I mean, that doesn't free my will up any for appreciating the beauty of life, you know what I mean God?"

Falubio doesn't answer. He has decided to interpret the role of God as an unresponsive deity. Either that, or he is fast asleep. Either that, or Falubio is the kind of God who thinks that we should all stop and just appreciate the beauty of life, the beauty being himself. Frankly, there is no telling what Falubio thinks, because he is as silent as a horse clam. Brad waits a moment, and then lets out a scream of frustration that has us all diving for our ears.

"I want answers to these important questions!" screams A Guy Named Brad.

Floyd Little clears his throat in the corner of the room. "Do you think maybe these are questions that your God can't answer?" he asks gently.

Falubio just grins at that one.

A Guy Named Brad mutters, "If I was the God, I could answer them."

"God forbid," someone whispers. It takes a moment for me to realize it was Poodle.

We all laugh, except A Guy Named Brad, who merely screams more mosquito sounds in frustration. He gets up and locks himself in the bathroom, and we hear, from the shower, him screaming, "Why must there be pain? Why won't anyone answer me?" Over and over, until Costas brings the pre-dinner appetizers and wine.

Brad really wants answers. But all we have to give him is more story, and we come up with this next part without him.

Chapter Four
SOCIAL services, memos FROM THE heart, systemic STIFFNESS, SAD SACKED-ness

The week that the news came out about the three boys and the stolen car was also – and this is not coincidental – when Ray began to notice some new things about his community. He thought he knew everything there was to know about Morongo, but now he began to have premonitions about when many of the people around him would die. If the truth be told, he wasn't entirely happy with this new wrinkle in the domestic fabric.

At first, he blamed it on his father, and on the Jensen predisposition to growing faulty hearts. One of the side effects of his medication was an infrequent feeling of impending doom, but then, that was one of the side effects of his life. Heart attacks have a curious afterlife. They don't end with the prone body of the victim, who may have never even felt it coming, the death report, the burial or the check from the life insurance company. The people who live with a suddenly fatal heart attack are the children of the victim, and they see it around every stress-filled corner; they picture it intertwined with the fat in every slice of bacon; they hear it singing out to them like Frank Sinatra when a set of stairs leaves them short of breath; they imagine it crooking its little heart attack finger in their direction when they wake up in the middle of the night with heartburn.

A quick digression: In fact, at one time or another during his life, a child of a heart attack victim – the kind of heart attack victim who was asked to pass the syrup at breakfast but failed to appear at lunch due to systemic stiffness – might experience all, none, quite a few or a couple of the following clinical symptoms of an impending heart attack. He has no problem identifying these symptoms, because he has memorized them since he was thirty years old.

Shortness of breath. A dull or very sharp pain in the arm, neck, shoulder blades or chest that appears to radiate upwards, downwards or to the side. A crushing, substernal pain. Irritability and/or disorientation. Coughing up a pink, frothy sputum. Trouble sleeping. A deep, lingering dread accompanied by feelings of doom. An inability or marked disinterest in exercising. Catecholamine responses, such as coolness in extremities, perspiration, anxiety and restlessness. Infarction. Thromboembolism due to infarction. Fatigue, dyspnea and palpitations, usually accompanied by fever. Cough and pallor. Crackles. Wheezing. Elevated blood pressure, possibly in conjunction with jugular vein distention.

Possibly not.

There was no telling if Farrell Sr. had experienced any of the above symptoms, but Ray was reasonably sure that at one time or another, he had imagined having them all. He was more than a little aware that the pain of a heart attack could clinically range from the mildest discomfort – as if struck on the back of the head by a playful kitten – to profound and excruciating pain that is frequently likened to having one's chest gripped in an enormous vice and being at the mercy of a crazy carpenter who continues to tighten to the point of tissue shredding and bone splintering. With that clinical definition in mind, any random pain, even the pain caused by hiding from one's ex-wife, might be the precursor to the big one, and might be properly dreaded if one were in a certain mood.

More symptoms: Indigestion. Rampaging arrhythmia. Sudden death.

Add to these a pronounced apathy. A certain fatalistic point of view. A lingering fear. A demurring of life. Coughing up sputum, in Ray's experience one terrifying winter's day, and only imagining that it is pink and frothy. Which in turn makes the alleged victim scare the crap out of his loyal girlfriend Donna, have her fumble for the phone to call emergency services, and then spend an anxiety-filled day at the hospital until the doctors pull out the big "False Alarm" flag and wave it over Ray's bed.

Aftershocks: A willingness to go quietly into that good night. A certain heightened awareness of the inviolable nature of genetics. A mooning, hangdog disposition. Sad Sack-ed-ness, where you mope around for days and bore the crap out of everyone with your sighing and what's-the-use-edness.

Then, a tendency to read everything about heart disease and smile ruefully at the number of risk factors one has inherited. A tendency to ignore the "things you can do to make sure it doesn't happen to you" sections of the same articles and books. Conversations with one's sweetheart where one can't, for the tenth time, answer the simple question, "Why don't you just stop worrying and go for a walk once in awhile?"

A quality of being extremely, annoyingly vague about one's longevity. Inability or unwillingness to make long-term plans such as the purchase of property, timeshares or annuities. A propensity to ponder the existence of one's offspring and sigh at the years never to be shared, the grandchildren – as yet unconceived and unimagined -- never to be dandled, the ballgames unattended, the marriages and divorces unwitnessed and uncounseled. A tendency to "let oneself go." A giddy sensibility that leaves one prone to cheap joke-making, pratfalling and scatological humor.

At Truman County Social Services, Marjorie Corcoran Disbrow appeared in Ray's office and cleared her throat. How long had she been standing there? His hands were still shaking, so he tried to busy them by moving papers on his desk.

She reached out tentatively and touched him gently on the shoulder. "Are you okay? I heard you make a sound like you were in pain."

Ray raised a small smile. "As good as ever," he said.

"Should I call a doctor for you?"

"No, I don't think that's necessary. Just say that you love me, Margie."

"Oh, Raymond," she said, and blushed.

As Marjorie stood fussing over him, Ray made an observation that he had never before made in a dozen years of working together. She would die within ten years: Complications from Alzheimer's disease. The most prominent complication was that she would forget the simple concept of seasons and would walk out onto the frozen lake one February morning dressed only in her thin nightgown, and would not be discovered until hours later when it was too late.

It was Ray's turn to show concern. "Are you okay, Margie?"

She withdrew her hand from his shoulder. "Sure, I am," she said. "Why do you ask?"

Ray looked at her oddly. "I have no idea," he said. "What do you have?"

She slid a memo onto his desk. "Missive from his royal highness," she said. "It's not the best news." As was her custom, she was eyeing the doorway, instinctively measuring the distance to her escape and angling her body sideways to provide as narrow a target as possible to Ray. He always had an urge to grab her by the wrist when she did this.

"Thanks," he said. "I'll look it over in a minute."

"I got one, too," she said. "Everybody did."

Ray glanced quickly at the memo, afraid that if he looked away too long Margie would vanish. "To all staff. Something, something, something about meeting notes and action points and agency goals." Ray's eye stopped on the final sentence: "In short, why are you here? Have written responses on my desk by noon tomorrow."

"What's the dickwalter up to now?" Ray asked Marjorie. He was referring to Richard From Rochester, as Ray called the boss, who was the new head of the agency. Marjorie's shoulders instinctively drew up and she closed her eyes tightly at the suggestion of his name, and at Ray's rudeness. Her hands fluttered helplessly, and she shook her head tightly in response to his question, as if to say that the walls had ears, the ears belonged to RFR, RFR stood between her and a peaceful retirement, and she mustn't linger another moment.

"The dickwalter – I mean Mr. From Rochester -- is kind of on the warpath today," she whispered.

"Then I suppose we should circle our wagons," Ray whispered back. Seeing Marjorie freeze, unsure if she was supposed to advocate any action from Ray, he quickly added, "Just a little joke, Margie. A bad, bad little joke."

She took a sparrow step towards him and patted him awkwardly on the head. "Someone, somewhere would find it funny," she offered. "Help me with mine?"

Ray had already forgotten about the memo, and when she saw the puzzled look on his face, she tapped the piece of paper that had dropped onto his desk. "My response?" she asked. "You know I can't write. He needs it by noon tomorrow."

"Sure."

At noon, Ray stopped in the records department and found his brother's file. With only a slight feeling of guilt for snooping on Farrell Jr., he read it. Out of work for four months. Fired from yet another construction job, this one with a roofing company with which Farrell had had one of his typical disputes. "Refused to work overtime," was his explanation for the reason that he had left the company. Current job prospects were dim. Prospects for future employment were uncertain, due to chronic pain suffered in a back injury some years back.

He put his brother's folder on the top of the pile of applicants. Farrell would at least get an immediate answer from the agency on whether benefits would continue. A moment later, Richard From Rochester, a small, bustling, officious man, passed Ray in the hallway and nodded hello. Ray said hello, but then stopped abruptly and just stared at his boss's back as RFR walked away from him. Ray could not help but stare, because the man had cancer growing inside him like a blooming black rose. As Ray watched him, the cancer cells that would ultimately kill RFR were sleepily awakening on his prostate gland and stretching their malicious little arms. They would take their time waking up, yawning, adjusting their little jaws with pincer-like hands, stretching their necks to this side and the other, and having a second cup of cancer coffee before getting to the work of multiplying exponentially. They would convene a big cancerous hoedown on his baseball-sized gland.

"In about two years," whispered Ray.

He felt terrible. He walked back to his office and sat down hard. He suddenly wanted very badly to talk with his girlfriend Donna, but she had left earlier that week for her weeklong stay in Syracuse, where she was studying for her master's degree. She usually called with the number of the housing unit to which she was assigned, but hadn't yet, and Ray had no way of contacting her. He made a note to himself to check the dosage of his medicine and make sure that he had taken it correctly that week. One of the side effects was a mild depression, and Ray could not think of anything more depressing than having sudden visions of how everyone around him was going to die.

The phone rang, and he reached for it. He hoped it was Donna, who could turn around practically any mood of his, including morbid ones. But it was Janice.

"When were you going to tell me?" she asked.

Ray didn't know what she meant, and as usual, Janice had put him on the defensive, almost without even trying. If Ray were forced to summarize his quite complicated relationship with his ex-wife in one sentence, it would be this sentence: He often did not understand her questions.

"When was I going to tell you what?"

"Where Daniel was the other night. The night those boys crashed the car and almost died."

Ray wracked his brain for the right answer. With Janice, the right answer was crucial, but was rarely apparent.

"I thought he was with you."

Janice snorted. "Nice one, Ray."

There was a pause, and Ray was unclear if he had been asked another question. She spoke first. "He said he was at your house. It was a Tuesday night, and you're supposed to know where he is on Tuesday nights."

And then Ray remembered the night. He had an airtight alibi. "I had a meeting," he said triumphantly.

"When were you going to tell me?" she asked again.

Another pause. Another feeling that some crucial data was missing from Ray's brain, and he searched and searched and searched for it. "I told Daniel," Ray finally said. He felt a familiar anger begin to well up inside of him. "I thought he told you."

"Well he didn't, Ray." Janice paused and took a breath. She heard the catch in Ray's voice and did not want to fight, although she would, nay, she must defend herself and her progeny. She tried to soften her voice, and resented having to do it. "Next time, make sure that I know. Because he could have been out doing anything."

"I'll try to do that." Ray was unwilling to give up so easily. "Why, what did he do?"

"It's not what he did. It's what he could have done."

"But he didn't actually do anything. You're calling me to complain about something that I forgot to do that resulted in Daniel's not doing anything?"

There was a pause, and Ray could hear her breathing heavily, trying to calm herself. "I hate when you do this, Ray," she said, and hung up.

Ray looked at the phone blankly, and hung it up. The rest of the day was consumed by meetings and reviewing notes for the year-end report, and when he left the office at five o'clock, he had completely forgotten what it was that he had promised Janice.

That was not the only thing that Ray forgot, or missed. When he returned to his car that afternoon, there was a sheet of paper stuck inside the windshield wiper on the driver's side. He ignored it, because similar sheets of paper were stuck in all of the windshield wipers in the parking lot and on the cars parked down Elm Street, and they seemed to negate each other. Ray removed his sheet of paper and crumpled it into a ball without looking at it. He threw the ball into the backseat of the car and drove off.

The flyer said, "Want to live forever? Want to stop aging RIGHT NOW!!!?? Call this number on a Tuesday night. Cash money only." The flyer gave a phone number. The phone number was Ray's.

Chapter Five

POLICE BLOTTER

from the Morongo Express newspaper

A tenant of the Morongo Marina reported that his boat had been vandalized during the winter. He discovered the damage when he returned to retrieve his boat for the spring. Police are investigating.

Police were called to a home on Elm Street when neighbors reported a domestic disturbance. The tenants said that they were simply cheering loudly over a basketball game on television. No arrests were made.

Police were called to a disturbance at the Morongo Moose Lodge when arguments and fights broke out during a senior citizens' event. Attendees reported a strange feeling of euphoria and empowerment during the Bingo, which led to unwelcome sexual advances on the part of some attendees, as well as aggressive behavior on the part of others. Two adolescent youths were seen fleeing the club by the back entrance. Police are investigating; no charges have been filed.

Professor John Piczak, retired Dr. Emeritus of Chemistry at Morongo College, reported that bottles were missing from his basement and warned that they contained a substance that was potentially toxic and should be returned immediately, no questions asked.

One hastens to point out that the Police Blotter in the Morongo Express doesn't always get things right. The notes of crimes and events, so hastily scribbled by Police Captain Wendy Corcoran as her shift is ending and she's late to pick up her kids at the Bide-a-Wee day care, are not only an incomplete literary form, but shoddy journalism as well. The editors of the Express, who are under their own deadline pressures, never check the items, much less question them. Nevertheless, the Police Blotter is the most popular and widely discussed item in the paper every week.

One might take the first item, for example, about the tenant who returned to the Morongo Marina to find that his boat had been vandalized over the winter. Stroking our long, gray beards, we might reasonably ask, "How did he know that the vandals had struck in the winter? Did they pee their names in the snow that collected on the awning of the marina above the boat in question? Did they leave heavy woolen mittens and a mysterious black scarf at the scene?"

It's just one of many possible conclusions suggested by the template that is the Police Blotter. How about this one: Clearing our throats and waving our cigars at the jury of our peers, we might continue, "And [furthermore], what was the nature of this alleged act of vandalism? Was the boat ruined? If so, could it be that the affable, but dim-witted dockboy at the Morongo Marina had mistakenly unlatched the stay on the boat hoist of the vessel in question, causing the hoist's iron lifting wheel to spin crazily and out of control, which in turn caused the boat to crash down hard on the dock and crack its polymer keel? That only happens about twice a year at the marina.

"Or [we conclude, wheeling to face the tenant with an accusing finger jabbing at his chest] could the damage have had anything to do, your honor, with the fact that the tenant of the Morongo Marina had recently received disastrous news of his aluminum-siding business failing in Waterloo, and needed some fast insurance money to forestall the leg-breaking efforts of a certain Marino, DiFlaccio and SanFillipo collection agency in the tougher part of inner-city Rochester?"

Just asking. It's always good to ask.

As with most things Police Blotter, there is a story behind the Moose Lodge incident, as it came to be known in the days and weeks following the publication of the preceding item in the Express. Since neither embellishment nor explanation was offered by the police, the newspaper or the Moose themselves, it was left to the patrons of the Morongo Diner, the Wagonwheel and Bucky's to fill in the meaning of the story. They needed a few factual details to make sense of the item, so they made them up themselves. This they did unhesitatingly and with a kind of sense of civic duty. Their stories were, of course, rumors. But this is what really happened.

"Nice of you to show up," Jodi Bullock said to Daniel in the field behind Knapp & Schlappi Hardware. It was a week after they had become a couple thanks to a shared, bitter-orangey swig or two of John Piczak's home-brewed snops. What a lousy week! Daniel was having visions all week long of people dying and Jodi was SO EMBARRASSED that her new boyfriend was acting so – she wanted to give him the benefit of the doubt, but is there any other way to put this? – weird. She loved him as dearly as life itself, but doubts had begun to creep in, and she had no choice but to consider dumping him. Her friends, and they were many, were thrilled for her, yet watchful, ebullient over her good fortune but suspicious, hopeful for her lasting happiness and a large and vocal family to spring forth from their union, yet fairly clear that Jodi could do better. I mean, they said, he's SOOOO good-looking, but this weirdness of his is a new thing that merits careful consideration. All week long at school, by means of passed notes, furtive conversations, subtle hand and facial expressions and gestures, and shouted communications from one end of the hallway to the other, they discussed the permutations and possibilities of the Bullock/Jensen coupling at length, like diplomats with guaranteed contracts.

Daniel's friends, many of whom wrestled interscholastically, were less interested in exploring subtle details. They grunted, "Didja bang her yet?" He growled, "What do YOU think, shitferbrains?" They punched each other on the arm several times, and then slunk off to borrow lunch money from the punier of the freshmen. This was money, one might add, that would eventually be paid back not by the borrowers themselves, but by future generations of puny freshmen.

The federal government works much the same way. But one digresses…

The upshot was that Jodi was charged with divining his true intentions, not to mention his relative sanity, and squeeze a proclamation of unending *amour* from Daniel's thin lips, as the students in Miss Finnerty's French 201 class might put it. And if no such proclamation were forthcoming, she was to drop him like a greased chihuahua. She set the terms of their meeting: The old soccer field behind Knapp & Schlappi Hardware. On Friday. Weapons? Sarcasm and sexual allure (in the form of Flaming Passion Red lipstick, filched from the cosmetics department of the Wal-Mart in Geneva). Rules? No rules, baby, this is love.

When she said "Nice of you to show up" as a way of greeting him, a reasonable person might conclude that Daniel was late. Actually, Daniel had arrived before Jodi, and was surprised to feel a glow of warmth emanating from the rusted old incinerator can that had been sitting behind the hardware store for time immemorial, a warmth that seemed to suggest that he draw nearer to it. There was nothing but a pair of sodden, old athletic socks and a wad of blackened aluminum foil in the bottom of the can, but it seemed to hold a residual warmth – the memory of past fires. Daniel slouched against the can and enjoyed the feeling that seeped through his blue jeans and black hooded sweatshirt.

Jodi didn't know this herself – didn't even much think about it -- but her greeting was not so much about punctuality as it was about tone. She had decided instinctively that theirs would be a relationship based on sly suggestion bordering on accusation, on near-constant challenges and denunciations that were intended to confuse and irritate, followed by glorious reconciliations that allowed love to blossom in its fullest form. The strategy had worked well enough for her parents, who couldn't seem to stand being in the same room together yet had been married and inseparable for nearly a year longer than Jodi had been alive, and she reasoned that what was good for the Bullocks would be good for the future Jensens. She would proudly make Daniel's name her own, and she had already decided that as a tribute to her family, a nod to her past, their children would all receive B names: Brady, Brianna, Beth and (should they consider a fourth) Buddy.

Let's start again: Jodi arrived at the incinerator can behind Knapp & Schlappi Hardware and said, "Nice of you to show up" to Daniel, who was slouched against the can warming himself.

Daniel said, "Yeah."

But it was a heartfelt "yeah," a "yeah" that registered relief, a touch plaintively, because Daniel had things on his mind, too. Number one, he was relieved to see her, because the betting had been heavy on the corner where the boys smoked that she wouldn't show up, with odds approaching three to one. Also, he was relieved upon seeing her that he was receiving no advance notice of her death, because after a week of imagining teachers keeling over from heart attacks and liver failure, parents expiring in flaming car wrecks and the odd classmate slumping over from a drug overdose and making a mess of his World Civilizations notes, the news of his girlfriend's longevity -- or absence of demise, which was practically the same thing

-- was more than welcome. It wasn't that Daniel saw the fates of everyone whom he encountered, but he had had enough disturbing visions in the last seven days of friends and strangers alike that he had begun to fear what he might see next. He was eager to see if Jodi was having the same visions, and wondered how she was handling them so cheerfully.

Jodi looked at him quizzically, her almond eyes narrowing, eyebrows raised and an expectant, if challenging smile on her lips. "What IS your problem?" she asked. Coming from some girls, the tone of this statement might have been construed as harsh and mean-spirited (Becky Sorrentino, a field hockey player and fellow sixth-period Language Artist, comes instantly to mind), but Daniel heard the lilt in Jodi's voice and the implicit suggestion that he need only to play along, be the straight man in her routine.

"Problem?" he said like a tough guy. "I don't have no stinking problem."

The reply delighted her and her eyes narrowed as her smile grew, and then she stepped forward quickly and lightly and kissed him on the mouth. She stepped back just as quickly and told him a lengthy story about a bracelet that she had misplaced earlier that morning and the responses of a half-dozen girls whom she had enlisted to help find it.

When she seemed to be finished, Daniel took her by the wrist, pulled her close, which took a moment because she squirmed but then capitulated, and wrapped his arm around her lithe waist under her fur-lined parka, where his fingers came to rest on the inch of bare skin above the loops of her jeans. She craned her face away from his but watched his eyes closely and didn't try to escape his grasp, because they were a couple. Then he said something weird and ruined everything.

"Do you ever think about people dying?" he asked.

She studied his eyes for a moment, her heart sinking because it was all true, he was hot and he was weird and perhaps she should see what Jimmy Delamore was planning that weekend (he had a knack for scoring beer).

"I have snops," she replied, "want a drink?"

The reply made sense to Daniel. He made a gesturing motion with his hand, and she opened her knapsack and pulled out a plain, green wine bottle from John Piczak's basement. The bottle was full and was sealed by a cork that was pushed down flush with the lip of the bottle.

Daniel had told himself that he wasn't going to touch the stuff again; it indeed did make him weird, and he didn't like the taste of it, and he had reiterated so many times in conversations with friends that he would never stoop to doing something he disliked just to curry favor with a girl…no girl was worth it, the popular wisdom went…and he told himself that he just wanted to see and heft the bottle again and reassure himself that it was real. Despite all this, he wished very much that the cork protruded enough for him to be able to bite the end of it with his teeth and pull it out, because that might please Jodi enough to make her kiss him again and perhaps linger a moment or two near his face so that he could kiss her back this time. He noticed too that when he held the bottle of snops in his hand, Jodi's eyes studying him expectantly, the incinerator can behind him seemed to go up a noticeable ten degrees and be almost too hot, but not quite, to slouch against.

New and not entirely clear about this particular path of seduction, Daniel wondered if he was expected to have a wine opener on his person. Did the junior and senior boys carry corkscrews? He made a mental note to find out, and decided that honesty was the best policy.

"How are we supposed to open this?" he asked.

Jodi's eyebrows flickered up. "Why don't you tell me?"

He was stymied by this lobbing of the ball into his court, this topspin return of love, and looked around as if he might find a corkscrew lying in the weeds behind Knapp &

Schlappi Hardware. He thought briefly about trying to smash the bottle down quickly and incisively on the edge of the incinerator can to knock off its last two inches and allow them to drink deeply of its contents, but the thought of jagged glass flying, jagged glass raised to his lips in an invitation to drink and all of that bitter snops in his mouth and in his mind stopped him.

"Doesn't this stuff make you feel like crap?" he asked her.

This time Jodi did pull away from his encircling grasp. This was entirely unacceptable, she thought hotly. He doesn't like to drink? She felt her love slipping away. "What do you mean?" she asked. She was reluctant to reveal that the snops had not in fact, made her feel anything at all. It was a drink, you drank it, you got drunk together on whatever it was, and then you talked for a week about how drunk you had been.

Daniel's cheeks flushed for two reasons: Because he thought it was obvious, and because he had been caught making a genuine statement. He looked away and tried to salvage some semblance of being cool and mysterious, and he mumbled, "I don't know, it just makes me feel, like, weird. Like I see things in people that I don't want to see. It's nothing. It's just stupid."

Christ!, feelings are so instantaneous and so annoying. She liked him again because he was being sweet, although she dared not return the sweetness. She giggled. "It just makes me feel sexy," she confided.

Daniel suddenly remembered something else that made her feel sexy, and he reached into a zippered pocket on his parka and pulled out a cigarette and a lighter. He expertly lit it and took a drag, and then wordlessly handed the cigarette to Jodi. Or rather, he turned the cigarette and tried to put it to her lips, which had always seemed to him the very height of nuance and unspoken yet sizzling attraction when he had seen it done in the movies. But Jodi quickly moved her head away and reached for the cigarette with her hand. She grasped it and took a long, expert drag, which she blew out from the side of her mouth while locking eyes on Daniel. She didn't offer the cigarette back.

It was then that Daniel looked up and saw, as if for the first time, the Moose Lodge that had always been there, next door to the hardware store, but had been studiously ignored by the young people of Morongo for so many decades that it may as well have been a mirage constructed solely for the pleasure of people over forty. "I'll bet they have a corkscrew in there," he said knowingly. Jodi looked over her shoulder to see what he meant, saw the Moose Lodge herself for the first time ever, and without another word, Jodi took the bottle of snops from him, put it back into her knapsack, took a hasty last drag of the cigarette, threw it into the incinerator can, and turned her back on Daniel and began to run towards the Lodge's rear entrance. Daniel watched a moment, a slow, weary smile making its way onto his lips, and then followed her at a trot calculated to catch up with her in time to encircle her waist with his arm for the last twenty yards before the door. Mission accomplished, and she laughed when he reached her and kept running as she leaned against him.

  The door was cracked open and propped by a chair that had been pushed against it from the inside. It was a service entrance to the Moose Lodge's kitchen, a large industrial space that was rented out to community groups for picnics and gatherings and was rudimentarily stocked with odd lots of silverware, donated aluminum pots, kettles large enough to make chili for a hundred, and stainless steel racks and countertops. There was nobody inside the kitchen, but the door was opened that revealed the meeting hall inside, which was set with rows of tables and had begun to fill up with Moose and other elderly Morongans.

  Bingo Night: A Morongo senior citizen wouldn't miss it for the world.

  Trespassing is so much easier on the second date. Like many young couples, Jodi and Daniel had found something that they liked to do together, so they did it often and well. Holding hands and nervously looking into the shadows of the room, they slowly walked into the kitchen, each constructing an alibi in their mind should they be confronted by a Mooseian officer or elder. Daniel's was, "Is this the meeting of the baseball team?" because he had friends who played on the Babe Ruth league team sponsored by the organization. Phil Chapman, for example, was a Moose and had been since he was twelve and was bumped up to Babe Ruth from Little League because of a premature ability to grow facial hair and terrify the younger batters with both his above-average fastball and his whiskered glower.

  Jodi's excuse was, "I'm just with him and he said it was okay." Both of them were ready to flee on the slightest provocation.

  But no provocation came. They never do in these kinds of stories. Using non-verbal signals that they'd learned from the movies, they fanned out and began to case the room, opening drawers and cabinets. The only sounds were their breathing, the click and scrape of stainless-steel cabinetry and the murmur of voices from the meeting hall. On his way to one set of cabinets, Daniel pressed himself against a wall, stealthily reached out to the top of the door that separated the kitchen from the meeting hall, and gave it a tug that allowed it to swing shut. Jodi was so thrilled that she opened her narrow eyes as wide as she could and bit her lip as if to stifle a whoop of triumph. At the moment, every single thing seemed to her to be the funniest thing she'd ever seen or done.

It was Daniel who found the drawer that contained an old, rusty corkscrew, and he triumphantly held it aloft over his head and waved it. Jodi flew across the kitchen and jumped on him, almost knocking him into a stack of pans on a shelf that would have made a terrific crashing sound had they fallen. Trying hard not to impale her with the corkscrew, he held her with his free arm and regained his balance and they both cramped the roofs of their mouths with barely suppressed shouts of laughter.

"Open it, open it," Jodi stage-whispered as she danced around him and pulled the green bottle of snops from her knapsack. The corkscrew was old and barely up to the task, and Daniel had to re-screw it deeper into the cork twice, and then put the bottle between his legs and pull with all of his might before the cork released its grip and slid out with a popping sound that made them wince back laughter again. He held the bottle to her triumphantly, but she flapped her hands at him excitedly.

"You try it. Go on."

Daniel cocked his head and made an if-you-insist motion with his left eyebrow, tilted the bottle back and took a cautious swallow. Same old snops: Bitter, orangey, ashes. Highly overrated as a beverage.

Satisfied at his level of commitment, Jodi reached for the bottle and took a long pull herself, made a face and wiped her mouth with her sleeve. At that moment the door swung open and Miss Finnerty, the French teacher, walked into the kitchen with an anxious bustle. She didn't recognize the children (Daniel took Spanish, Jodi was undecided about her language requirements) and seemed only mildly interested in their presence in the kitchen.

Jodi thought, "Oh shit."

Daniel thought, "You're going to go into the hospital for gall bladder surgery and come out with a staph infection that will kill you."

Jodi stood as still as one can stand, and her eyes narrowed as she studied Miss Finnerty. She had long suspected that she could make herself invisible to adults by willing them to ignore her as she observed them carefully. Daniel, who had no such powers, chose a different tack.

"We were just getting the punch ready," he offered.

Miss Finnerty, who was looking in the refrigerator for something, looked at him as if she were seeing him for the first time. She saw the green bottle that was in Daniel's hand, Jodi having adroitly slipped it to him when the door opened, and her eyes flickered behind her glasses. Her mind registered, in this order, students, bottle, corkscrew. It all added up to an unwelcome duty that had been thrust upon her as an educator in the community, much like a volunteer firefighter must leave dinner and ballgame on TV when the siren blows.

"Is that wine?" she asked. "Are you children drinking?"

Daniel made motions and facial expressions of the what?-this? variety. Jodi spoke up quickly. "We don't know what it is," she said in a wheedling tone. "We were trying to find out. For the punch."

Miss Finnerty walked towards them and held her hand out for the bottle. Daniel reluctantly handed it to her. Jodi eyed the outside door. Miss Finnerty sniffed the bottle and made a face, and then delicately touched a drop of the snops on the rim of the bottle and tasted it. She handed the bottle back to Daniel.

"This juice has turned," she said. "I wouldn't put it in the punch. You'll find the rest of the ingredients in the refrigerator. Cups and trays on the counter over there." She opened a drawer and found what she had been looking for, a pie server, and left the kitchen without another word.

Of course they put the snops in the cups. Wouldn't you? But only a little bit, a few drops in each cup with the ginger ale and fruit juice. They had just finished filling the cups when two elderly men came into the kitchen and took the trays with only palsied shakes of the head and wry smiles by way of greeting to the two children, and they didn't stick around for the ensuing night of bingo, fistfights and unwelcome sexual advances on the part of certain patrons who were suddenly feeling young and frisky again, the degree of youth and friskiness [this was never reported or even suspected] in direct proportion to the amount of punch consumed.

Before they left, Daniel pointed to an elderly man who was sitting at the table nearest the kitchen door. The man was looking around vacantly, watching the action of bingo night with a kind of drooling, dim awareness that suggested a strong possibility that he believed himself to be home watching television. Daniel stared at him intently. "Watch that guy," he said to Jodi, pointing to the old man. "Look, you see that he's going to die soon, right? Now watch." Somebody handed the old man a paper cup of punch and he absently drained it.

"Now you can't tell how he's going to die," Daniel said triumphantly. "Did you see that?"

Jodi looked at him with an expression bordering on rapture. She didn't have the faintest idea what he was talking about, but he was more handsome and dashing than any boy with whom she'd ever broken and entered. "See what?" she asked.

"The stuff," Daniel said impatiently. "You don't know how they're going to die after they drink the stuff. That's the great thing about it."

Jodi shook her head, alarmed and suddenly cognizant of the amount of work her new boyfriend would take to be broken in properly. "No it isn't," she said firmly. "The great thing about the stuff is the way it makes me feel when I'm with you. And I'll prove it to you."

Daniel stared at her. "Are you telling me that the snops doesn't make you see things? How could that be?"

Jodi made a flirtatious face. "Guess I'm just lucky that way," she said.

"We have to get this stuff to every single sick person in town," he said.

She looked at him and shook her head. "God takes care of sick people," she said. (Her upstate accent made God rhyme with "awed.") She raised her eyebrows conspiratorially. "Why don't we sell it? If we gave it to the doctors, they would just sell it, right? My mom says they charge a fortune for medicine that doesn't cost a dime to make."

Daniel had to admit that she was right.

The police blotter is so wrong sometimes. The two teenagers in question – the persons of interest, as Chief Corcoran might put it -- did not flee the club at all by the back entrance. Fleeing implies flight, menace, and an intention of malice. These two teenagers simply propped open the back door wider with the folding chair and walked out, deliberately and arm in arm, laughing hysterically and all the while shouting, "That was so great!"

WHEREIN our narrators CRUISE TO Alaska And experience ALASKAN SPLENDOR, which includes a CHAMPAGNE RECEPTION with the CAPTAIN

The cruise to Alaska, when I first boarded the Royal Precious Platinum, was nice. I saw a bear. I bought a t-shirt in Skagway that said, "Whiskey: It's not Just for Breakfast Anymore" on one side and "Skagway: Gateway to Gold" on the other. I didn't know it at the time, but it would become my wedding gift to my new wife, Irmi. At the open market in Anchorage, I bought an ulu – "The legendary knife of the Yukon" – for my mother, who loves kitchen gadgets. It rained a lot, but in Glacier Bay National Park we had a clear view of the Marjorie Glacier – to my mind the pin-up girl of glaciers, with her bright white façade coyly revealing toothpaste-blue depths. As we exited the park, I remember eating an obscene amount of pasta primavera, short ribs, osso buco and chocolate cheesecake, and perhaps that is where the idea came to me that I could just stay on the ship and become a bigger person.

I recall from that first cruise the feeling that the Royal Precious Platinum was very comfortable, and the food was sensational. Of course, I was able to move about freely on board the ship, and leave it for shore excursions at every port, because I was a paying customer that week. I became a freeloader the week after, when the ship headed south from San Francisco to take in the sights of Baja Mexico. When all of the Alaska passengers disembarked, overfed and over-entertained from nights of ballroom dancing and Broadway musical revues, I stayed on. I wasn't satisfied. If good food and good wine, comfortable shelter and the company of likeable people are the stuff of life itself, then I was indeed intent on stuffing myself with life, until life made me burst.

I'm funny that way. I have an unusual affinity for cruise-ship life.

They try to sell you on new cruises all the time when you're on board, so it wasn't hard to simply book myself on the next six sailings in a row, and then a dozen more after that. I knew that my credit card would eventually throw up its mercenary hands at some point and say, "No mas!," but I figured that I would just deal with that when I had to. I became something of a fixture on board the Platinum, and a kind of tubby mascot to the crew, which was used to never seeing the same faces two weeks in a row and offered me that instant fellowship that comes from living in close quarters in a tight community.

They were either very generous or very sloppy in their bookkeeping, because I had the run of the ship for far longer than I imagined. In fact, it took the ship's purser about two months to figure out that I didn't have any money. They politely slipped an invoice under my door every night after that for a solid month. And then another month passed with almost no mention of my situation before the First Mate, manning the gangway in Hong Kong on a sparkling November morning, kindly informed me that I was not allowed to leave the ship until my bill was settled. They were afraid that I might bolt, Shanghai-ing myself to China. Even after that, fully three more months and a dozen cruises passed before they threatened to kick me off entirely, thus forcing me into the solitary, if utterly comfortable confinement of Penthouse Suite #1125. I believe that my tab is roughly $300,000 right now, not counting port taxes and gratuities, but to be honest, I haven't been keeping track.

I think that in this regard the Royal Precious management has been more than generous; Carnival Cruise Lines, for example, will kick you out if you get two weeks behind on the rent, I hear.

Can you believe me now when I say that I weighed just one-hundred-eighty pounds when I boarded the ship that first week? I know that it's hard to imagine. The archives of my weight gain are now being kept by the ship's photographers; I suspect I've become something of a documentary project for them. It started with the obligatory pictures that they try to sell you of your cruise. They snap you in front of a dopey set consisting of a life ring when you first board the ship, and then again a few days later at the Captain's Welcome Cocktail Reception, smiling hugely in your tuxedo alongside a florid Dutchman in a uniform. The snapshots are posted for all to see in the photo studio on the Tiffany Deck, and if you don't buy them, as I never do, they can stay there for months.

    This went on for the six months that I could move freely about the ship, my comings and goings documented by pictures that I never bought. Somebody – no doubt an aspiring documentarian among the shipboard photographers – had the bright idea of displaying my photos sequentially, and here we see the portraits of a man who is undergoing a startling transformation. The man who boards the Royal Precious Platinum in San Francisco for the Alaskan Splendor cruise is lean and (dare I say it?) handsome, even. A few weeks later the photos show that the same man at the Panama Canal has grown chubby, his eyes *puffy, his jawline lost to a rime of fat. In Valparaiso two cruises later he looks sweaty and jowly, his shirt bulging over his inflated chest. From jowly we go in successive portraits, from successive voyages, to round-faced to florid to fleshy, and finally, to ponderous, with a balloon-sized face sagging into an open-collared shirt that is clearly four sizes too small. In the final picture, taken at the last Captain's Cocktail Reception that I was allowed to attend, the Dutch captain, who serves as a constant in the photographic series and has nearly the exact pose and expression on his face each week, is nearly dwarfed by a fat man bulging out of a tux, the living caricature of the slender man from just a few photos back on the shelf.*

That's some syndrome, that Cruise Ship Syndrome. Skinny people in, fat people out.

And that was just in the first six months of my weight-gain experiment, my unprecedented embracing of the Syndrome. The photographers now come to my cabin to snap me -- sometimes naked, sometimes wearing props that they bring, sometimes in the robes and caftans that are now the only things I can wear. I think that they're making a book about me. (I'm reasonably sure that they're not displaying these images on the Tiffany Deck; bad for business.) Which is nice; it brings some art to their dreary, ship-board existences. It's not easy being a cruise ship photographer. Art is one thing worth living for, I suppose.

And so is food. Oh, my goodness, the food. When I had the run of the ship, I went to every buffet, and besides getting utterly hooked on coconut rice pudding, I ate delicious terrines of quail and aspic, mowed my way through the Asian Delights tables laden with pancit, satays, trays of sushi and sashimi and crab Rangoons, and asked for seconds on everything from the beef Wellingtons to the baked Alaskas that were borne, flaming and triumphant, through the dining room by liveried Filipino waiters. Sometimes I would graze the luncheon buffet on the Lido deck, arriving early and eating my fill of Veal Oscar, Steak Frites, fresh-baked rolls and four kinds of pie, and then go quickly, with a fat man's comic, urgent waddle, to make the last luncheon seating in the main Dining Room on the Crystal Deck. Walter, the Austrian Maitre d'Hotel would graciously seat me and I'd force myself to eat turbot in hollandaise sauce, spatzle and chocolate souffle. And then I'd stop in the Cappucino Café on the way back to my cabin for a handful of the delightful custard tarts that were always out and available.

Yes, Mr. or Ms. Disapproving Reader, Mr./Ms. Temperance & Discipline (you Frugal Fannies, you Lean Whippets, you Lap Runners on the Promenade Deck and

Treadmill Gerbils in the Salon & Spa) I did overindulge. I did want to get grotesquely large, and if the truth be told, I couldn't get fat fast enough. I wanted my health to fail, and I rejoiced when walking up the stairs from the Penthouse Deck to the Lido Deck made me wheeze, and when I began to make the elevators groan from the strain of bearing me up and down. You see, from that first week of Alaskan Splendor, when I was utterly in despair and unsure of what to do with my unraveling life, I was evolving a plan. And the plan grew directly out of the buffets. I decided that I needed to become a larger person in order to live my life to the fullest. I wanted to process a lot of calories. And frankly, I wanted to give my heart every opportunity to fulfill its destiny, whatever destiny that was. Finally, I wanted very badly to not talk myself into jumping off my balcony into the ocean, and eating myself to death was the most satisfying way that I knew how to do that.

  I take all of my meals in my cabin now, of course. Costas, my loyal Portuguese butler, brings me anything I want, but it's not the same as the total abandon suggested by buffet tables brimming with attractively packaged calories. I miss being able to go to the dining room now, and my goodness, how I long for the buffets. Walter sometimes comes by late at night after his shift is over to play cards with me. He often brings a slice or two of the best dessert of the night. For my birthday, he even sent a procession of three liveried Filipino waiters to my cabin with fully domed Baked Alaskas that they doused with brandy and lit on fire once they were inside and the door was closed. He would have caught hell from the officers if they carried flaming anything down the ship's hallways, but in my room, with the lights off, the desserts burned merrily and it made for quite a show. Costas sang me the birthday song in Portuguese.

It was nice. I served everyone myself, and then ate as much Baked Alaska as I could possibly stand, but even I couldn't get through three of them. My cabin was a sticky mess of melted ice-cream and little browned gobs of meringue for a week afterwards.

A Guy Named Brad finally emerged from the bathroom and attended another story conference. He had a furtive look about him and we all knew he was up to something. He kept biting his lip and nodding, all the while making sharp, pointed mosquito sounds that had the rest of us slapping the air in front of our noses.

"I've got it figured out," he said. "I know how to get rid of the pain."

"Wish I could get rid of the pain," grumbled Floyd Little. "The pain in my ass that is you."

Brad ignored the insult. "I'll take care of the next part," he said. "I'll be God."

So we let him. What did we have to lose? It was just a story, after all.

Chapter Six
FARRELL JR. MEETS A GUY NAMED BRAD

    To call what happens at the Wagonwheel between the hours of five and seven p.m. "happy hour" is being a trifle optimistic. For one thing, the place isn't exactly the Rainbow Room at Rockefeller Center. A kind of gloom descends over the bar and dining room of the Wagonwheel as dusk arrives in Morongo, a heavy realization that nothing has changed through breakfast and lunch, the men's bathroom still has a suspicious puddle on the floor, the toilets still want to be resealed, the yellow floor will still reflect up a yellow, dingy light from the yellow overhead lights, and Charlie Sheen and Rebecca Romjin, accompanied by their friends Bruce Willis (wearing a porkpie hat and carrying a harmonica) and Elle MacPherson (exuding Australian supermodel cheer), will not burst through the door spreading Hollywood buzz before them like shotgun pellets.

    Nor will love blossom between a rich Morongo College girl whose family owns a significant waterfront parcel on Long Island and a plucky local boy whose dickwalter family pumps out the septic tanks of Dundee. Sure, it could happen, but not tonight.

Nor will anyone, man or woman, suddenly slam his mug of Genesee Cream Ale down onto a table, smite his own forehead at how OBVIOUS it was, shout for pen and paper in the form of a cocktail napkin, and jot down an equation/mission statement/chemical formula/first sentence that, some years later, will lead to a non-polluting engine that runs on dirt/an international relief agency that fixes Africa/the cure for cancer/a novel that changes everything. Not tonight; not in this gin joint in this town.

What this Happiest of Hours does feature is Farrell Jensen Jr. sitting at the bar, sopping up pitchers of discount-priced suds with A Guy Named Brad, who is one of the core group of Wagonwheel regulars.

A Guy Named Brad was born and raised in Morongo, but not on the lake. Resents the hell out of anyone from Rochester; he figures they're all snots. Somewhere between the age of twenty-five and thirty-five; somewhere between $8,000 and $25,000 annual income, depending on the local need for roofing. Married shortly after high school to a girl who didn't remain a cheerleader for long. Smokes like an AMC Gremlin. Wears a greasy

John Deere cap over his longish hair, a parka, dirty overalls over a t-shirt, and work boots.

Having skipped the usual pleasantries about family and work -- both of them have too much of the one and too little of the other -- they have jumped right into the larger issues of life.

"I've got one," says A Guy Named Brad. "Here it is. I knew this guy? He's a cook, right, down to the Antique Inn. Lost his nuts to cancer when he was a kid. He's like eleven years old and he gets cancer in his nuts and they cut the damn things off. Guy never wants sex, never gets any tail, don't even know what he's missing. He has to go through the rest of his life without the jewels. And then a few years went by when he was okay? And then when he's like twenty-five, the cancer comes back, but this time it's in his tongue, and they cut half of it off to save his life again. He's a trained chef, but now he can't even taste the food he's making. And now the guy walks around with no nuts and half a tongue and he can barely swallow so he drinks all his food with a straw, even his beer. Wonders every single day why he hasn't died. And I'm just wondering, what's up with that? If God is so goddamned benevolent, why did he do that to that guy?"

Farrell takes a long drink of beer and nods, appearing to mull it over. "That's fucked up," he finally offers.

"Why would God do that to a person?" asks Brad. (His flat, mid-Atlantic accent makes God rhyme with "odd.") "Why would he do that to humanity? I mean, what's the fucking point of that? Guy walking around with no balls and no tastebuds. If God's looking out for all of us, he sure dropped the ball with this guy. You believe in God?"

Farrell shrugs his shoulders and pours more beer. He feels an odd, tingling pain in his left bicep, a soreness that runs down to his elbow. He wonders where it came from, because he hasn't done any work in a month and his muscles shouldn't be sore. In answer to Brad's question, he believes in the pain in his arm.

"If you do," says Brad, "then answer me this. Why the fuck do babies and little children die? What good does that do anyone; how does that serve humanity? What's up with cancer? If we have to die, okay, so be it. Everything dies, I suppose, but I don't really understand why it does me any good to know it. The dogs are better off than us. One minute they're taking a crap in the yard, the next minute they're dead, and they don't even know what dead is. But if you believe in God, then I have to ask you. Why does he make us die painfully? What good does it do anyone to feel excruciating pain, especially before they die? It's not like you learn some kind of lesson from the pain."

Farrell burps, a long rolling belch from deep down that sounds like, "Free will."

A Guy Named Brad refills his glass. "Don't give me that line about free will. I just don't need to hear about free will. So imagine you're God, right?"

Farrell nods.

"So you're omnipotent, right? That means you can do anything that you want to do. You created the fucking word omnipotent, right? So couldn't you have made free will exclusive of tremendous suffering? I mean, intense physical pain doesn't free my will up any for appreciating the beauty of life, you know what I mean? It just makes me hurt, and I don't learn a thing other than I hope it won't hurt anymore soon. You say that we all have to experience suffering in order to appreciate our lives? Okay, how about you make it so that at sixty-five years old we all stub our toe, and it hurts and we cry, and that's the suffering that we experience and it's over with. Know what I'm saying? Suffering doesn't have to, you know, make you suffer."

Farrell nods. He's thinking about the cemetery that he visited with his brother and his mother. He's thinking that the pain in his arm is getting worse, and wondering if he fell off a barstool or something that he doesn't remember that made his arm hurt so bad. He's thinking that he hopes it won't hurt anymore.

Brad is seized by a practically divine inspiration. The answer to the problem of pain is merely a design flaw. He waves his hand. "You're God, right? So when you made us, why didn't you just put a red light at the end of our nose? And instead of feeling pain or anguish, be it physical or spiritual suffering, the red light just goes on when something bad happens. Then it wouldn't hurt – we wouldn't actually experience the feelings of physical pain, or anguish, or suffering, or enormous grief as we do now. But everybody would say, 'Oh, look, the red light on his nose is lit up. He's hurting.' And grieving would just be a matter of waiting for the red light to fade out over time."

Farrell Jr. mulls that over, and nods his head. "A red light at the end of your nose," he repeats.

"Sure," says Brad, "something like that."

Farrell Jr. purses his lips and nods his head slowly. "That could work."

"Damn right it could work. I'll be damned if I know why God himself didn't think of it first."

Farrell puts his last five dollars on the table and lurches to his feet. His arm hurts very much at the elbow and he clutches it. He's sweating and feels shaky on his feet. He walks out the door of the Wagonwheel, pauses in the light, because he expected it to be dark, and then, holding his arm, he walks down the street in the direction of where he thinks he left his truck.

POODLE PLAYS God
HE STAYS

Floyd Little was one unhappy cardboard narrator. At the next story meeting, convened over a platter of crispy spring rolls, for we were steaming towards Vietnam, he lit into A Guy Named Brad.

"Lemme get this straight," Floyd says. "If you break your leg from a hard tackle, you don't feel nothing. A red light at the end of your nose just starts glowing like a damn reindeer."

"Yeah, something like that," mosquito-screams Brad. He is looking pretty pleased with himself and his new plot twist. Of all of us, he likes playing God the most.

"So how do you know that you broke your leg?"

"You can't walk, your leg swells up. You just know."

Poodle pipes up. "So your boyfriend breaks up with you just before your shift. And you go out there and wrap yourself around the pole, and you're not feeling a thing one way or the other, but a red light at the end of your nose is glowing, so everybody else knows?"

"Precisely."

Falubio chips in, "You just want to be happy all the time, and not feel sadness?"

"Why not?" asks a Guy Named Brad.

"What a boring life."

"I'm just saying," says Brad, and his voice is beginning, dangerously, to go up in pitch. "I'm just saying that there must be some other way. I'm just saying why does our heart have to break every time He farts? Why must we cry because our dad dies and we miss him? Why should we feel such pain when everybody dies, and it was just his turn?"

"Hey, how about this," says Falubio, grinning. "What if you break your leg AND your boyfriend breaks up with you AND your father dies on the same day. Sounds like the red light on your nose will explode then." He and Poodle crack up.

Floyd Little pretends to mull this over. "Sounds to me," he begins slowly, "that as your God, I recommend that what you need is to pull the red light out your butt."

Well, everyone is beside him or herself over that one. Poodle and Falubio high-five each other. I hide my snickers behind a ham-sized fist and a mouthful of spring roll. It takes a moment, but A Guy Named Brad finally realizes that we're laughing at him, not with him. Furious, he withdraws to the bathroom, screaming like a battalion of mosquitoes.

    I told you. Floyd Little is one sarcastic God.

    Three days later (and thousands and thousands of calories filtered through me) we are just leaving Sri Lanka, I believe, judging from the I ♥ Ceylon t-shirts that I am seeing out the window on my fellow cruise passengers. It is a Wednesday afternoon, time for my weekly story meeting, and this week the part of me that is Poodle gets to be God. She is very excited about this. She keeps clasping her hands in front of her and squeezing them.

    She turns to me and says, "I'm not going to last forever either, am I? Narrators die too, just like everyone else. How long do I have?"

    My other narrators pretend to look away or study their nails, but I can tell that they're interested in this, too. I can see that Floyd Little's grip on his football tightens a little, and Falubio's studied disinterest is a little too…method. I shrug my chubby shoulders and say, "I can't answer that. I don't know the end of the story yet."

    She says, "Certainly no longer than this book will last. And maybe even less than that, right?"

I nod and say, "People die in books all the time. It stimulates the plot, you know. So yeah, that's probably a pretty good bet."

And she says, "And you're okay with this power that you claim of just creating characters and then leaving us behind, killing us off in one way or another?"

And I say, "That's what fiction is. I can't change what it is."

And she says, "In your fiction, you feel like you can make anything happen, can't you?"

And I nod, pleased with my powers of creation, and say, "Yes, I do believe that. Within limits."

She says, "Could you make the moon split into four pieces and rain down molten gobs of flaming, smelly cheese onto North America?" Here, Falubio snaps to attention and says, "Yeah!" at the same moment that A Guy Named Brad shrieks from the bathroom, "No!"

And I say, "Why in the world would I want to do that?"

Poodle says, "But you could, couldn't you?"

And I say, "Yeah. If it really was necessary to the story, I suppose I could."

Floyd cuts in here. "What Miss Poodle appears to be saying, if I'm getting her right, is that the only chance *for us is maybe to introduce some new characters, tell a bunch of stories and make this book go on and on, isn't it?"*

I just look at him and make no-no-no motions with my head.

Poodle takes a deep breath. She has clearly been thinking about this for quite some time. "And I can make the world exactly the way that I want it, right? I'm God today, and I can create the world to be the way that I want it, and make my life be a dream of happiness and satisfaction and fulfillment, right?"

"I suppose," I say nervously, reaching for a cookie. I don't like where she is going with this. "It might be nicer if you did something for humanity, not just for yourself."

"The hell with humanity. Do you know what I want more than anything in the world?" she asks.

I don't bother to answer. I already know what's coming.

"Hello, Daddy," she says. She bursts into tears.

The patio door opens by itself, which is fairly terrifying when you're hundreds of miles out at sea, and in walks Professor Farrell Jensen Sr. He's wearing his professorial get-up of creased trousers, flannel shirt, sweater vest, blue blazer, Top-Siders. Without so much as a nod or a word, he walks over to the easy chair in the corner of the suite, sits down and opens a book and starts reading.

He looks every bit the fifty years old, two months and four days-old distinguished professor of literature from Morongo College that I remember from the day that he died. I should know what he looks like, after all. He is my father. And the part of me that is Poodle has brought him back.

At that moment, my heart breaks. I feel tears come out of my eyes, and I say, "Oh my God, Dad! What's it like to be dead?"

Farrell Sr. shrugs, puts his hand out flat in the air and waves it up and down, indicating to me that he can take or leave being deceased. He looks around the cabin once, takes in the narrative group, the sliding glass doors leading to the balcony, and the minibar and basket of fruit that Costas has replenished. He nods his head, satisfied. He can live with Penthouse Suite #1125. He doesn't say a word. In fact, we gather that he can't say a word. He has no physical presence, no ability to manipulate the air or the space around him. No sound is made when he sits down; the cushion of the easy chair doesn't dent. He makes a "just carry on" motion with his hand to all of us and continues to read his book.

Which is pretty much how I remember my Dad from childhood, his nose always in a book.

A Guy Named Brad screams from the bathroom, "You can't do this! You can't just bring back dead people."

Poodle is still crying, but they are happy tears. "Not dead people," she says. "Our daddy." She kneels down on the floor and hugs her face to the side of dad's incorporeal leg. "And sure I can bring him back," she says. "It's my turn to be God. And he's staying."

What can we do? He stays.

Chapter Seven
CHISPADORES (a dish of the GAUCHOS) and TELEMARKETERS

Why do I feel such pride, wondered Ray, that my son grew up? Why does this come as such a pleasant surprise, endlessly satisfying?

It was mid-afternoon, a Tuesday, and Ray had come home from work early to find Daniel eating cereal. Ray stood quietly at the kitchen door and watched his large boy shovel tablespoonfuls of grain into his trap until Daniel finally looked up.

"What are you looking at?" Daniel asked Ray with an accent he was trying out from old Robert DeNiro movies he had rented at the video store. A tough-guy accent, inflected with the streets of New York and beatings that left blood draining out of a guy's ears and eyes, although Daniel had never traveled farther from Morongo than Syracuse and the state fair. He was thrilled to see guys get punched in the face in movies, a reasonable response from someone who has never been punched in the face.

"I'm looking at a perfect eating machine," said Ray. "The ultimate cereal consumer, a beast that devours all that lies before him."

"You should be a writer, Daddy."

"Make me," said Ray.

Daniel grunted something unintelligible and resumed his feeding.

And what can you say to this? thought Ray. This feeling of paternal pride and love, this satisfaction over having accomplished something – the feeding, watering and growing of a human boy – despite everything? Through sheer dumb luck, stubborn determination, modern antibiotics and sanitation practices, and resisting all of the crap that had come between himself and Janice over the last dozen years – all of the clear outs she had provided for him, big doors with flashing neon EXIT signs through which Ray could have easily walked and left behind parenting duties and responsibilities – through these random forces of nature, Daniel had somehow grown up, and Ray was partially responsible. At fifteen years old, he was two inches taller than Ray, faster afoot than Ray had ever been and was ever likely to be, and by the way Daniel consumed grain and milk it was likely that he was not finished growing.

Ray remembered how his grandmother, during the last five years of her life, could sit for hours at the kitchen table of his aunt's house, gazing happily and with full beneficent senility at Ray and Farrell Jr., and repeat, "What a beautiful boy. Look at those shoulders," to no one in particular. Ray wondered aloud many times if perhaps Grandma might be better served by getting a hobby (not to mention a hubby, for Grandpa had been another early defector from life), but now he knew that she indeed had had a consuming interest, and it was in him. Or rather, in herself, and in basking on what she had achieved and begot, and would leave when she was gone. Almost as if having children and offspring made dying appear to be a personal choice, an option for the mature, spent organism to make at its leisure as it surveys the biological landscape that it has marked.

When Daniel was born, Ray remembered holding him and being visited by the thought, "When you grow up, baby boy, I die," as if the baby had suddenly and irrefutably placed Ray in a natural world of which he had only been vaguely aware. It was the conceit of parentless couples that they simply did not recognize the aging process, as if they had refused to read the clause, highlighted in our earthly owners' manuals, about the withering and dying of the human organism, absolutely no exceptions or substitutions allowed. But as any decent lawyer will tell you, not knowing the law does not make it waived for you; it just makes you ignorant of the law. Daniel made time begin for Ray, but it wasn't an unpleasant sensation of looming mortality. For Ray, it was more of a calming metronome sound ticking inside him that Daniel's gangly, ravenous presence allowed him to hear, a sound that reminded Ray to get on with his life.

The phone rang and Daniel answered it. As Ray read the mail in the living room, he heard, but did not listen to Daniel's conversation: "'lo? Yeah? That's right, s'long as you want to live. Immediate benefits. Huh? Fifty bucks. Cash money. Downtown, tonight. Christian coffee house. Yeah, that one. 'kay. Later."

And Ray thought: Homework. Friends. Rap music. Sophomore history of ancient Greece. Quiz on Friday. And then he forgot all about the phone call.

Daniel hung up the phone, put his spoon into the empty bowl and stood against the kitchen doorframe. "Dad, can I ask you something?"

"Sure, Dan, shoot."

"Why did Grandpa Farrell die?"

Ray was surprised by the question. They hadn't discussed his father's death, or his life for that matter, for several years. "He had a heart attack," said Ray. "He died suddenly of a heart attack."

Daniel wrinkled his nose. "Well, why? He must have had some symptoms or something. Did you ever find out why he had a heart attack?"

Ray shook his head. "Actually, we didn't. It happened so quickly. I was too young to ask any questions and Grandma Caroline was too upset to investigate it."

Daniel nodded his head. "I wish we knew."

"I wish so, too."

"How old was he when it happened?"

"He was fifty. The same age as your uncle."

"And you're, what, forty-eight?"

"Forty-seven."

"Dad?"

Ray looked up, surprised. The last time that Daniel had initiated a conversation was…well, Daniel had never initiated a conversation. "Go ahead."

"If you could have saved him, you would have, right? I mean, what happened on that day, that nobody could save him?"

Ray smiled sadly. "You know, I really don't remember. That whole period of my life is like a blank. Sure I would have saved him if I could have. He was my dad, and I loved him. Why are you thinking about this tonight?"

Daniel stood up and stretched, touching his fingertips to the ceiling of the kitchen. "I don't know. Probably thinking about those stupid kids in the car who almost died the other night." He turned his back to Ray and stretched again, and then surprised his father once again by turning back to him.

"You would save anyone you could, right? I mean, if they were sick or hurt or even dying and you could do something about it?"

"Sure. I guess I would if I could."

"And you're okay, right? I mean, you take that medicine for your heart all the time."

"I'm fine," said Ray. "I have a very mild heart condition, and the medicine is more of a precaution."

"That's good, Dad."

The phone rang again, and Daniel moved to answer it, but Ray was closer, and picked it up before the second ring.

"I want to live forever," said the caller.

Ray paused a moment to absorb this information. "And I want to kick a 65-yard field goal that wins the Superbowl for the Bills," he said. "Can you help me do that?"

There was silence on the other end of the line. "Thank you," said the caller, and hung up.

"Who's that?" asked Daniel.

"Telemarketer," said Ray.

"Weird," they both said together, and Daniel laughed.

"Shut up," he said, knowing that Ray had gotten to him with good timing.

"You shut up.

Daniel found a box of crackers and tucked them under his arm. "Got homework," he grunted. He turned and walked up the stairs, cracker crumbs flying from his mouth with every step.

And Ray thought admiringly, Look at the shoulders on that kid.

The phone rang again an hour later, but Daniel answered it before Ray could reach it, and Ray did not hear the conversation. He opened a bottle of red wine and poured himself a glass, found a frying pan and began to brown hamburger for dinner for himself and Daniel. He diced an onion and a green pepper and threw them into the pan, along with salt and pepper, and began to think of a name for the dish he was making, because Daniel always asked and Ray always had an answer. It was one of the games that they had been playing for nearly ten years, begun on Daniel's visitation nights and weekends.

As Ray cooked, the phone rang twice more, and he paused to listen, hoping that it was Donna calling from Rochester and waiting for Daniel to call downstairs, "Dad, it's for you." But Daniel never called downstairs, and Ray got through two glasses of wine before dinner was ready. He put four tortillas into the microwave and warmed them, and finished the hamburger with tomato paste, water and chili powder.

"What is it?" Daniel asked suspiciously when he came downstairs for dinner and looked at the frying pan.

"Beef chispadores," said Ray. "A favorite dish of the Argentine gauchos."

"Huh," said Daniel. "It looks a little bit like the Shlumberger Tacos from last week."

"I can see how you might think that," said Ray, "but there's really no comparison."

There was a giggle that sounded out of place from Daniel's gangly frame, and Ray looked up to see Daniel's girlfriend Jodi sitting at the kitchen table. How did she get in here? he wondered. Had she slipped into the cottage while he was cooking? While he was in the bathroom? It occurred to him that she might have been upstairs all along in Daniel's room, even before Ray got home. She was also wearing a hooded sweatshirt, with the Morongo Mustangs logo across the front, and a knit cap covered her short-cropped brown hair. Mousy hair, Ray thought, because there was always something about Jodi that he mistrusted. Her face was gaunt and white, with the barest glimmer of color in her cheeks, and she had narrow eyes of an indeterminate color that always made her look like she was squinting. She was thin and small, with faded jeans that were frayed and dirty where the pantlegs flopped over her black sneakers and dragged on the ground.

She giggled again. "Hello Mr. Jensen."

"Oh hello, Jodi," said Ray. "Nice to see you again." He put another tortilla into the microwave and warmed it for her. He knew from experience that she wouldn't eat, but would pretend to, tearing up the tortilla and pushing meat around on her plate, and that was yet another reason to mistrust her.

"You, too," she said. She looked at Daniel and giggled again, a conspiratorial laugh between thieves that established, it seemed to Ray, that of the three people in the room, one was clearly a witless dolt, and it was him.

"Would you like to join us for dinner?" Ray asked.

"I guess," she said.

Hey thanks, thought Ray, but he didn't say it. Thanks a lot. Thanks a MILLION. He got out a third plate and put it in front of Jodi. He put the tortillas onto another plate, and spooned the meat into a serving bowl, which he placed in the center of the table.

"The Argentine gauchos like to spoon a little of the beef chispadores onto a tortilla, roll it up and eat it by hand," he announced.

Jodi looked at Daniel and stifled another nervous laugh. She reached for a tortilla and gingerly put it onto her plate as if it might shortly grow tongues, and took the tiniest spoonful of ground meat. Daniel shoveled half of the bowlful of meat onto his tortilla, clumsily wrapped it up and began to devour it.

"How's school going?" Ray asked Jodi.

She looked up from her plate. "It's okay."

Ray flashed on the four base words from which spring all teenage communication: Cool, yeah, okay, huh?

"Got any tests this week?" he asked.

Daniel looked up from his chewing, as if aware of their presence for the first time. "We've got algebra on Friday. We were studying for it together."

Daniel began to rise from his chair, and finished his tortilla half-standing and leaning his face over the plate on the table. "Dad," he announced, "we have to go. We've got more studying to do, and all of the stuff is over at Jodi's house. Thanks for dinner." He looked at Jodi, and she stood up quickly.

Ray was halfway through his tortilla. He put it down on his plate. "You can't wait until dinner is over?" he asked.

"Dad, sorry, we're kind of running late," Daniel said. He came around the table and kissed Ray on the forehead. "I'll see you in a couple of days."

Jodi moved quickly towards the door. "Thanks for the dinner, Mr. Jensen," she said in her plaintive voice, the voice you use for obligatory communications with adults. She had learned that they were so easily appeased with formalities, that a girl just had to say the right thing in a chirping voice and they would get all sloppy-grinned and tell her mother what a good girl she was. The morons. The mental slugs. It was a wonder that anyone functioned after the age of thirty, as stupid as they got.

She picked up her backpack, and it looked heavy and awkward to Ray. Daniel reached for it and took it from her shoulder, and by the way it shifted Ray wondered if there might be…what?...bottles inside? Liquor bottles maybe, or wine? Or just books? He knew that Daniel and his friends refused to use their lockers at school to store their books, choosing instead to carry every book from every class all day long.

"That looks heavy," Ray said, as if that would allow him to look inside the backpack, to scrutinize its contents and make Daniel reveal everything to him, all of his secrets, all of his plans. But, of course, it would not only be awkward to ask to go through the backpack, but it wasn't Daniel's, it was Jodi's, and was even more off limits to Ray. Ray had an uneasy feeling that they knew that, too.

"I got it," Daniel said. "Bye, Dad."

Ten minutes later the phone rang again. "I want to live forever," said the caller.

"Join a health club!" Ray shouted, and slammed it down.

An hour later, while Ray was reading a magazine in the living room, the phone rang again. He hoped that it was Donna, and hoped even more that it wasn't Janice or another dying soul. He picked up the phone, said hello, and heard raspy breathing. He recognized immediately that it was another call that he didn't particularly care to take, but was stuck with. The breathing continued for a few more seconds, as if the caller was trying to catch his breath from the effort of punching in Ray's phone number, and then an elderly man's voice blurted out, "I knew your father."

Ray had heard this before, about three times a year for the last five years or so. It was John Piczak, a former friend and colleague of Farrell Sr. who still lived in Morongo. He was retired now, a professor emeritus of chemistry from Morongo College who attended graduation ceremonies every year in his bowtie and doctoral robes, looking a little older and more feeble each time. Ray rarely saw him outside of those functions, and never called the older man himself, but the memory of Farrell Sr. seemed to enter John Piczak's mind in some sort of semi-annual rotation that compelled him to call Ray, usually late at night.

The heavy breathing continued. "Hello, Professor Piczak. How are you tonight?" Ray asked, trying to keep the note of annoyance from his voice. He realized again that he wished the call had been from Donna, and hoped he would speak with her before bedtime.

"I knew your father," the older man said again.

"Yes, you were professors together," Ray said.

"Damn right we were."

There was another pause and more heavy breathing. Ray waited.

"I saw your son," Dr. Piczak continued. He said it in a tone that sounded accusing to Ray.

"Yes, he's getting big," Ray said, hoping that it might somehow be the key information that would allow the call to end.

"Very big." The heavy breathing continued.

"Is there anything that I can do for you, John?"

Pause. A gasp for air. And then, "Check the can," said John Piczak. "What you want to know, it's all in the can. I'm done with all of it. Stop bothering me. Keep your kid away from my house. I'm putting an end to all of this right now. Everything that you want to know, it's in the can." There followed a full thirty seconds of heavy breathing.

"I'm afraid that I don't know what you mean, John," said Ray.

"Damn all of you. Live forever." And then he hung up.

Remember the wine that Ray drank before dinner? Well, the first of those two glasses had a distinctive orangey, bitter quality to it that made Ray wrinkle his nose and inspect the wine bottle. He drank it nevertheless, and then drank the second glass, barely noticing the bitter taste by then. Why the sour grapes? There is a simple explanation: Daniel had crept down from upstairs with a small vial of the Piczak snops, aka the Fountain of Youth, in his hand. If Ray had seen him and said anything, Daniel was prepared with a story about the vial containing part of his chemistry homework, and an experiment was in progress. He would not have told his trusting old Dad that the experiment was on him, Ray. Daniel poured the snops into the wine bottle and swirled it around.

The experiment was a huge success. When Daniel came down for dinner with Jodi, and looked his father in the eye, he relaxed and smiled. He no longer knew how Ray was going to die.

THE NARRATORS
the WISDOM of the PORTUGUESE; fastball DOWN the PIPE

"We have a saying in my native Portugal," Costas is telling me, "that a man's words do not necessarily reflect his meaning."

He is standing expectantly by the door, and as usual, I don't know what the hell he is talking about. He lingers like he expects a tip from me or something, which we both know is ridiculous. And then it hits me all at once that he has been reading my manuscript, about Ray and Daniel and that little snot Jodi, and something is not sitting right with him.

"You have a problem with something in the book?" I ask politely.

Costas is the only person who has been reading what I write, and I appreciate anything he can offer. In fact, I cling to his observations as I would to a lifebuoy thrown out to me in the ocean. It had better be a pretty damn big lifebuoy, while we're on the subject, because I see that I have recently passed 520 pounds on the health-o-meter in my bathroom, a figure that both pleases and appalls me simultaneously.

"No, it's not a problem," he says. His butler training would never allow even the hint of a conflict between himself and a client (me), not even a whisper in the air of a disagreement. "It's no problem at all. I am just a little [he pronounces it 'leetle'] confused about the can. That is all. It's nothing, really."

My pleasantly round mug twists into something of a perplexed expression. I do not want to suggest anything here, but maybe Costas' English is not as good as I imagined.

"What can?" I ask. "Which can? What are you talking about?"

He takes a sharp little breath. He is on delicate butler ground here, I can tell. Uncharted waters, as it were, from his formal training. He does not want to appear to contradict me. "It is just there, at the end of the last page," he says respectfully. "The elderly man, the one with the heavy bad breath, is talking about the can."

"Let me see that," I say. I roll up to my feet, get all body parts centered and moving in the same direction, and waddle over to where he is standing. He formally hands me the manuscript as if it were a note from the Queen on a silver platter. Very elegant in all his movements, is Costas. And I'll bet he does not weigh one-fifty-five. Very graceful guy.

I flip through the pages and there it is right where he says it would be. "Would you excuse me, Costas?" I mumble. "I have to deal with something right away."

"Of course, Mr. Little," he says, and, with a bow, he slips out the door.

I summon the four component parts of my personality, the four narrators of my story. They take their sweet time showing up, but then there they are, slouching on the furniture of Penthouse Suite 1125. My father sits quietly in the big, comfortable chair, his book folded on his lap.

"Anybody know anything about a can?" I ask.

The part of me that is Floyd Little is perplexed. "I don't know nothing about no can," he says from the corner. Somebody has draped a towel over his stiff arm and he looks a little silly. He isn't pleased with the new development in the story. He generally likes to be in charge, to know that A will naturally be followed by B will naturally be followed by C in my story, a careful progression downfield, as it were. Football runs do not differ much, one from the other; you don't have to think about what you are doing, you just move forward and gain *ground. It would be a damn fool who tried to reinvent the very concept of running itself; they would be slammed to the ground by the defensive line while they were standing around, trying to reinvent running. You just run. That's it.*

He feels the same way about revisions.

Sitting on the floor and leaning against my father's chair, the part of me that is Poodle looks a little scared. She just wants everyone to be happy, to have a good time, to be titillated and not cause any conflict. She shakes her head quickly, fearful that she did something that is against the rules of the gentlemen's club in which she is employed. "It wasn't me," *she whispers.* "I don't do cans."

Falubio, too, looks vexed. He was mostly just chilling, trying to get his head cleared, just hanging with the vibe and going with the flow, and this invasion of his space is none too welcome. "Wasn't me, boss," *he grumbles, and you could just about see a stub of a cigarette dangling from his lip, just about smell the thin trail of smoke that glides above him and somehow stays out of his eyes. Smoking is not allowed on the ship, of course, and this is a rule that I respect even in the sanctity of Penthouse Suite 1125; I'm just saying that you can practically see this on him, because he is so awesomely cool.*

This leaves A Guy Named Brad. He never leaves his house. He rarely changes his socks. He has a voice like a mosquito. He raises his hand and quietly explains the following to the rest of us who are telling this story.

"The narrators of this story had all called it a night," he says. "I was the only one who was up. I never get much sleep. I have a restless nature. I walked into the bedroom and cried out, 'The can! The can! The incinerator can behind Knapp & Schlappi contains all of the wisdom of the world!' But nobody was listening to me. Nobody ever listens to me."

"All I heard was a damn mosquito buzzing in my ear," grumbled Floyd Little, and everybody laughed. Everybody but A Guy Named Brad, that is.

He continued. "So I decided to go this part alone. And this is what I wrote."

I put my head in my hands. "Tell me it's not a dream sequence," *I moaned.*

Brad just grinned.

Chapter Seven-A
A DREAM sequence

In a dream now, Ray Jensen is standing in the field behind Knapp & Schlappi Hardware. It was the field where he used to play Babe Ruth baseball on the Kiwanis team, where his coach, Joe Benulis, would jiggle his belly up and down twice if he wanted you to bunt, from side to side for a steal. Ray is standing at home plate admiring the arc of a hit he just made, a long, towering fly ball that went all the way to the warehouse behind left field and landed with a thud against the wooden siding.

Ray is alone in the field, and he spots the old incinerator can that sits out in deep right-center field. How can he miss it? The can is spewing showers of sparks and is alternately glowing red, white and blue. Ray remembers the can from his childhood. He and Mike Benulis used to throw rocks at it. Even back then it was ancient -- brown-red from rust, blackened from ancient fires, with round airholes punched into its sides, the better to burn excess paper and garbage in the days before air pollution. After heaving rocks at it, Ray and Mike Benulis walked up to the can a few times to see what was inside and were repulsed by the pile of half-burned garbage, milk cartons and gray-black ash, sodden with rain, that always inhabited the bottom third of incinerator cans in the '60s. Like most ashcans, it lacked true entertainment value, and they forgot about it.

In the dream, though, Ray is entranced by the can and its spewing sparks. He picks up a stone and throws it, and as if guided by radar, the stone flies right into the can through the tiniest of its vent holes. Ray picks up another rock, and then another, and then a huge boulder, chucks them all and they all go plunk!, right into the can. Ray is mesmerized by his good aim and good arm; he has always thought of himself as a hurler, and this confirms it. He walks up to the can and looks inside. Sitting plumply atop the ashes and sodden milk cartons is a book of some sort. It is bound in worn, etched leather. He reaches down into the can to pick it up, but the book gets deeper and deeper, the can growing larger and larger, and Ray is nearly headfirst and falling into the can. He is perched on its rusty rim and teetering as he reaches for the book, and then a jet of flame shoots straight up from deep inside the can, straight up past Ray's head. He screams and backs out of the can as fast as he can, leaving the book.

The dream ends.

THE NARRATORS (always the Narrators)

The other narrators are all on the edges of their seats.

"And then what happened?" Falubio demands to know.

A Guy Named Brad averts his eyes. "I don't really know."

"You don't KNOW?"

"I think the flame singed Ray's moustache or something," he mumbles.

Floyd Little snorts, "Ray don't have no moustache."

"I'm still working on what happens next," says A Guy Named Brad. He looks like he might cry.

"Well, I guess that's okay," the other three narrators grumble. "No harm, no foul. It's not a bad addition to the story. You just might tell us once in awhile when you're introducing a plot point. Don't assume that we read the memo."

A Guy Named Brad whines something along the lines of, "Okay."

"Hey," says the part of me that is Falubio. "What about the collarbone? What's up with the kid's collarbone? Ray does all of this business about Daniel's collarbone hurting, but I'm danged if I know why."

Floyd Little clears his throat. "I can help you out with that," he says. "Here's what I had in mind for that." And he tells this story.

Chapter Seven-B
Floyd LITTLE, a FOOTBALL PLAYER and FAST BACK, tells a flashback BASEBALL Story

In this little SportsCenter highlight, which happened six years before our story takes place, divorced dad Ray Jensen is standing on the same field, the one behind Knapp & Schlappi Hardware, with his own slugging first baseman, nine-year old Daniel Jensen. To paraphrase Casey Stengel, this kid has all the tools: Good arm, good reach, a real *good-looking* ballplayer, and if everything goes right, in about twenty years he has a good chance to be thirty. Daniel is nervously considering trying out for Little League and Ray practically breaks down the door of his ugly cottage on the lake to teach his son some of the finer points of the game. They go to the practice field of Ray's youth armed with a bucket of balls, their gloves and a new aluminum bat. Ray will pitch baseballs to Daniel all night if he has to, to groove the lad's swing and get him thinking confidently about hard shots past the shortstop, line drives that find the gaps between galumphing outfielders for doubles and triples, and that occasional sweet long ball, the one where you turn on an inside pitch and drive it down the line, where it disappears over the fence like the very distilled essence of joy.

But Daniel does not immediately grasp the lesson. He swings, in fact, like his mother, waving the bat with his arms. No weight shift. No head on the ball. No driving it into the gaps. When he makes contact, which is not altogether a sure thing, the best result is a weak pop fly that any self-respecting Moose or Rotary shortstop would gather in. With a smirk. Ray patiently adjusts his son's stance, offers loads of advice, points to the warehouse that he had once hit on the fly when he was roughly Daniel's age. Ray is talking and talking and talking, but Daniel does not seem to grasp a word of it. Ray slows down his pitches to the point where they barely reach home plate before dropping, exhausted, to the ground. His last resort, which he does not want to go to unless he absolutely has to, would be to pitch underhand.

"Look, let me show you," Ray offers. He takes the twenty-eight ounce aluminum bat from Daniel and sends him out to the mound to do the pitching. Daniel likes to throw the ball, and maybe he will be a pitcher, with sneaky heat like Mike Benulis had, and a curveball that Ray can teach him even though it is not recommended for nine-year olds to throw curves because it can hurt their elbows. But he can throw it until his elbow starts to hurt, Ray reasons, and get plenty of guys out with it. "Go ahead, wing it in here," Ray instructs.

Daniel starts to heave the ball. He misses the strike zone more times than not, but some of them come over the plate with a nice little hop. Ray is impressed with his son's good arm. If he can find the strike zone at nine years old with reasonable heat, he could be pitching for the Morongo Mustangs varsity by the time he's a fourteen-year old freshman. Be *worlds* ahead of the other pitchers by the time he graduates, and maybe even get a tryout for a minor league team. Ray takes little chopping swings at the first pitches, trying just to bunt them back to the mound for Daniel to pick up. A little game of pepper. This, now, is fun for both of them, and Daniel is winding up like a pro, like Roger Clemens in the exaggerated delivery that Ray taught him. Ray is talking about waiting on the pitch, and getting the fat part of the bat head on the ball. Ray is still talking and talking and talking.

Daniel is hitting the strike zone with more pitches now, crowing after each one. Forget Roger Clemens, a mere mortal; In his mind, Daniel is a Ninja Power Ranger throwing thunderbolts of pure, malicious molybdenite at the evil Zordon invaders played by his father. Right about now,

Ray gets the bright idea that it would be instructive to really swing at a pitch, not just bunt it back to the mound, so the boy can see what good things can happen when you keep those arms high, the head still, and turn on the ball, get your weight behind it and your wrists snapping at just the right moment. He takes a big rip at a nice pitch over the middle of the plate, but the Little League-sized bat fools him. It is too small and light, and he too pops the ball up to short, although it is quite an impressive pop fly, higher than the backstop, and Daniel runs under it from the pitcher's mound and almost catches it over his shoulder.

Both father and son are aware of the power that was in that swing, the speed that was unleashed in that bat when Ray swung hard. Now Ray really wants to hit one, not only to show Daniel but to feel it once more himself. He wants to hit a solid line drive all the way to the warehouse, or better yet, put one over the warehouse and into the lake. He wants it for Daniel, to create a moment that they can treasure, and he wants it badly for himself. Baseball was all the fun that he ever needed. Clearing the warehouse could make up for a mile of childhood fears and setbacks. If he could still play baseball he would be a happy man, especially if he could play against Little League pitching.

Daniel feels that they have entered a new game, too, and he tries too hard to throw a fast strike on the next three pitches. He overthrows them all and they go in the dirt, over Ray's head, two feet outside.

"Just relax and get it over," Ray instructs, holding the bat flat across home plate as a visual aid. Daniel nods and blows out a deep breath. He winds up.

Ray takes the tiny bat back and cocks it at his shoulder. The pitch is a beauty, belt-high and on the outside corner of home plate. This is a pitch that a man can have his way with, that a man can drive. Ray goes from stillness to motion in a heartbeat, an explosion of a swing. He steps forward, shifts his weight just like Ted Williams instructed so many years ago in the books on hitting that Ray kept at his bedside as a twelve-year old. The Little League bat whips around. But it is a trifle too late and Ray has forgotten that it is hard to hit an outside pitch deep to left field, to the warehouse, and doubly hard for a thirty-nine year-old man who has not played ball for decades. The best you can do with that pitch is take it up the middle, and Ray has done that with a vengeance.

The ball rockets off his bat in a head-high line drive up the middle. As instructed, Daniel's Roger Clemens-style delivery has left him facing home plate in perfect position to field the ball. That is, if you can see the ball, which Daniel can not. The ball hits him flush on the right collarbone, flies up in the air and caroms away.

Daniel wordlessly crashes to the ground and Ray's first thought is that the ball hit him in the face and has killed him. It is only when he is halfway to the mound, running, that Daniel's screaming begins, and he sees that the boy is trying to somehow get away from his right arm, trying to do anything to send away the pain of a shattered collarbone. The worst part for Ray is leaving the boy on the field, continuing to scream, while he runs into Knapp & Schlappi Hardware, which thankfully keeps late hours, to call the ambulance.

Daniel was in a cast, and then a sling, for the entire Little League season, the summer and the beginning of the next fall. He would long associate baseball with the not-so-pleasurable memory of watching a projectile hurtle mercilessly at his body. It soured him for life on sports in general and baseball in particular.

For his part, Ray received a reassuring letter from the law firm of Yoni, Tunnell & Trane in Rochester that their client, the former Janice Jensen, did not wish to press civil charges against Ray for the accident, charges which might naturally include the revocation of his visitation rights with his son. They added that it might be in his, Ray's, best interests to refrain from further "aggressive and inappropriate displays of competition" with his son in the future.

This letter was signed by an attorney named Nancy. Janice's first attorney, Holly, had apparently moved on to another firm.

THE NARRATORS (continued)
BREAKFAST with DADDY

"*Good story,*" says Poodle. *My father nods from his chair.*

I wish I could have agreed. I had forgotten all about the incident at the ballfield, Daniel's busted shoulder, the two years of frost with Janice that ensued. How did any of us survive that? It was my story, and I wish they might have left that part out. I'm about to make a formal notice of my displeasure, but Falubio pipes up, which is very uncharacteristic of him.

"*I wonder what happened to the ball,*" says Falubio.

"*Which ball?*" asks Floyd Little.

"*The ball that hit Daniel's shoulder. It caromed into the air. Where did it land?*"

Floyd frowns. "*What the hell does it matter where it landed?*"

A tiny voice from under the bed, the voice of a mosquito, answers. "*It's in the incinerator can.*"

The parts of me that are Falubio, Floyd Little and Poodle all break down in laughter. Even my father wipes a ghostly tear of laughter from his ethereal cheek.

"As if," someone wheezes, and they all laugh again.

Later that day – or maybe it's that week, time being different on a cruise ship -- we are sailing past the white cliffs of Dover on cruise #455 – A Spot of English Tea and Normandy Landing Beaches -- but it doesn't really matter to me where we are. As I had done in the Indian Ocean, at the dock in Cannes, and when the ship toured the great capitals of Scandinavia, I sit on a chair directly opposite my father and ask one simple question. If the truth be told, it has become a daily ritual between us.

"Now?" I ask.

He looks up from the book he was reading and frowns. I ask him again. "Now?"

He makes an expression with his eyebrows that ask a question in return: "Now, what?"

"Am I big enough yet? Is today to be my last day? Do I have to die soon? Is my time almost up? Is it now?"

See, I've assumed all this time that the reason my Dad came back was to harvest me. To escort me to the here-after. I mean, why else? But he seems to be taking his sweet time about it; he too appears to enjoy this cruise ship life.

He frowns and shakes his head and goes back to his reading, a trifle annoyed by the distraction. But I can tell in his manner that he is not annoyed because he doesn't know the answer to the question. He just doesn't like the timing. In other words, not now. Without looking up, he makes a flitting gesture with his hand that wordlessly indicates, "carry on."

"That's good," I say, "because Costas is about to bring us lunch, and I think we're in luck. It's a buffet day."

In fact, the theme of the day was "Flavors of Mexico," and my loyal butler, assisted by the divine chefs of the Royal Precious Platinum, does not disappoint. The door opens and Costas grandly supervises the delivery, on silver trays borne by a battalion of Indonesian busboys, of my own sumptuous buffet. Or rather, the sumptuous buffet for me, my father and the four component parts of my personality. Farrell Sr. has begun the practice of joining me for lunch. I no longer even have to set a place for him at my table. After a few days of doing so myself, Costas asked if I was expecting a guest and I explained that my father, Farrell Sr., was eating with me in spirit. So then Costas began to set an extra place.

With Poodle happily sitting on the carpet holding his leg and the other three narrators busy with a jigsaw puzzle, my father carefully marks and closes his book, straightens his tie and smoothes the leather elbow patches on his jacket, and joins me at the table.

As I mentioned, I love the buffets. There are silver trays of exquisite little botanitas of fresh dorado nestled in a perfect puddle of chocolate mole sauce and wrapped in thin strips of tortilla with toothpicks cunningly crafted from bacon. There are four kinds of ceviche – one that is entirely tentacles – and little spiced puffs of shredded chicken in cups carved from tomatillos and lined with pastry. Entrees include skirt steaks sizzling on a platter (Costas thoughtfully brought five) and the meaty, succulent thigh of a suckling pig that has been roasted slowly all night long. Five types of ocean fish have been prepared five different ways and assembled on a long platter to look like a swordfish that is chasing a tuna that is chasing a mackerel that is chasing – cleverly, I think – a painstakingly filleted and marinated herring that is millimeters away from catching a dab of caviar. The flans and fried ice creams, pies and pan dulces fill my entire desk and bar area and culminate in a two-foot tall ice sculpture of a Mayan pyramid that will melt to reveal a single, perfect scoop of agave ice cream at its center.

Farrell Sr. can not eat, of course, owing to his incorporeal nature, but he watches me eagerly, pointing with a surprisingly steady finger at the next dish that he wants me to consume. I take a careful, studied mouthful of the mahi-mahi, the squid or the roasted corn salad, chew it thoughtfully, swallow, dab napkin to lips, and then describe to him the flavors and textures. He in turn takes a moment to gather all of my words, sometimes closing his eyes and sighing softly (although inaudibly) at the memory of food, and then nods and gestures me to the next dish. I eat heartily and happily. I am well-stuffed, and two hours later, when I am finished, my father also appears to be satisfied with the meal.

"Now?" *I ask my father once again. He has returned to his book, and it takes him a moment to mark his place with a finger and respond to me. He shrugs his shoulders.*

"No really, I could use some guidance, Dad."

He puts his finger to his lips in thought, and then mimes the motion of furiously stuffing food into his mouth with both hands, and then points to me.

"I'm not big enough yet?"

He shakes his head.

"So how do I get bigger? I mean, look at all of the food I've socked away today."

He thinks about it for another moment. And then mimes the motion of pushing a pen through space.

"I need to keep writing."

He nods and points a finger at me in an exaggerated mime of affirmation. A trifle sarcastic, if the truth be told. He goes back to his book.

I sigh. This book, this story of my life, is not getting any easier to write. I thought that if I gave myself over to the cruise ship, all of my problems would be solved. That clearly is not the case. I call yet another story meeting. They show up grumbling and disinterested.

"People," I say, "let's get to work. Now who wants to be God today?"

We begin to write, and we start with the can. That incinerator can, which may or may not have a baseball inside, is never far from our minds these days.

Chapter Eight
THE CAN and the LAKE and a CHRISTIAN in a Christian COFFEE Haus

In fact, the incinerator can behind Knapp & Schlappi Hardware had Ray Jensen on its mind. Late at night, when nobody was there to see it, it grinned its toothy, air-hole grin and curled its rusted lip and belched out three identical puffs of gray-green smoke that wafted towards Ray's cottage. Inside of the can were nine inches of foul-smelling ashes, a pair of wet, ruined athletic socks, three bags of greasy packaging from McDonalds and the shattered green glass remains of a pint of bourbon. And an old baseball with the slightest curved dent, the imprint of a young boy's collarbone, beneath a line of stitches.

    The can shifted heavily and awkwardly on its concrete pad, moving a few inches around in a circle while making the sound of a hubcap rolling on pavement. Nobody heard it; nobody saw it move. It was going to have a little fun tonight. From one of its holes, it farted a thin, foul odor in Ray's direction, a come-hither call that wafted out into the Morongo night. Come and see what I'm burning now, Ray, said the can in its peculiar, canny way. Come and sift through my ashes.

By local traditions that amounted to community consent, Morongo evenings were generally left for teenagers to prowl and conduct their mating rituals, and for the Morongo College students and post-adolescent men and women of the community to congregate at places like the Wagonwheel and Lloyd's Limited, to drink beer and recall old stories and challenge each other to quests as deeply resonant as fighting for the hand of a woman (even if the woman was the Wagonwheel barmaid, a dickwalter who had already been divorced thrice; in certain lights her hand was still worth winning), as mundane as drinking a half-dozen shots of tequila straight from the bottle while reclining backwards with one's head on the bar, mouth facing upwards.

Rites of passage: One could write an entire book exploring them.

No, it was the incinerator can that roused Ray from his shock over the phone call with John Piczak. It crooked its rusty little finger and pursed its iron lip into a pucker, and said to come hither, Ray, come now. And Ray heard its call from where he sat in his living room, felt the need to find his shoes and turn off lights and find his keys where he had left them on top of the stove. His beef chispadores grumbling in his gut, he reluctantly went out into the Morongo night.

He knew that he had to find Daniel. The mention of his son's name by John Piczak, his father's former colleague, had stirred something inside Ray, something paternal and protective while at the same time being something suspicious and accusing. The yin and yang of fatherhood. Ray wondered what Daniel had done, and how much trouble he might be facing. He drove past Janice's house, and was relieved to see that the house was dark and there were no cars in the driveway.

He turned onto Water Street and drove downtown. The storefronts of Morongo's businesses were dark; the only lights came from inside the Christian Coffee Haus. He parked the car and went inside. The Christian Coffee Haus always looked like somebody had taken pains to keep things as modest and uncomfortable as possible. Rickety old chairs made of unfinished wood – no upholstery or adornment in the form of paint allowed – had backs that slanted forward slightly, positioning the occupant of the chair into a supplicant posture. The tables were worn and pitted, unadorned with cloths, and tilted abruptly when a hand, an elbow, or a full cup of Christian coffee was placed on the surface, with no shims offered or expected under the scraped feet, since all tables are upright and sturdy in God's eyes.

Ray scanned the room. In one corner were two young people and their Bible teacher murmuring over their Good Books; at the other end of the room were a pair of elderly women who were talking excitedly. Ray's heart sank and a chill ran through his spine, and it was not because Daniel was nowhere in sight. The morbid thoughts that he had been having – call them visions since we're in a Christian Coffee Haus – those visions of desolation and visible decline and impending doom were returning. The three Christians huddled at the table in the corner all had their demises practically floating above their heads in comic book thought balloons for Ray, and only Ray, to see.

She's going to be hit by a car soon, Ray thought of the blonde teenager with a ponytail who was reading her catechism. Terminated. Wiped out. Future prospects: Dim.

"For me, liver failure," responded the somber youth next to her. "I'll make it to about forty. Leave three kids and a wife behind and grieving me."

Their bible teacher at the same table would simply wither away, like a helium balloon from a birthday party that leaks its vital gases, gets lower to the ground every day and winds up sideways and flaccid on the carpet before being put in the trash.

Ray shook his head and closed his eyes as a wave of sadness seemed to wash through him, and then was gone. Ray looked away from the three Bible students and noticed that when he looked at the old ladies in the other corner, he felt nothing but a vague curiosity. They were talking loudly and laughing and slapping the table for emphasis, and the thought that occurred to him was not so much that they would die soon, but that they were a trifle noisy and annoying.

"Hello, Ray, can I help you with something?" It was Taylor David, Ray's old childhood friend. Twenty-five years earlier, while studying in Albany to become a lawyer, he had been visited by the word of Jesus, and it touched him in a way that no amount of fractious tortes could ever approach. He dropped out of school and returned to Morongo to offer his testimony on a daily basis. He had grown up to become a bald man with a frowning mouth. Ray found that every communication with Taylor since his illumination seemed to be fraught with dismay. He was the glummest person in the world who had been visited by the spirit of eternal joy.

(Quick story: When Ray saw Taylor David, he was always reminded of old Mr. Snook, who used to own a record store on Main Street when Ray was a kid. If you went into the store to kill a few minutes after school, Mr. Snook would look up warily from his stool behind the cash register, wearily rise to his feet, shuffle over to you and have this conversation:

"Can I help you, Son?"

"No thanks, Mr. Snook, just looking."

"Then get out.")

Ray looked closely at Taylor David, and into his mind popped the words "infection of the lungs, bronchial pneumonia."

"About ten years from now," Ray murmured. "You've got lots of time."

David looked at him oddly, and Ray realized that he had been caught thinking aloud. "Oh hello, Taylor," he said. "Do you know if my son Daniel was in tonight? He probably would have been here with his girlfriend, Jodi."

Taylor nodded. "Yes, they were in here about a half-hour ago. They served the tea, in fact, to that table full of ladies." He pointed to the pair of raucous old women in the corner.

"Did they happen to say where they were going?" asked Ray.

"Do any of us truly know where we are going?" asked Taylor mournfully. "I've been meaning to discuss this with you for some time, Raymond."

Ray held up a hand with one finger pointed skyward. "Hold that thought, Taylor," he said, and turned around and quickly left the Christian Coffee Haus.

He returned to his car and drove to the lake. He remembered that John Piczak lived alone in a cottage facing the lake on the north-facing shore near Indian Pines Park, a pretty and peaceful area where Ray's friends, Jim and Gloria Long, also lived. Ray had not been to John Piczak's house for forty years. He remembered a summer party held there when he was a child, a clambake on the lawn when Farrell Sr. and Caroline and John Piczak were young and vibrant and happy, in the prime of their academic and personal lives. Ray and his brother Farrell had played on the lawn and swam and eaten while the adults drank beer and played horseshoes. The only thing that marred the festive day was when Ray wandered off into a nearby park and burned himself on an old incinerator can behind Knapp & Schlappi Hardware that looked a hundred years old and never used, but was smoldering and hot to the touch when Ray looked inside. He had run, crying, back to the clambake, and John Piczak salved his burn with a cream that he mixed up himself in his basement laboratory.

There were no streetlights on that side of the lake, and it was dark enough that Ray had to drive slowly to identify Piczak's house, turning around once in a driveway when he went too far and wound up at the back entrance to the park. When he recognized the house, it was also dark. The house was a large, two-story cottage with an attached garage and a long lawn, overgrown with weeds and thick grass, that angled downwards to the lake, where a bulkhead wall made of railroad ties separated the lawn from a thirty-yard wide swath of pebbles and gray dirt that passed as a beach. A long dock was moored in the lake, at the end of which was a covered boat hoist.

Ray cut the lights and parked the car. He walked up to the house and knocked on the door, calling John Piczak's name, but there was no answer. Unsure of what to do next or where to go, he walked around to the side of the house, for no other reason than that it offered a pretty view of the lake at night, with lights twinkling on either side of the narrow lake for miles.

It was quiet and cool, with the lake's surface rippled by a breeze. There were no lights on in the neighboring homes, or sounds of cars or people. The lake seemed to glow dully, reflecting the light from the cottages on its banks, and Ray was startled to see the silhouette of a man standing at the end of Piczak's dock, a hundred yards away from where Ray was standing. Ray could not make out who the man was, but he was seized by a terrible thought: Whoever he was, he was about to die. Severe head trauma. Possible asphyxiation. Possibly both at once.

Ray moved a few steps closer and saw that the man at the end of the dock appeared to be holding something large and bulky, a heavy weight. The man was tall and lean and appeared to hold the weight gracefully. Ray was confused, thinking at first that the man was John Piczak, but the appearance was all wrong. Piczak was in his seventies, gracefully stooped over the last time Ray saw him. Ray had an uneasy feeling that he was trespassing, that the man on the dock might have something to say on the subject and that he wanted to find Daniel more than ever. He stopped and watched.

The man on the dock looked up and saw Ray across the lawn, and that seemed to stimulate the man into action. He moved heavily away from Ray, to the far edge of the dock. The weight that he carried seemed to be very heavy, and he had to shuffle his feet to move. Ray could see from the movement that something – a rope, a cable – was attached to the weight that the man carried. The other end of the rope or cable was attached to the man's ankle.

The man screamed, "Leave me alone, Jensen! You've done quite enough. All of you. Everything I told you, everything you need to know, it's in the can."

It was John Piczak's voice, Ray could be sure of that, and it sounded odd coming from the youthful figure on the dock. Ray began to walk quickly towards the dock, but stopped when he saw the man's figure make a throwing motion in his direction, and Ray heard the sigh and thump of a rock landing in the grass near him. Ray stopped again.

"John, is that you?" he called out. From where he stood, he could see more clearly that the weight that Piczak was holding was a heavy cinderblock, and that it was in fact attached to a rope that was connected to the old man's ankle. The dock was a long one, extending fifty feet out into the lake to accommodate the boats of visitors and neighbors, and Ray was still a hundred feet away from the man. As Ray watched, astonished, John Piczak threw the cinderblock into the lake with a heave. Still facing Ray, he made a military salute in Ray's direction, waited a few seconds for the cinderblock to adjust to the water and play out its length of rope, and then was summarily and almost comically yanked foot-first into the water. The last thing that Ray saw of John Piczak was the older man's head disappearing under the water.

Ray began to run to the dock, his heart racing. He had taken a half-dozen steps when a movement flashed past him, tripping Ray and knocking him to the lawn. Ray rolled to a stop and made out the figure of his son Daniel, racing past at a full sprint that Ray could not begin to match, outdistancing him even after Ray had had a twenty-yard head start.

Daniel never broke stride as he reached the end of the dock. He dove headfirst on the pier, but stopped short of flying straight into Morongo Lake. He reached his arm under the water and strained for something, moved closer to the end of the dock so that his head and shoulders were off the end of it, almost touching the water. A full minute passed as he groped in the water, and then Ray saw Daniel's back and shoulder blades stiffen as he held something heavy. He began to back up on the dock, still lying on his belly, and with all of his strength he heaved John Piczak's limp body onto the dock. The older man was unconscious; surely drowned. He had been under the water for more than two minutes by Ray's reckoning.

Ray ran to the edge of the lake and stopped stupidly, as if the water were a barrier that he could not cross, as Daniel dragged the lifeless body of John Piczak, still attached to the cinderblock, towards him. That is,

Daniel dragged the upper half of Piczak while the lower half, weighted down by the block, floated through the water.

"Dad, get me that bottle," Daniel called out to his father, and Ray was puzzled for a moment, not only by the request but by the calm authority of his son's voice, like an emergency room doctor who could not be flustered by something as routine as life and death.

"Get me the bottle, Dad, it's in my backpack," he repeated, and Ray dumbly walked to where he saw the backpack sprawled on the weeds and rocks at the edge of the dock, just as it was generally thrown to the floor of the living room in Ray's house. He opened it up and found inside a wine bottle of plain, dark glass with no label. A cork was shoved halfway into its top, and the bottle was half full of a clear liquid.

"Dad, goddamnit, hurry up," Daniel swore, and the voice made Ray jump. Daniel was sitting at the edge of the dock, cradling John Piczak's head in his lap. The concrete block was still tied to his ankle and John was stretched out, like a fakir being levitated, like a dead man, his feet pointing to the middle of the lake, his head in Daniel's lap.

Ray brought the bottle to Daniel and was shocked to see that John Piczak, who was at least 75 years old, the age that Farrell Sr. would have been, looked somehow youthful. His hair was gray turning to white but his face was smooth, unlined, and in repose he could have passed for thirty.

"Give me it, give me the bottle, Dad," Daniel said again, and Ray dumbly handed it over. Daniel pulled the cork out with his teeth and quickly poured a splash of the contents of the wine bottle into John Piczak's mouth. He waited a moment and repeated the action.

The older man began to sputter and cough. He looked up wildly, trying to understand where he was and where he had been. He started to scream an unearthly scream, of terror and pain and fear.

"No," he wailed, "No you can't do this to me. Not once more."

He tried to stand up but the cinderblock pulled him down, and he fell with a splash headlong into the lake. Daniel had to fish his head out one more time.

"Now calm down Dr. Piczak," he said. "It's going to be all right."

"No!" he screamed again. "I will decide how to do this."

He sat down in the lake and began to cry, holding his head in his hands and weeping into them. The sounds were of an old man, but Ray could see that the hands were smooth and firm. "It doesn't matter," said Piczak. "It's all lost. All lost." He pointed to the lawn and beyond, to the park beyond his house. "My life's work. It's up in flames," he said.

Daniel looked up and said, "Oh shit." He leapt to his feet and began to race across the lawn without another word. Ray looked past him and saw, in the distance, flames shooting out of the old incinerator can in the park, the can that had once burned Ray's hand. He looked at Piczak sitting in the water, and then Ray too got up and ran, following Daniel across the lawn and towards the park.

Arriving at the can, Ray found Daniel trying to reach for something inside the burning incinerator can. It was too hot, and yelping with pain, he withdrew his hand. He began to take off his shirt to wrap it around his hand, but Ray, arriving a few moments later, saw what he was after, and instinctively reached into the can. He ignored the heat and the pain of the fire, and pulled out a leather satchel from inside the can. It was an old briefcase, with a leather flap that cinched the briefcase shut with a brass clasp that was charred black from the fire. The underside of the briefcase was also charred, but the top was only mildly singed. Ray could smell gasoline and saw rags in the bottom of the can that were still flaming.

Ray said, "Daniel what is this?"

"No time to explain, Pop."

He stood up and began to run back towards the lake and Piczak's house. Ray, who was winded and was still holding the briefcase, settled for an easy jog. When he reached the edge of the lake, he found Daniel frantically searching up and down the shore. John Piczak was gone.

"Dr. Piczak!" called Daniel. "Goddamn it, where are you?"

Ray looked towards the house, but the lights were still off and the house was still, the doors closed. He looked to the dock and realized that something was different. The boat hoist had been lowered and the speedboat that it had cradled was gone.

That was when they heard the whine of a revving engine and saw the speedboat in the lake. John Piczak was at the wheel. In a tight, fast circle, he turned the boat away from the dock and raced away from shore. Fifty yards away, he wheeled around in an abrupt circle. He glared at Ray and Daniel, gave them the finger, and then wheeled the boat again and sped off towards the center of the lake.

Ray stood dumbly at the shore end of the dock watching the boat. Morongo Lake was formed by glaciers that scraped out a deep basin like a giant backhoe. It fell to depths of five hundred feet or more only a half-mile or so off-shore, and many fishermen had vanished into its cold, icy depths. In the moonlight, he watched as John Piczak's boat slowed to a stop, and then silhouetted against the moonlight, a man stood on the transom, threw something heavy into the water, and then himself was jerked off the boat. Ray could barely hear the splash from where he stood. The boat began to drift downwind, away from him and Daniel.

Ray leaped to his feet, intent on another rescue, but Daniel stopped him with a firm hand.

"There's nothing we can do this time, Dad," said Daniel.

"We've got to help him," Ray said wildly.

"It's what he wanted, Dad. It's awfully hard to die. I tried to save him, but he didn't want it."

Ray stared at his son, and saw the bottle still in Daniel's hand. Unthinking, his nerves shot through with adrenaline, he grabbed the bottle, uncorked it and took a long, deep drink. It tasted of oranges and ashes and bitterness.

"To your health and long life," Daniel muttered.

"What is this?" Ray asked, brandishing the bottle.

"It's a long story, Pop."

Daniel reached over and gently took the bottle from Ray's hand. He carefully corked it and put it back in his backpack. He gripped Ray's shoulder and shook him. "Do you have the briefcase, Dad?" he asked.

Ray cleared his head and saw that he was still holding the briefcase from the incinerator can. He nodded, still speechless.

"Then let's get out of here, Dad," Daniel said. He helped Ray to his feet and they walked across the field where the can was still glowing, past the place where Ray played baseball as a kid, and where Daniel's collarbone was shattered by his father's best hit ever. They walked through the parking lot of Knapp & Schlappi Hardware and crossed the street to the McDonalds.

"Burger?" Daniel said.

Ray shook his head, dazed. "Get me some coffee," he croaked.

"Money, Dad? They don't give this stuff away."

Ray reached into his pocket and found a five-dollar bill, wet but intact.

"I want change," he said, handing the money to his son, his sophomore, and then collapsing on a picnic table, exhausted.

"Make me," said Daniel.

Chapter Nine

(more) MORONGO

such a dickwalter; ORANGES & ashes

At McDonalds, Daniel was halfway through his second quarter-pounder with cheese when he paused for air. He noticed that Ray's Big Mac was untouched, and thought he'd put in a good word on his own behalf to become the rightful heir and owner of the sandwich.

"Aren't you going to eat that burger that I bought you?"

Ray shook his head and slid the sandwich across the table. He took another sip of coffee. McDonalds, he reminded himself, always has good coffee. His hand reached towards the green, unlabeled wine bottle that Daniel had removed from his backpack and placed on the far side of the table. Daniel quickly took two more fast bites, finishing his quarter-pounder with cheese, swallowed them hard, and reached for the bottle before Ray could take it.

"I think you've had enough, Dad," said Daniel. "Go easy on this stuff."

"I only had that one drink on the beach," complained Ray.

"No, you've had more than that." Daniel explained that over the last week that he and Jodi had been in possession of the bottles of John Piczak's snops, he had been giving Ray small doses of the liquid in his morning cereal. Just to see what would happen.

"You've been dosing me with chemicals in my morning cereal?" asked Ray.

"If you choose to look at it that way."

"Why?"

"Try it, Dad, and then you tell me."

Daniel handed the bottle back to Ray, who uncorked it and took a long swig. He winced at the bitter taste, like something that you want badly and know that you should not have.

"So what?" asked Ray. "It tastes like really horrible wine."

"So look at the guy in the corner," said Daniel.

At the corner table, an unshaven man in a filthy, green, down-filled parka gave Ray a dirty, what're-u-lookin'-at-numbnuts? glare over his Happy Meal. It was Vincent McWalter, aka the original Dickwalter.

"What do you give him?" asked Daniel. "One year? Maybe two?"

"Maybe two," Ray murmured.

"How about the girl at the counter?" asked Daniel.

Ray reluctantly looked, afraid of what he might see. The girl behind the counter was no more than sixteen years old, wore braces and her hair pulled back in a ponytail. A junior in high school by Ray's reckoning; in his mind, he watched her grow old and haggard, her blonde hair turning to gray strings and her face collapsing over lost teeth.

"A ripe old age," said Ray.

"No, that's not right, Dad. Crystal meth. When she's about thirty."

Ray instinctively reached over and gripped Daniel's shoulder with his hand and looked intently into his eyes. "My God," he said, "how have you been living with these visions? I mean, isn't this just about breaking your heart? I'm so sorry, Daniel."

Daniel just smiled. He did not pull away from his father's touch. He picked up a french fry and ate it. "It's not so bad, Dad. The visions go away quickly. And you want to know what else is hella cool about snops?" He reached for another fry before continuing. "When you give it to someone, you don't know how they'll die anymore."

"You've given this to other people?"

"Only you, Mom and my history teacher. She was about to have a brain tumor or something, but now she's okay."

Ray put his head into his hands and moaned. The taste of oranges and ashes and bitterness lingered unpleasantly in his mouth, and the night's events were making him feel sick. Nevertheless, he wanted more, and he had to stifle an urge to rip the bottle away from his son and chug the contents. He could tell that all was not right in the world of Ray. He was shaken from the experience with John Piczak and the sight of a man stepping off of a boat in the middle of the lake to end his life.

The sound of Ray's moan startled Daniel. He reached over and patted Ray's head awkwardly. "It's going to be okay, Dad. The feelings don't last long."

Ray chanced a glance at his son and was relieved to see only Daniel and the remnants of hamburgers. He found that if he focused intently on his son's face, he could block out the visions. "How come I don't know when you're going to die?" he asked.

"Beats me. I think it's because either I'm not going to die for a really, really long time. Or I'm going to die after you. Don't worry, Dad. Those thoughts were hella scary for me. I went through what you're going through now. But it got easier to take."

"You knew how and when I was going to die, didn't you?" asked Ray quietly.

Daniel nodded. "Yes, I sure did, Dad." He began to continue, but Ray raised a hand to stop him.

"Do I want to know this?" Ray asked. He was asking himself and Daniel at the same time.

Daniel patted his head again. "You have a long life ahead of you, Dad. And you know what else is cool? Your future might change. I've already seen that three times with Jodi."

Ray reached for the bottle and pulled it away from Daniel, who reluctantly let it go. He uncorked it and sniffed the opening. No odor. He carefully tilted the bottle and released a few drops onto the white tabletop. No color. He dipped his finger into the small pool of snops and tasted it, and his mouth flinched from the bitterness, but his finger reached right back to the small pool as if by its own instruction and swiped up the remaining drops and delivered them to Ray's tongue. He motioned to Daniel, and the boy corked the bottle and put it out of sight into his backpack.

"Let's look in the briefcase, Dad."

"No, let's start saving lives," said Ray. He looked around the McDonalds. "Him," I guess, he said, nodding to Vincent McWalter, who was still chewing on his hamburger.

"You want to save the original Dickwalter?"

"I don't think it would be fair of us to decide."

"We can't save everybody, Dad."

Ray realized that he was right. He had been in possession of the powers of a God for ten minutes and was already stumped. "I guess we just save who we can," he said. "Whomever washes up at our feet, so to speak." He looked again at Vincent McWalter, who glared a look back that said, in effect, "keep lookin' and I'll tear you a new asshole, shit-fer-brains."

"How do we save him?" asked Ray. "I don't even want to talk to him."

"I'll show you how," said Daniel. He opened the lid of his cup and poured a small dribble of snops into his Coke. He closed the lid again, stood up and walked over to Vincent McWalter.

"You want this?" asked Daniel. "I can't finish it."

McWalter eyed him warily. "You spit in it?"

"No, dude, I just don't want it."

McWalter picked up the cup and drank from it.

"Tastes like shit," he said. But then he took another drink, and another after that. Thanks to that, not to mention his inclusion in this story, he would continue to live and laugh and love in his dickwalter way. He would also be the first one to sell crystal methadrine to the girl behind the counter, but that would be years later.

"Pretty cool, huh?" said Daniel, returning to the table.

"God help us," said Ray.

Chapter Nine-A
VOLUME 5 and a flugelhorn

The satchel that Ray had retrieved from the burning incinerator can was an old briefcase from the 1960's that had a pebbly leather exterior and a brass clasp. When Ray got to it, it had been burning for several minutes, and the back and bottom showed holes where the fire had burned through the leather. Inside were five vinyl, three-ring binders that were filled with papers. The binders showed some discoloration from the smoke and fire, but had not themselves been singed, and the pages appeared to be intact. Ray carefully removed all five of the binders. The last volume in the satchel had its rings opened, but seemed otherwise undisturbed. Each binder was filled with lined notebook paper onto which were written hand-inked notes in a small, disciplined, if wildly effusive hand. The notes began in the upper-left corner of each page of paper and crabbed across the page to the right edge and then down, completely filling each page.

In life, John Piczak had always been something of a windbag. Ray remembered that as a child, he had thought Dr. Piczak was a lot of fun, a droll, talkative man who seemed to always be telling jokes and kidding around. But as he grew older and the contacts between his family and the Piczaks had grown less frequent, Ray began to notice the forced smiles on his father's and mother's faces when Piczak was in the room, telling stories and jokes and dominating the conversation. He sensed their exasperation, and noticed the measured looks that Farrell Sr. and Caroline gave each other, sometimes across an entire room, when Piczak stood in a room and loudly expounded on anything and everything from campus politics at Morongo College to the science of NASA and the space race. It was confusing to Ray to slowly gather that the Piczaks and the Jensens had long since stopped being friends.

John Piczak's penchant for never quite knowing when to shut up was evident in the notes. The first notebook began with a lengthy and bitter denunciation of the Morongo College administration, circa 1977, when funding was cut off for a pet research project that Piczak, then head of the chemistry department, wanted to pursue. This went on for several pages in the tight, crabbed handwriting as Piczak cursed and ridiculed everyone from the Dean of the College of Arts and Sciences to the janitors who swept the floors in the nursing school. Lengthy digressions expounded on the superior wisdom of scientists, the writings of Plato and Socrates, the pitching rotation of the Rochester Red Wings, the ethical dilemmas faced by Einstein and Oppenheimer, and proper techniques and practices for landing trophy-sized pickerel in Morongo Lake. Ray tried to wade through the notes, but a diatribe is a diatribe.

"Even the story of eternal life requires a story," he muttered.

"What Dad?" Daniel was thinking about more french fries and patiently watching his father read. It was a school night and he hoped that Ray would not ask him how much Spanish homework he had done, because the answer was, "Nada, Señor." He borrowed two more dollars from Ray and went to buy fries.

Ray began to randomly flip through the remaining pages of Volume One and learned little more than that Piczak had had an affair with a graduate student and that he had begun to make wine at home from the local grapes.

In Volume Two, begun in the early '80s, Piczak was making some progress towards creating a better bottle of wine. At the same time, he was trying to quantify the healthful aspects of wine drinking through a series of experiments. The research was carefully reported and annotated, but the journal's science was somewhat overshadowed by the author's notion to intersperse sections of an autobiographical novel in progress wherein he cast himself as a dashing scientist whose name was Chuck Mangione.

The novel began with Chuck Mangione sipping wine at a bistro alongside Morongo Lake and trying to make time with a comely young graduate student, but petered out at page one-hundred-and five after he slept with her after seducing her with his homemade wine.

Volume Three, begun in the mid-'90s, was composed largely of experiments about the botany of wine grapes and the chemical properties of their vines and their fruit. Piczak was studying *vitis labrusca* vines that produced hardy, fruity grapes like Concords, Catawbas and Niagaras, the staples of New York winemaking for generations. He was trying to differentiate their chemical characteristics from *vitis vinifera,* the vines that produced the cabernets, merlots and chardonnays that constituted the great wines of Europe. It seemed to be a productive time for the professor, because the experiments and the writing were more lucid than in the previous volumes. The work was still credited to a Mangione, but this time it was Gap Mangione, Chuck's brother and another accomplished jazz musician from Rochester. Gap was credited at the beginning of each new experiment, and his name even appeared in two published works in scientific journals. Volume Three ended with several pages of chemical formulas and a large collection of photographs of the Mangione brothers that had been cut out of magazines and pasted onto card-stock.

Daniel, who had grown bored by this time, picked up the fifth and final volume and began to idly flip through its pages after closing the rings. He thought it was cool that the pages in the back of the book were singed at the bottom, like a pirate's treasure map, and he ran his finger across the binder and enjoyed the trail of ash that it cleared.

Ray was wading through synopses of Gap Mangione's experiments when Daniel interrupted him.

"It's called extra-Resveratrol-plus."

"What's called extra-Resveratrol-plus?"

Daniel tapped the green bottle in front of him. "This stuff. That's what he calls it. That's the chemical inside of it that's making all these weird things happen."

He handed the fifth journal to Ray. During a rare and treasured period of clarity, Piczak had found his life's work and was able to focus his research. The journal, which was more than three hundred pages thick, began and ended and was interspersed with an article from the New York Times. Copies of the article appeared every forty pages or so throughout the Piczak journal, generally after the conclusions were reached from strings of experiments, and across the articles Piczak had written angry comments like, "LIES!" "LIARS!" "ABSOLUTELY NOT TRUE," "WHO YOU CALLING A MOUSE?" "WHAT ABOUT MORONGO?" and (Ray's personal favorite), "UNSEEING, UNCOMPREHENDING FOOLS" in a bright-red marker. There was no mention of the Mangione brothers in Volume Five.

The article from the New York Times explained that scientists had isolated a compound called resveratrol that was present in red wines, particularly red wines whose grapes were grown in cool climates, such as the ones in New York state. The chemicals excited biologists and chemists alike, not to mention tipplers, because they mimicked the effects on the body of extremely low-calorie diets, which in turn had been shown in experiments to prolong life. Laboratory rodents who had been put on such diets showed life spans of thirty to fifty percent longer than average. In short, the consumption of resveratrol tricked the body into believing that it was living on a subsistence amount of calories, and triggered its anti-aging mechanisms.

"A chemical that makes you live forever," said Ray.

"I told you you should let me drink wine," Daniel said, tilting the red French Fries box to his mouth and enjoying the scratching sound of the fries sliding against the cardboard into his mouth. "Keep reading; it gets better."

"You're too young," said Ray. "You don't need to live forever yet." He read on. Piczak was trying to find a way to accelerate the properties of the resveratrol that he was able to isolate from concentrates of wine grapes. He conducted hundreds of experiments, sampling the grapes from dozens of vineyards in the region. He found the highest concentration of resveratrol to come from the grapes grown at the Swedish Hill Winery on Cayuga Lake, twenty miles from Morongo. It was the same winery that advertised its red wine as "great to wash down a pizza or a burger." Modesty is a quality that is noticeably absent from the marketing materials of most vintners, but Swedish Hill had it in spades. If they learned that their wine, when distilled to its very essence, could make you live forever they would probably say, "Great to wash down a pizza or a burger when you're 150 years old."

It was an accident in the laboratory that led to Piczak's breakthrough, for he was not only a loquacious man, but a clumsy one. He accidentally spoiled a sample of resveratrol with an industrial hand cleaner that had been scented with the essence of oranges. Then he nearly burned down his home laboratory by tripping and turning the acetylene up way too high. When he threw a handful of fire retardant into the burning compound to retard the gathering fire, chemical magic happened, baby. The resulting molecule had successfully accelerated the resveratrol properties a million-fold. It took him six months of night and day experiments to figure out what he had done, but he finally successfully recreated the conditions of the experiment. He had invented a fountain of youth.

Piczak dubbed the resulting compound ERP, or extra-Resveratrol-plus, when he isolated a batch of it and bottled it. Mouse and yeast tests be damned: He tried it on himself straight away and began to document changes to his very cells, watching them strengthen and mutate under his microscope. At first he had to drink bottles and bottles of the Piczak Snops to achieve even a glimmer of the reversal of aging process, which gave him severe headaches and a wicked halitosis. Over the course of two years, he was able to continually increase the strength of the compound and its affects on his cells until the latest version of snops was so loaded with ERP that a single drop could begin the anti-aging process, and a thimbleful could make a bed-ridden octogenarian stand up and dance an Irish jig.

The formula for ERP was supposed to be at the end of Volume Five, but when Ray got to the section, he found pages missing. Puzzled, Ray flipped ahead several pages and then back again through Volume Five. The pages were numbered, and it took him three passes to understand what he had only sensed. Pages two hundred fourteen to two hundred twenty-four, with precise instructions for synthesizing ERP, were missing. Ray looked through the binder, and then quickly flipped through the other binders and searched inside the seared satchel.

"Did you see any loose pages?" he asked Daniel, who shook his head.

"Something missing?" Daniel asked through a mouthful of the last of the fries.

"Only the secret to how to create eternal life," said Ray.

"Damn."

Ray carefully closed the binder on Volume Five and returned it and the other four volumes to the briefcase. "This is important. You know that, right?"

Daniel rolled his eyes. "Yes, Dad, of course I know that."

"You brought a dead man back to life before my eyes tonight. And then we watched him die again."

"Duh."

"Are you and your girlfriend the only ones who know about this?"

Daniel's face darkened. He looked away from Ray. "Soon to be ex-girlfriend," he said.

"You broke up?"

"She is being really stupid," Daniel said, and tried by looking away from Ray long enough and avoiding the subject to make it go away.

Ray waited him out. After a few minutes of silence, he said, "So what happened?"

Daniel sighed heavily. As if Ray or any adult could possibly understand the intricacies of the heart. As if talking about it could do anybody any good. Some personal things – no, ALL things personal – were always left better unsaid.

"Tell me."

"She was stupid," Daniel repeated. "She doesn't believe in the snops. She says that I'm crazy that you can see how people will die. She apparently doesn't see it. And to prove me wrong, all she wants to do is give it to a bunch of old people. I say that it makes them feel younger; she says that it just makes them drunk."

"Why doesn't she see the effects it has? Why doesn't she get the visions?"

"I have no idea, Dad. Maybe she's just stupid." Daniel moodily looked away.

Another thought occurred to Ray. "Does your mother know about this?" he asked.

Daniel shook his head. "I haven't told anyone about it, Dad. It's too important to trust with grown-ups."

Ray reached his hand across the table and laid it against his son's smooth cheek. He held it there and Daniel didn't pull away. "You saved my life back there on the beach when that boat was coming at us," Ray said. "Thank you. I was very proud of what you did to try to save Dr. Piczak, too."

Daniel shrugged. He smiled and leaned his face into Ray's hand and then turned his head and pretended to bite it. "So what do we do now, Dad?"

Ray said, "We start to save lives."

more NARRATORS
a reasonable explanation of HAUSFRAUS and
HOLLANDER JURISPRUDENCE

You are no doubt wondering how it is that I was never thrown off of the Royal Precious Platinum. I owe it all to a magnificent confluence of circumstances, not to mention the sweetest little chambermaid in the history of the hospitality business. This is, of course, my lovely Austrian wife Irmi, my schnecken, my liebesfrau, my world.

Irmi and I actually met on the first week of my tenancy on board the Royal Precious Platinum. Way back when I was slim. We could hardly miss each other, since she was my chambermaid. How well I remember her lovely blue eyes, her sturdy back and round bottom hidden under a gray uniform, her blonde hair tied back and her wide mouth opening to a grin when I passed her in the corridor.

"Half a GREAT day, Mr. Little," she would call out, and I responded, every time, "Thank you, Fraulein." In my cabin, she arranged my shoes in a line, made the bed just the way that I like it and kept the bathroom spotless.

That in itself is a kind of intimacy, isn't it? I know many people who wish they had even that much from a marriage. We barely spoke to each other, and I could not honestly say that I noticed an attraction in either direction, but still, she was there for me twice a day, to clean my room and turn down my bedclothes at night and leave me a little shaw-co-LOT, as she pronounced it, on my pillow. If nothing else, she was one great chambermaid.

She was only nineteen years old, on her first job away from home. I could never remember the name of her little town in the Austrian Alps -- Oosterlichenbad or Badenoosterlich, I can never get it right. Her English was minimal, and I spoke no German, so there wasn't much to talk about rather than the mutual wishing of a GREAT day, but in those days, that was all the communicating that I needed.

But just because Irmi was barely educated did not mean that she wasn't perceptive. As the months wore on and everyone came to realize that I would not be leaving the ship, it was Irmi, along with my wonderful butler Costas, who cared for me and smoothed my way. When Tennis de Jong, the ship's purser, came prowling around looking for me, his dignified European manners breaking down a little more each week that my bill went unpaid and my shipboard tab continued to soar, it was Irmi or Costas who would find me at whichever buffet venue at which I was camped and warn me to go hide in the children's daycare until Tennis gave up searching for me that day.

And it was Irmi who uncovered my secret and provided the opportunity for me to complete my plan of staying on the ship until I ate myself into oblivion. It was Irmi who found my secret notebooks and my slim collection of orangey-ashey fluid and, in the time that it takes to change a bed and tidy up a sloppy man's room, managed to piece together, bit by bit, my little secret. Even when she discovered and verified the truth -- that despite my immensity it was going to be heroically difficult for me ever to die -- Irmi did not act. She still passed me in the hallways and offered the sunniest of smiles and wishes for the greatest of days. Or, when I was confined to quarters, knocked on my door and asked me if I could use more towels, and maybe a little light fack-ume uff my carpet, as she put it.

It wasn't until Tennis de Jong was bearing down on me with a final eviction notice, a notice that would have dumped me onto a quay in Civitavecchia, Rome with only the undersized shirts on my back and scant means to overeat, that Irmi sprang into action.

Appearing at my door one morning with Costas at her side to act as an interpreter, Irmi wished me a good day, and I responded in kind. They hemmed and hawed in Austrian-German and Portuguese-accented English for a few minutes, because they are polite people, and I asked them if there was something that I could help them with.

"Yes," said Irmi, with a directness that seemed to spring directly from her blue eyes into my brown ones, and which I've always adored. "Zey are making you to leaf the ship soon, yes?"

"Yes, I'm afraid that's true."

"And you half no place of your own to go, yes?"

"Also, true. You're two for two, Irmi."

Costas interrupted. "Yes, of course. Fraulein Irmi has a way to help you. Allow me to explain."

And that was the first time that I heard about the Law of Maritime Incumbency. It was a law peculiar to Dutch maritime commerce that dates backs to the 18th century, and can be summarized like this: If you are both married to a crewmember of a Dutch-registered ship AND have somehow completed thirty successive weeks residency on board that ship, the ship in general and your cabin in particular become your official and lawful domicile until you willingly relinquish it or otherwise remove yourself from its area. The intent of the law was to give merchant sailors' spouses a legitimate address and domicile for legal purposes, if not for practical ones, since in the 18th century *no spouses were actually allowed to travel on the ships. Apparently, during a particularly painful economic period when people were losing their homes and jobs, the maritime industry tried to protect its sailors' and seamen's interests and pushed through the law that allowed families to claim a legal, if not a practical, domicile. Sailors would lie and say that their wives had completed residency on the ship, and the captains and administrators would back them up. The practice lasted a few years until the economy picked up again, and the law faded into anonymity.*

Irmi had done even more checking on the internet and during her brief hours allowed off the ship in ports, where she would head not for the bars or shopping areas, but to the local library. It must have been painstaking work when you can barely read English, much less Dutch, but she persisted. She found that the law had been subsequently invoked only once in the history of the Netherlands, and that to a ship's surgeon and his wife in 1895, but their right to cohabitate and claim their cabin as their legal home had been upheld by the courts, and the law was still on the books.

"And of course, the Royal Precious Platinum is registered under Dutch law," Costas concluded.

"That's great, and very interesting," I said. "But I'm not married to a crewmember."

That was when Irmi stepped forward shyly and took my hand. The moment, I must admit, sent a thrill shivering up my spine that practically made my back fat quiver with it. "Ask me ze kves-chun," she said fetchingly. She looked at me again, and somehow I knew in her frank gaze that she knew everything about me, and knew the secret that I had dared not reveal.

I rubbed my thumb across the top of her soft hand. I asked her something that I had vowed I would never ask anyone again, ever.

"Do you want to live forever?" I asked.

She smiled shyly and nodded her head quickly. "And maybe you can teach me how to do zis?" she asked. "Maybe zis formula or secret zat you half, it vill become ze property uff your vife alzo?"

I nodded my head in return. "Yes, all for one and one for all."

She rubbed my hand affectionately. She really was a sweet girl, if a trifle opportunistic. Young people: Always in a hurry to make their fortune. I'm pretty sure that she had figured out my other secret: That I was eating myself to a late grave.

"You vill marry me?" she asked.

Costas, who was an ordained minister as part of his butler training, did the service on the spot in Portuguese.

My deceased father was a witness of sorts; he did put down his book and watched the whole thing with the faintest trace of a smile on his weathered face. I wore my brightest caftan, and Irmi wore the t-shirt that I had purchased in Skagway. Afterwards, Costas served us cake and coffee, and when Irmi left to clean her afternoon rooms, the narrative group convened and offered congratulations.

None of your business about the consummating the marriage part. Don't even ask.

You should have seen the look on Tennis de Jong's face later that day when he came knocking with the final eviction notice, and I handed him my wedding certificate and claimed domicile in Penthouse Suite #1125. He turned the color of Heineken and swore to get me if I set so much as one large toe outside of my room. In one of the funniest things I've heard lately, he said he'd starve me out if there was no other way, and I picked up a gob of Baked Alaska from a tray and offered it to him.

I must admit, with a boyish blush, that it was the happiest day of my life.

Chapter Ten
in the hills, CREEPING BEWILDERMENT; EAGLES to penguins to EAGLES

Where, you might ask, might we find our hero on the morning after he discovers the secret of eternal life? What does our Mr. Jensen do upon holding in his hands the formula that will give us all that for which we so fervently pray?

Does he hurry his slender butt on down to the pediatric oncology ward at Strong Memorial in Rochester to make-a-wish for every child in residence and buy them all a few more years with a swig or two from his green wine bottle?

No. Sorry.

Does he offer to brighten the days, not to mention the long-term outlooks, and provide some soothing relief to the tracheas of the emphysema-addled smokers at Morongo Hospice?

Nope. Nein. Nichts.

Does he even slink off to the Lap Song Lounge in Dundee with the intention of improving the longevity of a favorite interpretive dancer or two (NOT Jackie)? Many guys secretly hope that their lap dancer will live forever, you know. It's called projecting.

Not our boy. Our fella sleeps in.

He sleeps in, and then he returns a few phone calls.

[Oh, for the love of Francis Ford Coppola, he does *what*?]

Just listen.

On the day after Ray discovered the secret of eternal life, a Sunday, he slept late. When he awoke, light was filling the second floor of his cottage, and through the curtains of his bedroom he could see a sliver of the lake gleaming sea-green. It looked to be a beautiful day. He instinctively reached his hand out to Donna's side of the bed and came up with only her pillow. He remembered that she hadn't been home when he arrived, exhausted, the night before, and that he had forgotten to check his answering machine to see if she had called. He thought about getting up to go downstairs and find the portable phone, but lay back down a moment to gather his thoughts. He brought Donna's pillow to his side and hugged it, imagining the curve of her back and hip and two inches of her neck that he affectionately bit nearly every day that they woke up together. Then he fell back asleep, and didn't wake up again until noon.

He went into the kitchen and started a pot of coffee. Daniel's backpack was on the floor, and Ray opened it, found the bottle of ERP (aka the Piczak Snops), uncorked it and sniffed it, and then closed it tight. He brought the charred, leather briefcase into the living room and checked it to make sure that all five volumes were still there. The events of the previous evening came back to him, and the satchel, as well as the bottles of snops, seemed dangerous and illicit to him. He wondered if he could be in legal jeopardy for possessing either one, particularly given the circumstances of John Piczak's disappearance and death. He decided to hide the satchel under an upholstered recliner, but only after he first wrapped it in two garbage bags and sealed them tight to prevent any moisture damage to Piczak's work.

Ray lingered by the phone, hoping that Donna would call, but it never rang. At two o'clock he left the house, armed with the bottle of snops and Daniel's backpack. It occurred to him that he couldn't very well go anywhere without his life-saving juice anymore. What if he encountered an accident on the street? What if someone he knew was minutes away from a deadly heart attack?

He drove to his brother's house in the hills above the east side of the lake, where a grubby child in denim overalls, no shoes and no shirt was pounding on a rock with a hammer when Ray arrived, and didn't stop as Ray crossed the front lawn and knocked on the door of the old farmhouse.

His sister-in-law Bump came to the door. Her maiden name was Peggy Bump, but Bump she had become during high school and Bump was the name on her wedding invitations with Farrell Jr., and Bump she would ever remain. "Ray," she said at the door. "I didn't know you was coming over."

"Sorry I didn't call," Ray said, leaning down to kiss her cheek but then thinking better of it when Bump turned away from him. "Kind of moving slow today."

"Your brother isn't home," she said. "He went out. Make yourself comfortable if you want to stay." She walked away from him into the living room and sat down on a plaid couch that was covered by two black and red afghan blankets that Ray remembered from his childhood and had been knit by his grandmother. A small television set in the corner of the room was on and flickering, and Bump watched it intently. "Help yourself to a beer," she called out. "I don't wait on nobody on my days off."

You don't do no housework, either, Ray thought. There were dishes piled up in the kitchen sink that showed crusted layers of what appeared to be refried beans from at least the night before, possibly longer, and a pan on the stove had congealed traces of bright orange macaroni and cheese from a box, which was conveniently present and empty on the floor by the stove, as if wolves had hurriedly cooked dinner before moving the pack. Breakfast dishes remained on the table and suggested (to the scholarly observer) that a seismic event may have taken place under the table that scattered six-to-eight participants to the farthest reaches of the house approximately four minutes after having been served a hasty combination of scrambled eggs, bacon and three kinds of cereal. A half-gallon milk jug flung into the corner was emptied and flattened rudely by a foot. All things considered, beer seemed to be a good idea to Ray, and he opened the refrigerator and pulled out a bottle, unscrewed the cap and, finding no clues as to where the garbage can might be kept, dropped the cap into a cereal bowl on the table, where it floated nicely in the remaining puddle of milk and Cheerios.

"Do you know where he went?" Ray asked Bump. She was sitting on the edge of the couch with her hands clutching her knees and her chest almost bent over double to hug her thighs. The pose of a child, thought Ray. She watched the television intently, and Ray gathered at a glance that it was a talk show where half the audience was shouting at the other half, with the occasional encouragement of four dickwalter people on a stage who had apparently decided to mate, but couldn't figure out how or with whom. An unkind thought flashed into Ray's mind: "They will live lives of hopeless ignorance and then die soon."

He wasn't sure if Bump had heard him, so he repeated the question. She seemed almost catatonic, biting her lip and hugging herself as she stared at the television, and the only vision of her demise that he could sense was that Bump would be overcome by sadness, and her life would be replaced not by death but by bitterness and a creeping bewilderment over the conditions that life placed upon her.

(*Beats getting run over by a tractor. Beats it three ways to Friday. You offer me the choice of bewilderment and dismemberment, I'm taking bewilderment every time.*)

She bit her lip and shook her head quickly. "No, he didn't' say nothing," she said. She looked up nervously, as if seeing Ray for the first time. "Ray," she said, "you need to find him. He's not well."

Ray felt a little jolt inside him, a small pang of fear and worry well up. He moved closer to Bump, but she didn't move from her knee-hugging pose, and it was slightly maddening to him that her attention seemed to turn back to the show. "What do you mean?" he said. "Is he sick?"

She shook her head again. "He won't say. He's just mad all the time, and he's stopped talking to us or playing with the kids. Gets up from the table and just leaves the house without a word. And then some days he don't come back. Ray," she said, and she ventured another quick look at him, "we're broke. He hasn't worked in over a year, and my shifts are being cut back at the diner."

"I know that he came into the agency earlier this week and registered for benefits. I didn't know that it was so bad, though."

Bump seemed to stiffen and bristle, a tremor of indignation straightening her back. "Yeah, like the agency ever does anybody a lick of good," she said. "You can register all you want and there isn't a job to be had in this county." Bump started to cry and Ray could see that it wasn't so much from sadness, but because she was seething, furious, and if he had tried to sidle up to her and offer a brotherly embrace, she would have elbowed him in the choppers. He decided quickly that it wasn't a good time to explain that the agency's mission really wasn't to dole out money to every Morongan who couldn't be bothered with learning a new job skill or keeping the jobs that they did get for more than two weeks at a time. Bump didn't seem especially interested in the theories and practice of public assistance and its evolution since the Great Society was formed.

"I'll try to help him," said Ray, "but you know, he usually won't even talk to me."

She waved her hand dismissively. "Join the club."

Ray noticed then that something had been missing since the moment he stepped into the house, and it wasn't only Farrell's absence. The house was unusually quiet and had a sort of vacated feeling. The ten little wildpersons who were Ray's nieces and nephews were conspicuously absent, not counting the one with the hammer in the front yard whose name eluded Ray at the moment. "Where are your kids?" he asked.

Bump waved again and shook her head, and Ray noticed a new look of fear in her eyes. "Older ones are out with their friends," she said. "Baby's sick. Been sick for a week, and we can't even afford to take her to the doctor. Your agency don't cover that."

"Well, actually it does if you apply and qualify for the right kind of assistance," he said. "I could help you with the paperwork. Can I see her?"

"She's upstairs in my bedroom. Go ahead," said Bump, and when Ray hesitated, unsure of where to find the stairs, she added, "Same place they've been the last twenty years, Ray. Over there by the corner."

He walked to the corner of the room, pushing past the piles of clothes on the uneven, slatted floor that had been painted black for as long as he could remember. There was a door in the corner that he had always assumed was a closet, but when he opened it he found a narrow staircase that was lit by a single, bare bulb hanging from a wire. He went up and came out in a landing that was larger than a hallway and smaller than a room. There was a twin bed on the floor in the corner onto which were heaped sheets and blankets and a child's clothes, and more clothes were hung on hangars on a wire rack in the corner of the space, which showed four doors. One of the doors was opened to reveal a bathroom with an old claw-footed tub that had been rigged with wires and a curtain to make a shower. Rotted drywall panels had been torn away in places to reveal bare studs and the inside of the house's outer siding, and the floor was the same wide, uneven boards from the living room, only painted industrial gray this time, which was the same color as most of the walls. Somebody at some time had apparently given thought to adding flourishes of green in spots, but had apparently given up on the idea or run out of paint, and the green remained in patches on two of the walls. A rusted tin mirror unit was hung above the sink, its hinges rusted open to reveal shelves that were crammed with medicines and beauty products. Two of the other doors opening into the space were closed, and Ray could hear faint strains of radios or televisions playing inside the rooms. The fourth door was open, revealing a corner of Bump and Farrell's queen bed on a frame that Ray remembered from the old house on Main Street where his family had lived before moving to the cottage. He heard sounds of sniffling and followed them into the room.

A baby girl of somewhere fifteen months old was lying quietly in the center of the queen bed. Her eyes were open and they studied Ray's face when he came into the room, but moved away. Her chest was rising and falling steadily and her breaths were punctuated by the movement of heavy mucus in her nose and throat that seemed to be moving into her chest and causing a rasp with every third or fourth breath. Ray sat down on the edge of the bed and touched the little girl's arm gently. She was terribly hot. If she was the youngest of Farrell's kids then her name would be…Molly…he guessed.

"Are you sick?" he asked.

Her eyes returned to his face and she scanned his face and eyes. She nodded and tried to say something, but the attempt made her cough so hard that Ray instinctively reached behind her head and lifted it until the coughing stopped. He found a tissue in a box on the night table and tried to blow her nose, but she didn't know how to do it and just blew on the tissue from her mouth.

Ray pictured no future for her, and nothing but sadness. He had to do something. "I have something that can make you better," he said. He opened his backpack and removed the bottle of snops, and carefully opened it. "Will you drink some of this?" he asked.

She shook her head and eyed the bottle nervously.

"I think you'll like it."

She shook her head again, but didn't pull away when Ray gently supported her back with his hand. He carefully brought the bottle to her lips and tipped it until the clear fluid formed a line against her upper lip. She jerked back and a violent cough exploded from her throat, followed closely by a wad of mucus that shot from her open mouth and narrowly missed Ray's left ear. She struggled for breath for a moment and then began to howl a full-throated cry that seemed to have the capacity to fill the volume of the old farmhouse.

Bump arrived moments later while Ray was searching for the cork to the bottle. "She seems to have perked right up," Bump said. "What in the world did you do?"

Ray tried to act surprised. "I just gave her a little taste of this juice. It's very healthy. Donna drinks it all the time."

Bump reached for the bottle and eyed it critically. "You gave wine to a baby?" she asked. She sniffed it and then raised it to her lips and took a drink. She grimaced, and then took another swallow, and grimaced again. "Jeez, this stuff tastes awful. This is the worst wine I think I've ever tasted. I think it's gone bad, Ray. You shouldn't give stuff like this to a little kid, Ray."

The child reached for her mother and pointed to her lip, which was still wet from the drink. She wailed again, but it was a wail of shock more than of pain. Bump gathered her in her arms and held her.

"You shouldn't give stuff like that to a child, Ray," she repeated.

"I was just trying to help. And it seems to have cleared her head up pretty good."

Bump studied her child. A long trail of yellowish snot began to peek out of the girl's nostrils and then disappear back inside her nose with several breaths, and then it gave up the game and flowed out of her nose. Bump found the tissue on the side of the bed and wiped it clean. "Well, her fever seems to have broken. And her head looks like it's trying to drain, finally. I'll give you that much."

Ray watched them blankly, and then reached for his wallet and pulled out forty dollars. "Let me at least try to help you out. Grocery money," he said. Bump wordlessly accepted the cash and held it tightly in her hand. "And I'll try to find Farrell," he added.

"You do that, Ray," she said, and watched him turn and leave the room.

Outside, the little boy was still pounding the rock with the hammer. He looked to be about five years old. He paused for a moment when Ray neared.

"Hey Mister," said the little boy. "You're a fuckhead."

Ray stopped and stared. He could not for the life of him remember the child's name. The little boy stood up, made a face, and ran off towards the house.

An hour later, Ray was at his mother's house watching Caroline pick up her collection of ceramic penguins and move them to where the carved eagles were, pick up the eagles and move them to the shelf with the antique spoons. She looked small and tired to him, and he realized as he watched her that she had entered a period of mourning to which she always returned at this time of year, at the anniversary of Farrell Sr.'s death. She would walk around the cottage restlessly, touching every object in the house, as if to feel her world in her hands and clarify her place in it.

Ray pointed out what she was doing, and she said that it was part of her cleaning.

"Usually, cleaning involves a duster or rag or paper towel," he said.

She didn't appreciate his tone of voice. "Then I'm rearranging my things," she said. "Is there something wrong with that?"

Eagles to penguins, spoons to eagles. She reached for the fountain pen stuck in a faux-marble holder with Farrell's name stamped into a gold plate, spun it twice between her thumb and index finger and put it back. "Did you come over here to give me a lecture?" she said.

Historically, the mourning period would last from two weeks to two months, and then she would get sick with a flu or bronchitis and be bed-ridden for a week before her penance was completed and she could resume her life. This usually coincided with the beginning of summer, and sitting in the sun watching the lake was what brought her back to the land of the living. This time, Ray pictured clearly in his mind that the illness that was bound to come over her would be her last one, and would put her in a bed at Soldiers & Sailors Memorial Hospital from which she would not leave.

"No," said Ray. "I came over here to ask you about John Piczak. Do you remember him?"

"Sure. Chemistry professor. Bit of a flake. I never liked him."

"Friend of dad's?"

"I'm not sure you could call him a friend. He was an oddball. He had or tried to have numerous affairs at the college, and after awhile, everyone steered clear of him. The last time I saw him he was wearing an ascot and wanted to be called Chuck."

"So what did you do?"

"I called him Chuck. What else was I supposed to do?"

Ray made an attempt to keep his voice even and casual. "He calls me sometimes."

Penguins to spoons. Eagles to spoons. Spoons to the top of the refrigerator. "He calls me, too," she said. "I hang up on him. He's crazy as a carp."

Ray took the green bottle out of the backpack. "Mother," he said, "I want you to try something."

"What is it?"

"I can't tell you."

"You can't tell me?"

"No," said Ray. "All I can say is that it is good for you. It will improve your health."

She took the bottle and sniffed it. "So what's wrong with my health? Besides the fact that I'm old and everything hurts."

Ray took a deep breath. "Mother," he said, "what if I told you that I have discovered a miracle. And this miracle can keep us all alive forever. You don't have to do anything for it, or pay for it, and the side effects are very mild, and you'll never be sick or be put in the hospital again."

She touched her finger to the rim of the bottle and placed it carefully on the tip of her tongue. "Keep me alive forever?"

"I think so."

"Can it bring your father back to life? Because, my darling, I don't see much point in staying alive forever like this. I'd rather be living where he's living. Can it do that, my darling boy?"

Ray blushed. "No, of course it can't do that."

"Then come back and ask me again when you find a miracle that can bring your father back to us. That would be a miracle that I'd be interested in."

Penguins to eagles, eagles to spoons, spoons to the desktop.

Ray excused himself and went into the bathroom. He poured an ounce of snops into the glass on the sink where she kept her dentures at night. He returned to the living room and kissed her on the cheek.

"Have you spoken to your brother lately?"

"No, not since the other day, when he dropped by the office," said Ray. Talking with Caroline often had the quality of counterintelligence agents exchanging information in a wired room. He was never quite certain of what she knew, and she liked it that way. Gathering data had become the sport that suited her retirement years.

"What did he say?"

"Nothing."

"Oh." She sounded disappointed. "Well I haven't heard from him for a week. So tell him to call me if you see him. His baby's sick, by the way. You might send Bump a card or something."

"Which baby is that?"

Caroline thought for a moment. "I don't know. I can never keep them all straight."

"Me either."

"So what are you going to do with your miracle bottle of wine?" she asked.

"I don't know," said Ray. "Throw it in the lake."

"Good idea," she said. Penguins to penguins. Eagles to eagles. Spoons to spoons. She was eyeing the fountain pen on the desk when Ray left.

THE NARRATORS
what happened out by the PANAMA CANAL

Wednesday afternoon. Story meeting. Panama Canal outside my verandah, judging from the giant locks and all of the engineers on board.

The part of me that is Poodle raises her hand tentatively, lowers it, chews her lip, raises her hand again halfway, decides something and then raises it all the way and waves it. "Can I say something?" *she asks brightly.* "Can I have a turn?"

"I don't want to sound like I'm complaining or anything. But couldn't we make this a little nicer? A little happier? I mean, everybody's dying, or is going to die, and practically has thought balloons over their head about how they're going to die, and isn't the whole point that we should just enjoy the living part? Where do our characters say that they like the living part, and appreciate the fact that we've given them life in the first place?"

She looks around brightly at the other component parts of me, as if this fine speech should earn her a dollar tip placed daintily inside her leg garter. Everybody ignores her.

Falubio clears his throat. "I mean, what's the big deal?" he asks the room. "Life isn't so tough; Ray is just a big baby. You know what life is? You make a little money, you buy something to eat, you keep yourself in shape, you have a cup of coffee. Life just comes to you and you live it, and that's all there is to it. Somebody takes a picture of you and they send a big check to your agent and you buy yourself a new car. It's just that simple. I don't get all this stuff about waiting around and wondering about when you die. Like, what's the point?"

Surprised looks on the faces of the other members of the narrative group. This is the most we've heard from Falubio in three months.

Floyd Little waves his stiff arm and is given the floor. "You know, I agree with Falubio," he says. "This dying stuff, it's all in our head. We was made the way we was made, and nothing's gonna change that. Life is what it is; so is death. People a hundred years ago didn't sit around and worry about when they was going to die. They just died. They lived their lives and died. They died young sometimes. They lost babies routinely. They had seven kids, and if four of them showed up at the dinner table they thought they was doing pretty good. Their life span was *forty-five years old, and they didn't know any better. They didn't know about myocardial...itis...or something. They didn't know about cells dividing and cancerous growths. They had a lump on their neck and it hurt, and their stomachs hurt, and then they died. They didn't have time to worry about that stuff. They were busy living while they was alive. So could somebody please explain to me why we're spending so much time talking about it?"*

At that moment I happened to glance over at my dad, who had closed his book and was following the conversation. He nodded and tapped his forefinger to his lip and then pointed it at Floyd: Point well made.

Does anybody want to be God? I ask.

No takers. No answers. My father, I notice, smiles a small smile and then goes back to his reading.

And then A Guy Named Brad unfurls his scroll of questions and begins to read in his high-pitched, unnerving voice. Everyone else groans. This is going to be a long one. "Why is there so much pain?" he begins. "Why is there suffering? Why in the world do we need Lou Gehrig's Disease? People! Somebody has to ask these questions!"

Blah blah blah. We've all heard this before. Brad seems to think that if he asks the same stupid questions over and over they will be somehow validated, and then answered. If I were his God, I'd ignore him, too. Like most mosquitoes, he likes to hear himself talk. His voice takes on the aspect of an annoying drone somewhere deep inside our heads as we all drift off into our own thoughts, and Barry the Cruise Director comes on the intercom to brief us on that evening's exciting entertainment options, and Costas brings a plate of fatty hors d'oeuvres, and the ship goes clunk clunk clunk, and slips down lock after lock after lock. And then we're on the other side of Panama, and I don't hardly know how we got there.

more NARRATORS
MEXICAN HEARTBREAKER

Four days later we are trawling slowly through the warm, blue waters outside of Enseñada, Mexico on the eight-day "Wonders of the Mexican Riviera" cruise. The day had begun typically enough. A sumptuous breakfast at nine, a brief pause to let everything settle and then a stuffing session that had a special emphasis on dairy fats (crème brulees, milkshakes, full fat French bries and Camemberts). I don't remember feeling anything different than usual other than a mild discomfort deep in my abdomen that I generally associate with the kitchen running out of custard pies.

I awoke to find my father reading quietly, as was his custom, at his chair. I asked him the usual question.

"Now?"

He put his thumb on the page to not lose his place. And then he looked me in the eyes with a frank gaze that might even be construed as pity. He did not shake his head, as he always had before. He nodded. He mouthed the

[219]

word, "Now." And then my chest began to hurt as badly as a chest can hurt. I was having my heart attack.

I must report that it was every bit as crushing, vice-like, excruciating and terrifying as advertised. Mine was not to be a heart attack that was announced by the hoped-for symptoms of indigestion and a vague malaise of the spirit. Mine felt more like a quartet of sumo wrestlers had been instructed to carry a Steinway grand piano from their dojo, deposit it onto my chest and then stand atop it doing jumping jacks.

"I'll be damned," I remember thinking, "maybe I can die after all."

The last thing I recall, besides searing, blinding, liver-bursting pain, was seeing my father fold up his book, sigh, tap his chest over his heart once, and then make a what-can-you-do? gesture with his shoulders. By his gesture, I understood him to mean that I was having a heart attack. I concurred. I made a loud gagging noise and then collapsed theatrically and face first onto the coffee table, which splintered under my considerable weight and sent me to the floor in a jagged heap. I also vomited but (I'm proud to say) held my bowels, which was practically an Olympian feat of athletic skill under the circumstances.

The next thing of which I was aware was when I was dangling on a gurney high above the ship and staring up at the confusing sight of the underside of a helicopter, its skids scraped and pitted, its belly open and a begoggled Coast Guard officer beckoning me to ascend to him with one hand, his other hand on the wire that served as an umbilicus between me and the aircraft. When I glanced over the side of the gurney, I saw that the ship's uppermost deck was crowded with people who were watching my evacuation. From what I gathered, some four hundred drunks were on board and had been drinking ceaselessly since Acapulco. They were a raucous bunch, perhaps owing to the wine seminars that constituted a shipboard enrichment program, emphasis on California varietals and tequila. Their silence and concern after four days of unceasing noise was all the more striking when I looked out over the gurney, with a sweeping view of the ocean below me and the underside of a helicopter above me. They watched me being borne aloft with stunned looks on their faces. I'm fairly certain that I saw an attractive woman in her late fifties turn to a deckhand and mouth the words, "Is this included?"

    It must have been her first cruise.

    Most of the real fun had occurred before I came to. Upon hearing of my plight from a frantic Irmi and Costas, who heard me crash to the floor, the helicopter had been summoned all the way from San Diego by Tennis de Jong, which was awfully thoughtful of him considering that he must have reckoned (correctly) that I had neither medical insurance nor the means to pay for emergency airlifts. I gather that he finally saw a way to get me off the ship that would not conflict with the Law of Maritime Incumbency, and seized it. Upon arrival and a thrilling descent by two uniformed paramedics by means of the guidewire and a harness, the medics came barging in through my door to rescue me, loaded me onto the gurney with considerable effort and the assistance of three tequila-intoxicated paramedics from Cleveland who had won the cruise in a raffle, and then found that I wouldn't fit through my doorway, with or without the additional mass of the Coast Guard medic who sat on my chest and shoved at my heart with both hands, demanding rhythmia.

  Much low comedy ensued with my feet sticking out into the hallway of the Penthouse deck, my belly lodged against my doorframe and my head resolutely residing inside Penthouse Suite #1125. Thank God that my cabin not only had a verandah, but a full-sized sliding glass door, because the only other option was to wheel me straight outside and undertake a very tricky lift with a long cable that pulled the helicopter perilously close to the ship's stacks when the weight of me and the gurney caught on the cable, tightened it dangerously, and then lifted me, swaying crazily, over the blue Pacific.

When I peeked over the side of the gurney and saw all of those somber people, I also made out my wife and chambermaid, Irmi, my most wunderbahr frau. Her pretty pink complexion was red, and I could see that she was sobbing. She held a handkerchief in one hand and in the other she was waving a glass jar. It took a moment for me to recognize the jar, but it came to me just as my tongue and lips felt their first sensation return other than systemic pain. They registered a lingering, but definite taste of ashes and oranges and bitterness. Irmi had somehow managed to slip me a dose of snops as the medics cursed and unwedged me from my own doorway.

It was the last of my snops. She had given up her marital security deposit to keep me alive. It was also the last time I ever saw Irmi. Every time I asked Costas about her after that, he looked away and said that her contract had expired.

Irmi was waving the jar at me and by the looks of things and the way my throat felt, she had emptied the entire contents of it down my gullet. As I approached the open hatch of the chopper, my tongue peeked out and licked my upper lip, and I felt the lingering spice of snops as my first sentient sensation upon returning from the dead.

I wish I had a near-death experience to relate – something soulful and deeply poignant that alludes to mythology, religion, beatitude and glimpses of the after-life – but honestly, all that I gathered about death was that it hurt like hell and I was glad when it was over. The pain subsided all of a sudden, but only when, four feet from the salvation of the hatch, with the Coast Guard cadet reaching his hand out to grasp my gurney, I felt a quite unprecedented bubble of gas begin to move somewhere near my sternum, rush towards my diaphragm, quiver slightly and fill my belly as if gathering itself, and then come roaring out of me in what one might reasonably describe as a cataclysmic wind. Within seconds, the expression on the face of the cadet turned from concerned and duty-focused to horrified and repulsed, and he turned his head away involuntarily from the deep, musky smell that seemed to emanate in waves from beneath me. Forty feet below us, the noxious cloud that I had produced descended upon the ship thanks to the assistance of the copter's pulsing rotors, and a low moan of revulsion rose up from four hundred scalded throats. Show over: The crowd on deck scattered like mice from the crew's pantry, and sought the comfort of indoor ventilation.

By the time the medics had completed my journey and pulled me into their cozy lair, I was feeling many things, the foremost being relief. "How do you feel?" the cadet shouted, a trifle suspiciously I felt, as if I had been making the whole thing up.

"Quite good, really," I replied. "A little hungry." They asked and I answered queries about my name, age and where I was feeling pain, which I had to admit was completely gone.

They didn't seem to be happy for me. They conducted some tests, hooked me up to machines and took some readings, and asked me pointed questions about what I had eaten, and when. My answers, which were truthful and detailed, didn't seem to satisfy them, and I had to repeat myself several times, particularly concerning the questions about the quantities of food that I'd consumed. I wasn't the least bit upset about their courtroom-type interrogation. In truth, I was so thrilled to be out of pain and alive, and it occurred to me that if I cooperated fully and didn't cause the Coast Guard undue delays, I might still make it back to the ship in time for dinner.

"There's nothing wrong with him," the head honcho finally said in disgust to his cohorts, as if he were paid by the amount of dead-or-dying tissue that he returned to the mainland. Still hovering above the ship, which was turning slow circles a mile in diameter in the open water, they kicked around the idea of taking me to a hospital but decided, after a shrewd calculation of my weight divided by the fuel consumption characteristics of the helicopter, that it would be cheaper all around to leave me. In another brilliant technical feat of maneuvering, the pilot again brought the helicopter down low and they lowered me carefully on the gurney back to my verandah. The cadet unsnapped my restraints and helped me to my feet.

"Have a nice cruise," he said a trifle disdainfully, tugged once on the wire and then ascended back to his mother ship, which banked jauntily and headed back to the mainland.

Three hours after I had succumbed I was back in my easy chair with my slippers on, and Costas was nervously serving me a vodka gimlet.

"That was a close one, Sir," he said.

I nodded my head in agreement and assessed my condition once more. We were both slightly amazed and speechless at all that had transpired, and Costas left quietly after freshening my jug of ice water and tucking a blanket around me. My father, I noticed, refused to look at me. He studiously read his book, and I gathered a trace of malice from his shade, as if he were wondering why some people survive heart attacks and others don't.

It was several hours later that evening, as the ship resumed its journey and distant lights revealed the far-off shores of the Baja Peninsula, that the real heartache came. I realized all at once that something was missing, and it was Floyd Little. That is, the life-sized cardboard cutout of him that had accompanied me for so long was no longer in its customary place behind the easy chair, adjacent to the sliding glass doors.

"Where's Floyd?" I screamed to an empty room.

There was a brief, confusing rustle of voices. Then Falubio said, "We're sorry, boss." With a catch in his voice he added, "We lost the football player."

"How did we lose him?" I cried out, clutching a pillow to my ample belly.

The simple answer was that it was the wind from the helicopter combined with an open verandah door that caused Floyd to fly over the side of the railing and land headfirst in the drink. But there was more to the story than that, of course. Some say that Floyd saw me ascending towards the heavens in my gurney and suddenly recalled the sight of a huge blocker leading him into a hole. He tightened his grip on the ball crooked in his forearm, stiffened his stiff arm, and followed me to glory. Others say that he was looking after me like a padded guardian angel, and followed me airborne until he saw that I was alright, and perhaps it was my gigantic fart that dazed and flattened him and sent him into the ocean. Still another theory, *advanced by conspiracists among the narrative group, posits that someone (and here, all fingers point towards A Guy Named Brad) managed to loosen the football in Floyd's arm with a scissors or a knife, and when the verandah door was open and the winds came, the ball flew out of Floyd's grasp towards the open water. Fumble! His instincts took over and like a good running back, he leaped after it, and was gone.*

All I know is that he is gone forever, and I stayed up all night mourning him and wondering, now that we don't have a straight-line runner left among the narrative group, how we will ever finish this story. Everyone was a mess. The part of me that is Poodle cried all night. Falubio brooded like he was auditioning for Hamlet. A Guy Named Brad was uncharacteristically silent.

On my verandah, I stood with my hands on the polished teak rail and I shouted things to the sea, eleven decks below. It pains me to report that I was, in fact, railing at the ocean, but there is no other way to put it. I shouted my usual refrain: "I'm a lousy God!"

I also shouted, "I don't know anything! What kind of God doesn't know anything? A lousy God, that's what kind."

The ocean didn't answer, of course. The swell of it caused a tremor to appear in the floppy fat below my right clavicle and sent the tremor all the way around me in a clockwise manner, ending in a little bouncing motion over my still-beating heart.

Some God I am. Some divine deity.

For the first time all year I sat on my verandah and just watched the dark water rush past the ship, wondering about loss and pains both physical and emotional, and death and redemption. With every death, you lose part of yourself. Every football player and father who flies over the railing and goes overboard from life takes with him a piece of your heart, and for someone with an ongoing fear of heart disease, that's a piece that is sorely missed and can't be spared.

Costas found me there, asleep, in the morning, and politely rustled dishes and furniture loudly enough to wake me. I should eat a little something, he said, to have strength to continue. You should have fun on a cruise, and satisfy your urges, he said. He laid out the breakfast buffet, and with a heavy heart, I went to it. From the armchair, my father pointed to a nice-looking Belgian waffle that was slathered with whipped cream and studded prettily with raspberries and pitted cherries. Sadly, but with ultimate devotion, I slid it onto a plate and began to eat.

Chapter Eleven
Middle SCHOOL can be so TOUGH

I have a question: If God, or Falubio, who sometimes thinks he's God, wants us to die so easily and so unfailingly, why did he make us struggle so hard to stay alive? As my late grandmother, the famous philosopher Nanny, might have put it, "That self-preservation, it's really something, that self-preservation."

Question number two: If it happens to everyone, why do we see it as tragic? Why isn't it funny? Could it be that the Big Guy gets a good chuckle from our bull-headed struggles to stay alive in the face of overwhelming evidence to the contrary? If so, I wish to say this publicly; I'll shout it to the seven seas. "You're not funny!" I would shout. "You're sick if you think that's funny! You should see a divine therapist."

And finally, I wonder if it could be that the screenwriters are the only ones who are getting it all right. They, after all, can't get through a two-hour movie script without spraying crowds of people with automatic weapons, inflicting terrible viruses on mankind, dropping aliens from the sky to blow up well-populated parts of town, and derailing whole trains and somehow pretending that the screams aren't attached to pain. Could it be that they're all in cahoots and are trying to lighten our collective load a bit, and help desensitize us so that dying will one day become as funny and commonplace as falling down a manhole that (comically) was left opened on a busy street?

I'm just asking.

But now I detect a high-pitched whine of frustration filling up my penthouse suite. Our story has languished all the way from Mexico to Juneau, Alaska, and it's time to get back to work. So where were we? Oh yes, Farrell Jr. was missing, Ray had a snops problem, Daniel had a Jodi problem, Janice was trying to get Ray on the phone, and Caroline was puttering around her house rearranging the penguins and the eagles.

Here's what happened.

Ray took a different route downtown on Monday morning, passing in front of Morongo Middle School. It was early enough that the schoolchildren stood huddled in small clusters outside before the first bell, an astonishing variety of physical types between the puny sixth grade boys who were slow to develop, their female counterparts looming above them, skinny and awkward like Praying Mantises with braces, and the hulking eighth graders who by all rights should have been shaving twice a day and playing linebacker for the high school Mustangs.

There was still a morning chill in the air, a reminder that winter was not so long passed, and a cold front could sweep across Lake Ontario from Canada at any moment, rush down the glacial valleys of the Finger Lakes and bring with it a late snow. Despite the cool morning, the middle school children wore only t-shirts or midriff tops; no jackets or sweaters allowed in this particular fashion season. Half of them completed the ensemble with long, baggy shorts; the other half wore threadbare sweatpants, because Morongo was a poor community. They stood shivering and slouching, hands thrust into pockets, trying mightily to look nonchalant and somehow warm, as if inner heat were an adult trait that they all claimed.

Ray spotted two of his brother Farrell's kids, the younger boy and his sister. They stood in separate groups and seemed particularly ragged and cold, their thin shoulders even more hunched and vulnerable than the other kids'. A good uncle, Ray noted to himself, would remember the names of the children and would know stuff like which grade they were in and who had a birthday coming up soon.

Another characteristic of Ray's: He was not a good uncle.

Ray slowed down and considered honking the horn to catch the attention of his niece and nephew, but they were rapt in their groups, observing intently what the lead animals in their packs were saying and doing. He stopped the car and got out and approached the groups of children. Farrell's third-to-youngest son (Tommy? Leo?) was standing with his back to Ray and the second-oldest girl (Sheila? Marcie?) was facing him. Conversation stopped and a sheen of dullness slipped over the faces of the schoolchildren as they grasped that an intruder was in their midst; they instinctively moved away from Ray, leaving his niece and nephew isolated from the groups.

"Hi. You know who I am, right?" Ray asked the girl.

She nodded and looked at the ground. "Uncle Ray," she whispered.

"That's right." He had an overwhelming desire to feed them hot soup and give them a dollar. "I have to ask you something. Did your dad come home last night?"

The girl, still looking at the ground, shook her head. The boy took a step closer. "Who did you say you were, Mister?" he asked. His face was freckled and his hair was red. He looked like he might have a standing invitation to detention.

Ray faced him. "I'm your Uncle Ray."

"Well, Uncle Ray, why don't you get the hell out of here before I call the police?" asked the boy. "We don't answer no questions about our father."

Tough crowd.

The girl stepped towards him. "Be quiet, Tim," she admonished her brother. "Uncle Ray, I think he's at the college."

"Your dad?"

She nodded her head, and then without another word, turn and ran all the way to the schoolhouse.

Ray returned to the car and drove past the high school, hoping to see Daniel on his way to school. He trolled past the same clumps of boys, but not his son and, disappointed, Ray returned downtown. Halfway there, a familiar figure appeared in the sidewalk in his rearview mirror, and Ray pulled to the side to watch. Like a freight train from the Great Plains, like a dump truck full of gravel, Janice was chugging up the sidewalk in her morning jog. Cheeks puffed from the effort and hair pulled strictly back, she passed his car without comment.

Ray felt something cold and clammy seize his heart, and his breathing became short. He had had a vision about

Janice when she passed so close to him, and it was a vision that made him hopelessly sad.

She was going to live longer than he was.

Damn the luck. Damn the capricious nature of snops and its effects on different tissues.

An hour later, like a sylph, or a shadow, or the ghostly Grandma that she was, Marjorie Corcoran Disbrow appeared in Ray's office and waited beside him in a silent, looming way (if 105-pound grandmothers can truly be said to loom) until he not so much saw as felt her there and jerked to attention with a nervous start.

"How you terrify me, Marjorie," he said.

"Oh, pssht," she replied. "Are you alright, Ray?"

Ray frowned. "Now why does every woman I adore ask me that these days? Donna leaves me notes on the mirror asking if I'm alright. My mother and my ex-wife ask me what the hell is wrong with me on a regular basis. Do I appear to not be well?"

Marjorie patted his shoulder. "We're all concerned about you, Ray. We can never quite tell if you're in agony or just trying to be funny."

They looked at each other a moment and then Ray said, "You go first."

Marjorie eyed her exit and, satisfied that the path to the hallway was clear, eased a step closer to Ray and quartered herself towards him in order to present as narrow a target as possible. "Did you write my memo? The one about why we're here?"

Ray looked at her quizzically. "Why are we here, MJ?"

She shut her eyes and bit her lip to summon concentration. "I think that we're here because some higher power, in our case Albany, has put us here to do our life's work, and a deity, Richard From Rochester, allows us to stay here as long as we don't do anything to harm ourselves or others. That's the way that I understand it."

Ray nodded. "Beautifully put. How about I write that we're here because it is our lifelong calling to selflessly serve the public and help other people to be happy."

"Well, you're the writer. Your turn."

"Have you seen my brother today?"

"No, he hasn't been in."

"Well if he comes down to check on his benefits, or calls, would you call me right away?"

"Without delay," said Marjorie Corcoran Disbrow, and then she was gone from Ray's office with only a soft whispering sound of Wal-Mart fashions (purchased in Geneva only that weekend) to announce her exit.

Ray opened his computer to the word processing program and wrote two memos to Richard From Rochester in response to his missive of the day before, signed one from himself and the other one from Marjorie, made multiple copies of both, and as the last page sighed out of the printer, Marjorie reappeared briefly to collect them. She glanced at them, nodded appreciatively and said, "I'll file and distribute them. Thanks, Ray."

The concept of filing and distributing sparked an idea in Ray, and he turned to his computer, logged onto the state system, and typed in the name Jodi Bullock. Three responses came back, but two were in Poughkeepsie and one in Watertown. He rummaged through the bottom drawers of his desk and found the Morongo phone book, and turned to Bullock. There were eighteen listed, and he tried to remember where Jodi lived. By her bike riding, her bangs and the way she wore her jeans low on her hips and flared around her flip-flop sandals so that they pooled on the ground by her feet and frayed at the edges, he made her for a town girl. The farm girls of greater Morongo wore tight, colored jeans in yellow and purple that widened only enough to fit snugly around their riding boots. That eliminated half of the Bullocks, who lived in the outlying farming communities of Himrod and Naples and Dundee. Of the other nine, four lived out by the college in Morongo Park, and three were on the lake, both of which were too rich for Jodi's blood. The two remaining Bullocks lived near downtown Morongo; one in an apartment building that backed up to the alley behind Long's Bookstore and the Wagonwheel, and the other in a mobile-home park on the north side of town, where the houses turn dilapidated over the space of two blocks and the elm trees and green lawns that characterize much of Morongo give way to scrubby, yellow grass clinging to a hardpan surface, as if the water supply suddenly ran out.

    Ray opted for the latter address and typed in the names Kathleen and Stanley Bullock that came with the phonebook listing. The address came up on his screen and was followed by a ten-year history of intermittent benefits applied for and granted when the father was out of work or temporarily disabled. With the listing were details on four dependents, the last one of whom was misspelled as Jody Bullock, birthdate November Seventeenth, 1987. Ray wrote the address down on a slip of paper and put it into his pocket, and considered his options. Should he confront the girl in front of her parents and accuse her of…what? Prolonging the lives of Morongo's senior citizens? Possessing a colorless, odorless liquid? Corrupting the morals of his teenaged son? Should he demand that she turn over all bottles of legal and uncontrolled substances, under threat of his calling the cops, when he had the same stuff sitting in his refrigerator? This required more thought.

The phone rang and Ray was relieved to recognize his mother's number on the caller ID. "Don't ask me if I'm alright," he said in lieu of a greeting.

"Why would I ask you that?" Caroline said after a moment. "Is there something going on that I should know about?"

"No, mother, nothing at all. What's up?"

"Funny that you should bring up John Piczak. He passed away over the weekend," she said.

Ray made an attempt to keep his voice even and casual. "How did he die?"

"I don't know. He appears to have drowned. I just heard it from Mary Wilbur at the college. Some rotten kids burned up his boat over the weekend, too, but they don't think it's related."

"I'm sorry to hear that," said Ray. "Anything else? Because I'm kind of on the public's time here, you know?"

"Well I'm the public and you can keep the dime," she said tartly, and then hung up.

Chapter 12
Jodi's HOUSE

Ray found the entrance to the mobile home park, turned in and drove slowly past a line of mobile homes that had long since lost all ability to be mobile. They sat rooted and rusted and shedding their parts. The Bullock's trailer showed a rusted white exterior trimmed in lavender that had faded to a dull puce. A canvas awning was stretched from the long end of the trailer, over the door, and was held up by flimsy poles to create a patio over a square section of green vinyl carpet that simulated grass and held three molded plastic chairs surrounding a telephone-wire spindle that served as a picnic table. An ashtray on the spindle was overflowing with cigarette butts, and a glow from the window indicated that the television was on inside the house.

Ray knocked on the screen door, which made a thin, clanging sound as the door rattled against its frame. There was no answer, and he waited. He knocked again. He was about to open the screen door and knock on the inner door when it opened a crack and a woman's voice said roughly, "What is it?" The door was secured by a chain, which was at eye level to the woman.

"I'm Ray Jensen," he said, "and I was hoping to speak with Jodi. It's about my son, Daniel."

"Why would she know about that?" asked the woman.

Because they stole the fountain of youth together, Ray thought. Because they are dumb kids who have been handed an enormous power. Because weird things happen to good people, even in a town like Morongo. But he didn't say any of that. "I think they're kind of dating," he said. "But who knows? Look, I'm sorry to bother you, but this won't take long."

The door closed and there was a rattle of the chain being unlatched, and the door opened again. The woman standing there was petite, with gray hair pulled back in a ponytail, eyes lined from worry and a mouth that seemed to cave in on itself from years of relentless pulling on the brown ends of cigarettes. She looked old and tired, but oddly familiar, like a teenager who makes herself up to appear old. Ray realized that he knew her. They had gone to school together in Morongo as children. "Aren't you Kathy Rogers?" he asked.

She exhaled a sharp breath through her nose, and the lines around her mouth re-arranged into a thin, unaccustomed smile. "Was once. Hasn't been Rogers for thirty years, Ray. You're thinking about a girl from another life." She bared her teeth in a larger smile, and they were small and yellow.

Ray vaguely recalled a quiet, cheerful girl who sat in the back of the classroom in grade school at Morongo Elementary, and then appeared to fade into the background at the time that the classmates matured and stratified into college-bound academic achievers, athletes and others. What happened to you? Ray wanted to ask, but kept that thought to himself, too. He supplied the answer himself: She just got old. Life happened, and in Kathy Rodgers case it had had a bleaching effect. She matched the inside of the trailer. "Can I come in?" he asked.

"I guess." She stepped aside and held the door open, and Ray stepped into the close, dead air of the home. Peeling vinyl at the entryway gave way to a stained carpet and gave the impression, sensed through the feet, that the floor underneath was thin and unstable and might give way at any moment. The home was spare, but neat inside, with no clutter in the living room or kitchen. A small television set on a cheap, wire stand occupied one corner of the room, and the décor consisted of framed photos of Jodi, taken by professional photographers in studios, that were arranged sequentially from the time she was a toddler.

Kathy Rogers Bullock followed Ray's eyes to the photos. "They grow up fast," she sighed, and sat down gingerly on the sofa. "This one thinks she's ready to leave the house and go off on her own, but she isn't." Ray could see by the way that she moved that she was in pain, and realized that he was receiving no premonitions of her death. Of course not, he thought, Jodi has been dosing her with the Piczak snops. In the small space of the trailer, he could smell her. She seemed to be preserved in nicotine. "Now she's nearly finished with us and she'll be gone soon," she sighed. "But you're in luck, Ray. She's never home, but she is right now. Go knock on her door." She nodded her heads towards the dark, narrow hallway paneled in imitation wood. "You'll know which one it is."

Ray thanked her and walked that way. It had the feeling of going into a dark tunnel, and he instinctively crouched, although the ceiling was just tall enough to accommodate his height. A door with a large J colored onto it with permanent markers was closed, and the sound of music from a tinny boombox came from inside. He knocked softly, and from behind the door he heard a rustling of papers and then Jodi's voice screamed, "WHAT?" He opened the door and stuck his head inside, and the look on her face went instantly from confrontational to surprised, and then guarded.

"Hi, Jodi, it's me," he said. "Could I have a word with you?"

"I guess," she said. She reached for the boombox and turned the volume down, but not off. She was wearing faded jeans, a pull-over hooded sweatshirt with the Morongo High logo, and she was barefoot. Ray thought it odd that she was wearing the hood of the sweatshirt over her head and had tied it tight. Her small, angular face seemed to peek out of it. "But don't ask me where your precious son is," she said. "It's not my job to keep track of him anymore."

"Why not? Did you two break up or something?"

"There was nothing to break up," she snapped. "I never even liked him. I'm sorry to say this to you, Mr. Jensen, but your wonderful son is just plain weird. And that's the nicest thing I have to say about him."

Ray couldn't help it. His hand went to his mouth and he tried to stifle a laugh, but couldn't. His shoulders began to shake and he sat down on the side of her bed and laughed out loud. "Well," he said, gasping, "as you can see, weirdness runs in our family."

"I guess," she said nervously. She sat down on a stool next to a shabby, wooden desk. She moved some papers around, and Ray had the feeling that she was trying to hide something from him.

He stopped laughing and looked at her closely. "You don't see any of the things we see when you drink it, do you?"

She peered at him from inside her hood, and her almond eyes widened. "You mean the snops?"

"If that's what you call it, yes."

"I don't have any snops," she said quickly. "Daniel had it all. We drank it. It was terrible."

"Do you have any idea what that stuff can do? How precious it is?"

"Oh sure," she said in the cutting manner that high school girls, particularly underclassmen, can say "oh sure," a manner that leaves no doubt that they really mean, "not sure at all."

"Let me guess," she continued, "it makes you see stuff. It makes you younger. It makes old people jump up and down and dance and it makes young people know how their math teacher is going to die. Am I close on this, Mr. Jensen?"

Ray nodded. "Yes, that's just about right."

"And we should give it to everyone in the whole stinkin' town of Morongo so that they'll live forever and we won't have to know how they're going to die anymore, right?"

"You didn't get any of that when you drank it?"

"No! And do you know why, Mr. Jensen?"

"Why?"

"Because I believe in God. God is what keeps us all alive and decides if we live or if we die. Not some stuff that crazy old Professor Piczak, may he rest in peace, cooked up in his basement. I believe in God, Mr. Jensen, and because I do, I don't have to believe in anything else.

"Excuse my French, but you and your precious son are crazy. I thought he was weird, but cute, but this is too much. It's a drink, okay? It makes you a little high. Hasn't anyone ever given you a lecture about drinking, Mr. Jensen?" And here she took two steps forward and reached out her skinny arm and actually tapped Ray on the side of the head at the temple. "It doesn't solve all your problems," she stage-whispered.

Ray said it before and he would say it again: Righteous indignation is the best emotion.

"Look, can I show you something?"

Ray nodded, and Jodi turned back to the desk and pulled out a sheaf of papers that were bound together with a staple. They were covered in writing that began at one edge of the paper and went all the way to the other edge, from top to bottom. He recognized immediately the crabbed handwriting of John Piczak. "You took those from Dr. Piczak's house, didn't you?" he said.

"No," she said. "I'm not a thief. He gave them to me. And I have no idea why, but you should read them."

She handed the bundle to him, and Ray's heartbeat quickened. He thought he had found the missing pages from the Piczak notebooks, the ones with the formula for synthesizing snops. His disappointment rose as he read through the first sheet, and then the next two. The notes described a series of failed experiments for a synthetic wine that used oranges and the residue from seared grape vines as its flavor base. Piczak was trying to concoct a distinctive wine from the by-products of traditional winemaking, just as distillers use grape stems and seeds to make grappa, but his experiments were unsuccessful. In fact, the wine was terrible. After several tries, he had finally bottled a half-dozen liters of the stuff and left it in his basement with the hopes – never realized, as is so often the case with science and home winemaking – that aging might make it palatable.

Ray turned to Jodi. "According to this, it's only wine. And very bad wine at that."

"No duh," she said, and when Ray looked up, he saw that she was crying. She snatched the pages back from him roughly and slammed them down on her desk. When she turned back to him, tears were streaming down her face.

"I wanted to believe in it, too!" she cried out. "I really wanted to believe in it. You're not the only ones who need snops. But I couldn't. Now get out! And when you see your stupid son, tell him he's wasting his time. You're both just wasting time." Her hands flew to her face and she sobbed hard.

Ray hesitated. He wanted to comfort her but she had turned away from him. "You can still believe in it," he said. "I know that it works. It said so in his notebooks, but some pages were missing. I've seen it work with my own eyes. Did he give you any other notes, Jodi?"

She shook her head, still sobbing.

"Are you sure?"

"No!" she shouted.

"Where's Daniel?" he asked. "I know that you know."

She glared at him. "He's probably down by the college. He goes down there every week. You should know where your own son is."

"You're right. I should." Ray reached for the door, but before he opened it, he was reminded of something. "So why did you give it to your mother?" he asked gently.

Her voice rose in intensity. "Shut up!" she screamed. "That's none of your business! Get out!"

Ask a stupid question, Ray thought as he left the room, closing the door behind him. Kathy Bullock was sitting on the sofa in the living room, watching the television. She didn't stand up. "Fun to talk with her, isn't it?" she said. "Don't feel bad; I get that all the time."

"I'm really sorry," Ray said. "I didn't mean to upset her…"

She cut him off with a wave of her hand. "It's not you," she said. "Jodi got some bad news yesterday from the doctor, and she just needs some time. She'll get over it."

Ray lingered by the door. "I'm sorry to hear that. If there's anything I can do…"

She looked at him sharply. "Well you could tell that agency of yours to stop stalling on our benefits," she said. "You could help us figure out a way to pay for this latest round of doctors. If you're wondering, that's where her father is, out driving truck because we got a mountain of medical bills." Her body had stiffened and her eyes were hard, but then she let out a sharp exhalation of breath and her figure seemed to deflate into the cushions of the sofa. Her voice was soft when she continued.

"I'm sorry, that wasn't fair. It ain't you, Ray. She's just been a tough child to raise, and here we are so close to her being grown up. I don't know if you knew this, but we had a scare with her when she was little. Cancer. It was in her bones. They treated it up in Rochester and she missed a whole year of school from the chemo, but they got it. We thought it was over and done with. Her PSAs been clean since she was nine, but she had a test last week and now they want her to come in for more tests. That's all. It's probably nothing."

"I'm so sorry," Ray said again. "I didn't know." His glance went to the row of photographs of Jodi on the wall, a stop-motion progression of a girl growing up. In two of the pictures she was wearing a cap that covered her hair.

"No reason you should know," she said. "We're not worried. God will take care of us. You might not see it that way after what you've been through, but he does."

Ray nodded and agreed with her. He didn't see it that way. He thanked her and wished her the best with Jodi's tests, and then left the mobile home. At his car, he had an idea. He returned to the house and Kathy Bullock let him in. Ray found a cup and poured a half-inch of his remaining snops into it. "Give this to her in a glass of orange juice and she'll be fine," he said. Jodi had obviously drunk the snops, and he had no premonitions of her death, but he figured it wouldn't hurt to give her a little booster.

She looked at it dubiously and sniffed it. "I'm not even going to ask you what this is," she said.

"Good, because I'm not sure I could tell you if you did. Just give it to her."

"Whatever works," said Jodi's mother.

Chapter Thirteen

a cottage beside MORONGO LAKE wherein HOSES are LIFELINES

Jim Long greeted Ray at the door of his lakefront home with a bottle of beer and a friendly, if unsolicited opinion about Ray's general demeanor: "You look like shit, Ray."

"That's funny, I feel great," Ray lied. He took the beer and drank it, shuddering over the harsh taste of a Genessee Cream Ale (it's the water), but going right back for a second swig, and then a third.

"Come on in, Glo's got lunch ready," said Long. They had known each other since forever, since Jim Long moved to Morongo in the fourth grade and Ray promptly made him his best friend. They had spent their summers growing up at the Long family cottage, where the boys jumped off of the roof into the lake when Jim Long's parents weren't home. When he and Ray were teenagers, Jim Long was the best water-skier on the lake. He could barefoot from a dry start on the dock outside of his cottage.

Now you had the feeling that they hadn't yet built the Evinrude that could pull him out of the water. He had grown up to be a big man, six-foot-three and nearly 300 pounds when he didn't watch it, when his wife Gloria was in a pizza and pasta mood for a month or two. The athlete gone, what remained were warm, friendly eyes behind horn-rimmed glasses, and a frequent smile. A heavy Long, a Long with his Gloria and two young sons, was a happy Long.

    The Long's back door opened onto their kitchen, and then led in turn to a living room and a doorway that led to a broad, wooden patio overlooking the lake. Ray could follow the smell of something saucy and Italian from the kitchen to the patio, and he realized that he was hungry. Outside, the table was set prettily with a checkered cloth, linen napkins and a big bowl of pasta that shared space with an equally large and overflowing bowl of salad. Gloria, a small, cheerful woman with a pretty, unlined face, was sitting at the table with her father Elwood, and she was spooning food into his mouth with the rapt, delighted expression of a mother feeding a particularly adorable infant. The Longs' two sons were playing on the beach in bathing suits, water shoes and lifejackets, and for once Ray had the feeling that life was trumping death, nobody's end was near, and there was going to be a lot more energy expended than withdrawn from this particular group of mortals in the foreseeable future.

Except for Elwood. Elwood, who was eighty-seven, was something of a legend in Morongo circles for his sheer longevity in the face of a constantly looming demise. He had been losing his mind slowly for the previous three years, after they had found him wandering in his bathrobe in Geneva, thirty miles away, one frantic April weekend, but dementia was the least of Elwood's health concerns. When he was sixty, he had survived not one but two heart attacks. His enlarged prostate was plucked by Rochester surgeons and thrown in the garbage five years after that, and tumors on his lungs and kidney had miraculously given up the good fight and said, figuratively, of course, and in French, "Chemotherapy, *je t'embrace. Vous avez gagne.*" At sixty-eight and on vacation in Hawaii with his girlfriend, he had been rushed to the Maui hospital and implanted with a pacemaker. He had both hips and both knees replaced in his early seventies, and a cruise at age seventy-eight had so filled his earthly trappings with fluid that his heart and lungs nearly stopped and he had to be airlifted from the middle of the Mediterranean to Corsica. There, he peed a river over three straight days thanks to a relentless program of Corsican diuretics, and returned to the ship in time to win the bingo tournament. Since then, it really wasn't much of a year if Elwood didn't wind up in the hospital once or twice, with doctors performing miracles and Gloria and Jim taking shifts at his bedside.

Since the cruise, he had been living on around-the-clock oxygen that was delivered via canisters that loomed in the corner of the Longs' living room and connected to Elwood via long, clear tubes that revealed his whereabouts as they snaked throughout the house, forming a serpentine line from the canister to his nose. Lately, the lines had been necessary to find him, because he had taken to spending large parts of his days in closets and underneath the dining room table when Gloria or the boys weren't home to keep an eye on him. Throughout it all, Elwood maintained a slightly bewildered, but positive attitude that could be summarized by the phrase, "So what's next?" His hands and ankles were blue and the oxygen had long since been turned up to its highest setting, but he had a healthy appetite, a loving daughter and grandsons, and a hazy sense that he was entitled to whatever the next day brought.

"How's Elwood doing today?" asked Ray after he bent down to kiss Gloria's cheek. She was smiling and expertly catching dribbles of sauce from the side of Elwood's mouth with the spoon and returning them to his mouth.

Elwood frowned, confused by the question.

"Great," Gloria answered for him. "He's doing absolutely great."

And Ray thought, but didn't say, "A month or two left. Maybe six at the outside. Congestive heart failure. Deteriorating everything."

Gloria finished her spoonage and turned her attention on Ray. "Oh honey," she said, "you look like you need to sit down." She patted a chair next to her, and Ray sat down heavily, admiring the view of the lake and wondering if he could just stay on the Longs' porch and be fed by Gloria with a spoon for the rest of the week.

Gloria patted his knee. "I've been talking to Donna," she said.

The thought of Donna made Ray wince and miss her. "That's more than I've been able to do," he said. "I wish she would come home."

"It must be hard," Gloria agreed.

Jim Long sat down at the table and began to ladle spaghetti and sauce onto his plate, and motioned for Ray to do the same. Ray did and began to eat. "The lake looks beautiful today," he said.

"It's a blessing," said Gloria. "We're thankful for it just about every day. And for him, too," she said, pointing to Elwood, who had closed his eyes and appeared to be either napping or enjoying the sensations of sunshine and a gentle breeze on his skin. Gloria looked at Ray. "Your father would have enjoyed this kind of day, too. It's a shame that he didn't ever get to have a retirement. Just a shame that he died so young."

Ray agreed. Gloria had been a student of Farrell Sr.'s during his last semester at Morongo College and had attended his funeral. It was a detail that colored her relationship with Ray over the twenty-five years since Jim had introduced Gloria as his bride-to-be, and she and Ray had gotten to know each other. She referred to Farrell often and easily; it was one of the many things that Ray enjoyed about her. This time, however, she added something that made the small hairs on the back of Ray's neck stiffen. "God's ways are so mysterious," she said.

Are they really? Ray wondered as he dug into his pasta. Because they seem fairly straightforward to me, he thought. As soon as you're old enough to know better, you're handed a ticking clock that is your life with the explicit instructions that there is only so much you can do to keep it ticking, and any attempts to alter the mechanism will be harshly punished. Learning all you can about heredity, about risk factors, about disease and medicine and prevention, only gives you a better understanding of the clock, not the ticking. The truly mysterious thing is the way that people respond, and how they choose, either willfully or instinctively, to live out their days. Right or wrong, in sickness or in health, 'til death do us part. People's ways are so mysterious; God, you can read like a book.

The Longs were deeply religious, and were regulars at the Sunday services of St. Michael's Catholic Church in Morongo. Gloria volunteered at church functions, the two boys were in training to be altar boys and Jim Long's baritone voice had provided the steady, bottom line for a generation of hymn singers. Gloria had teased Ray about his intense disinterest in the church early in their friendship, and she almost got him to consider attending services after his divorce from Janice had left him shaken and feeling even more disconnected from the community than ever. He had managed to weather the storm of faithlessness, or at least the faithful storm of Gloria's entreaties, and she had not brought it up again in several years.

"Can I ask you something?" said Ray. "Excuse me for being serious for a moment, but this is something that's on my mind. You pray for Elwood, right?"

Gloria looked surprised. "Of course I do. I pray for everyone. Even you, Ray."

"Oh, thanks. What do you pray for? I mean, for him." Elwood at the moment was chuckling, still with his eyes closed, at the memory of something deep and fleeting.

Jim said, "We pray that his next operation won't cost us a fortune."

Gloria said, "Cut it out, Ray's being serious. I don't know, we pray for him to enjoy his days on Earth and for God to welcome him into the Kingdom of heaven."

"When?"

"What do you mean when?"

"Doesn't the question of when will he enter this Kingdom of heaven ever enter into it? I mean, every time he gets sick, you pray for him to get better, right?"

"Of course we want him to get better. I'm not sure I understand…"

"Why do you pray for him to get better if what's in store for him, and hopefully for all of you non-sinners, is an eternal and glorious afterlife? Aren't you grooming yourselves, so to speak, for death?"

"Have you been drinking?" asked Jim. "I mean, that's some buzz you got off of that one Genny Cream."

"Forgive me if I'm being weird here," said Ray. "This stuff has just been on my mind."

Gloria said, "That's alright Ray. The thing is that none of us knows how or when we're going to die, and our missions on Earth are to explore and appreciate and enjoy the lives that we've been given to the fullest, because that honors our Creator and thanks him every day for the gift of life."

Elwood opened his mouth wide and held it open, and Gloria carefully put a spoonful of pasta onto his tongue. He swallowed it and sighed and closed his eyes again.

"Would you say that Elwood is living a rich and fulfilling life?" asked Ray. "Let's take it a step further: Do you think that the people in the cancer wards, the children with birth defects who are on respirators and feeding tubes, and the people who can't get out of bed in the morning because of intense pain are leading lives of fulfillment? Do you pray for them to get better, too? Wouldn't it make more sense to pray for them to hurry up and get to the next level, so to speak?"

Gloria smiled, a trifle beatifically in Ray's opinion. "It's not for me to say. Everyone's life is different, and they can find satisfaction in their own ways. God has filled our world with pleasures. Maybe the pleasure is as slight as those people in pain finding just a moment of joy in their day. Maybe their satisfaction is just in bearing the burden that God chose to give them. It's not for me to say. But look at us and all of the joys that we have."

"Nicely put," Ray said, and drained the can of beer.

Then Ray opened his backpack and pulled out the can of snops that he was carrying. He set it onto the table.

"What if I told you that this bottle of wine has the power to allow us all to live forever? And if we gave Elwood a good, strong drink of it, he would live another fifty years in exactly the same condition that he's in right now. Would you give it to him?"

"I knew he was going to try to sell us something," Jim said. He reached for the jar, unscrewed its lid and sniffed it. "It can make me live forever? Sign me up for a case of it."

Gloria just smiled at Ray. "I don't have the answer to that either, Ray. We give daddy medicine every day that prolongs his life and keeps him with us. We take him to the hospital when he gets sick, and the doctors do what they can to keep him going. And thank goodness, it has worked so far and he continues to live a long and happy life. Or at least I think he's happy. I wouldn't trade these last five years that we've had with him for anything. And I'll bet he wouldn't, either. I would, and always will, choose the life I've been given. It's a gift."

"But wouldn't you like to live forever?" Ray asked.

Gloria laughed. She looked at her boys playing on the beach, at the lake and the sunlight and her father and her husband. "I think we already are living forever, Ray," she said. "This is all that there is, and all that I could possibly want. I guess I want to live as long as I'm supposed to live."

Elwood belched in agreement and reached out to hold his daughter's hand. She took it in both of hers and stroked the blue skin.

"Thanks for lunch," said Ray. "I'd want to live forever, too, if I had Gloria cooking for me."

Gloria reached out and squeezed Ray's arm. "You have a lot of blessings, too, Ray."

The phone rang and Gloria got up to answer it. When she returned to the room, there was a catch in her voice. "It's Janice," she said. "She said that she's been trying to reach you everywhere."

"Tell her the check is in the mail," said Ray.

Gloria shook her head. "It's not that. This is important. Daniel is missing. Ray, I'm so sorry."

Ray brought the phone into the living room. Janice's voice was tense and worried. No signs of Daniel…homework left out on the table…hadn't gone to school that day…she thought he was at Ray's…Ray so hard to reach by phone…and, in summation, what was Ray going to do about it?

"I'll look for him, make a few calls," he said, hoping that it was the right answer.

"You do that, Ray," said Janice in a tone of voice that suggested that Ray should have already known that Daniel was missing, and perhaps she was right. "And let me know what you find out, and I'll let you know if I hear anything."

When Ray returned to the porch, Gloria had left and was on the beach playing with her children. Jim was holding Ray's bottle of snops. He raised it to his lips and gave it a long pull. "Every time I drink this stuff I swear that I won't do it again," said Jim. "But then I do it again."

He looked at Ray and added, "I've got two little kids to raise, and nobody else knows how to run my store. I need all the help I can get."

He handed the bottle back to Ray. "What's your story?" asked Jim.

"I've got to find my son. And then I've got to beat the hell out of him."

"Come on," Jim said, "I know how you can find your kid." He led Ray back into the living room and picked up the phone. From his pocket, Jim pulled out a folded piece of paper that looked worn, as if it had been in his back pocket for more than a few pants changes. He unfolded it carefully and showed it to Ray. It was the same flyer that Ray had once seen on his windshield in downtown Morongo and hastily discarded, the flyer that promised long life. Jim picked up the phone and dialed the number, and before it rang he handed the phone to Ray.

The call was answered on the fourth ring, and Ray recognized Daniel's voice when he answered it by saying, "Yeah?"

Ray looked at Jim, who pointed to the flyer in his hand. "I want to live forever," Ray said.

"Meet me at the Point down by the college," replied his eldest and only son. "Eight o'clock tonight. Bring fifty bucks. Cash."

Ray was momentarily speechless, and then he said, "Daniel?"

"Dad?" And then Daniel hung up.

Jim's hand was on Ray's shoulder. "Fountain of youth," he said.

THE NARRATORS
NOT a pretty THING

 Poodle has locked herself in the bathroom for most of the morning, and Falubio is out sunning on the verandah. A Guy Named Brad has crawled under the bed and is, for a change, silent. It occurs to me that I have a rare opportunity to be alone with my father. I rumble over to where he is sitting and sit down easily on the floor alongside his chair. I clear my throat. And then I clear it again.

 He doesn't look up from his book. I clear my throat a third time. No response. I can see that he is ignoring me, because the book is upside down and backwards, and unless there are mirrors in the afterlife, there is no way that he is reading it. So I hit the floor hard with the palm of my hand, making a resounding CRACK that could probably be heard all the way down in the Horizon Lounge. He jumps in his seat at that, and then looks at me. His face is calm and serene, but guarded. He seems to be wary of me, and I don't know why.

"Dad," I say as gently as I can, because I have gotten used to having him around and don't want to scare him away. "What do you want me to do?"

He shrugs. He keeps his eyes on mine, and my heart races a little bit. As much as he's been around on this cruise, it still thrills me to see him here. He doesn't look away, but he refuses to answer.

"No, really," I continue. "What shall I do? What would make you happy?"

He raises his hand to take in the room and the ocean outside, indicating that he already is happy and staying right where he is would suit him just fine. With both hands, he mimes the motion of typing.

"There isn't much book left to write," I tell him. "I've done the best that I can, but there just isn't much more to say."

He makes a big sad face with his mouth and then puts his finger to his lips and cocks his eyes upwards as if he is mulling over the question. Then he points a bony finger at the tray of hors d'oeuvres that Costas had thoughtfully left on my sideboard in the hopes that some fatty smoked salmon with dill crème fraîche might rouse my appetite.

"I'm sorry Dad, but I'm just not hungry."

In fact, since my heart attack and Floyd Little's disappearance, I haven't been able to eat a thing. The Belgian waffle with strawberries was the last attractively packaged bundle of calories to pass my lips. And what has it been, a week since then? Two?

He sighs and just looks at me. I adore him. It is so hard to let him go. I know that I have to move on, to continue my story without him, but I don't know how or when. Final acts have just never come easily to me. In a screenplay, you just blow up the remaining bad guys and reunite the hero with the girl, but this, as we've taken pains to mention, is not a screenplay, but my life. And although everybody has suggestions, nobody really ever tells you how you should live your life in a way that makes sense.

We sit there a long time, just looking at each other, and then I hear a soft coughing sound behind me that makes me jump. I look up to see that Costas has been standing behind me; I have no idea how long he has been there. He is holding something on a silver tray. "There is an old saying in my native Portugal," he begins slowly, "that time can truly be measured, but only by a man who is born with a yardstick."

What the hell does that mean? I mean, honestly, can you make heads or tails of it? Because I can't.

Costas pushes the silver tray a little closer to me. On it is a calendar, and it is opened to the month of July. A date is circled. It takes me a moment to notice, but the year had also been highlighted in bright, red marker at the top of the page, and it isn't the year that I expected it to be. I have been on the Royal Precious Platinum much, much longer than I ever dreamed.

"*Is that today?*" *I ask, a trifle embarrassed by my fundamental lack of knowledge of dates.*

Costas nods. "*Yes, it is, Sir.*"

"*And this is supposed to mean something to me?*" *My general awareness level: Dim. Perpetual state of mind: Stumped.*

My father begins to make a furious, circular motion with his finger in the air. Now this is fun; I love a good game of charades. He makes a quick, tight circle in the air with his finger, and I say, "*Tickling. You're tickling somebody.*"

He shakes his head no. The circle that he makes in the air gets bigger. "*Oh,*" *I say.* "*You're making the letter O. O Henry. Ohmygosh. O say can you see...*"

He shakes his head harder and faster. He holds up a long finger in front of my face and keeps it there, demanding my attention.

"Wait a minute," I say. "Hang on. Pause. Hold your horses."

He points to me. I am on the right track. He waves the finger upright in my face twice more, but slower.

"The number one!" I exclaim, and he claps his hands together and makes a motion as if to high-five me, although of course he can't.

"One! One is the loneliest number. Number one with a bullet. We're number one!"

He shakes his finger excitedly. And then makes the circular motion in the air. Once, twice, three times.

I still don't get it.

"Hula hoops," I say. "Circles. Round the world. Round the world in eighty days."

Costas coughs politely into his fist. "Zero," he says.

Dad points at Costas and sits back in his chair, his pantomime done. I look quickly to Costas, wondering if he can suddenly see my father. Costas studiously avoids my gaze. He stares straight ahead, the platter still held before him. I have to watch closely to see that it is shaking slightly.

"Zero," I repeat.

Dad points at the calendar on Costas's silver tray and makes an "okay" sign with his thumb and forefinger. I look from Dad to Costas and back again. Could it be that my Portuguese man-Friday, my valet to the stars that are me, detects the presence of Old Pops? Costas just stands patiently holding the tray, not letting on a thing. I to this day don't know if he was there because he knew or because coincidence is such a vital force in my life, and always has been.

"Zero Day," breathes Falubio. I wasn't even aware that he and Brad have come out from their places and are standing behind me, watching the game of charades.

And then I get it. Zero Day for me has passed, about a week before. My birthday has come and gone with it. I am now fifty years, four months and a week old: Older than my father had ever been in life. And, heart attacks in Mexico and sudden snoppish revivals and massive weight gains followed by massive weight losses notwithstanding, it looks like I might last at least a few months longer. "I've made it past Zero Day," I say. "And I'm still alive."

My father just nods. Costas politely bows and leaves the room, very-good-sirring all the way out.

I start to cry. "So what am I supposed to do now?" I ask my father. "What do you want me to do?"

He shrugs again. He obviously hasn't been thinking about it. He puts his hand to his chin and cocks his head to the side, as if he were giving the subject his full attention. He begins to mime a desire for pen and paper.

"He wants us to keep writing," says Brad. "I have some suggestions for new characters and sub-plots to throw in..."

My father shakes his finger violently at Brad and mimes a throat-cutting, can-it-clown gesture. He makes the gesture again for pen and paper and points, pointedly, at me.

"You want me to write the rest in longhand?"

He shakes his head violently.

"You want a pencil?" I ask.

He nods his head fast and scribbles his finger in the air quicker. "And paper!" shouts Falubio.

I jump to my feet and look around the cabin. It is like I am seeing it for the first time. Under the desk and heaped in corners are piles of clothes, interspersed with stray socks in places where socks should not be kept. I open the desk drawer and the vanity drawers and the drawers of the night tables on either side of my bed, and am shocked to see what is inside each and every one of them. They are filled with butter: Butter pats on little squares of waxed paper. Sticks of butter. Butter balls that had been scooped out by a decorative tool. Butter in neat rectangles on gleaming white porcelain plates, an impression of the Royal

Precious Platinum stamped into the smooth, yellow surfaces. Butter in wrappers from France, from Ireland, from the English countryside. Land o' Lakes, Tillamook, Darigold. My cabin – like my belly and (some might say) my story – is like a museum of butter.

There is butter everywhere in my cabin. But apparently no pen and paper.

I get on my hands and knees and pull the suitcases out from under my bed where they have been since the day I arrived on board ship and Costas unpacked and stowed them. And deep inside one of my bags I find it: An old pen from Long's Cards & Books and a sheet of paper that contains the details of my itinerary.

I hand them to my father, or rather, drop them into his lap. And then he does the most amazing thing. With ultimate effort and will, his brow knit and his teeth clenched, he somehow manages to manipulate the pen in space. Which is to say, he picks it up in his unsubstantial fingers and shakily, with unbelievable determination, makes it move across the page. He writes me a note, and I have never been without it on my person ever since. My father writes:

And then he drops the pen on the floor and sits back heavily in his chair, exhausted but very pleased with himself.

"Be okay? Is that all you want for me?"

He raises and drops a shoulder, indicating that it would suffice.

I am dumbfounded. It occurs to me that I don't have the faintest idea of how one can B-O-K. And, if the truth be told, I am the slightest bit unhappy that this is the best advice my father can offer from the Other Side.

It is about this time that Poodle emerges from the bathroom with a sheepish look on her face. "Do NOT go in there," *she announces pleasantly.*

Falubio just smiles, but A Guy Named Brad looks up suspiciously. "Why not?" *he mosquito-screams.*

"Are you sure you want to know?" *she asks.*

"Try me."

"There's a tiger in there," she says. "A five hundred and fifty pound Bengal tiger. And it appears to be very hungry."

I open the door a crack and glance in and, sure enough, I am greeted by the intense, green-eyed glare of a full-grown male tiger.

Funny how you can forget about a tiger in the bathroom when something that your father does upsets you. Funny how instantaneously the last six inches of your colon can chill. The tiger growls, deep and low and in a way that I feel in my bones and my belly. I close the door quickly.

A Guy Named Brad screeches, "Whose idea was this? We never discussed this!"

Falubio says, "Well, all of the best stories have a tiger on the boat."

A Guy Named Brad mosquito-screams his displeasure. "We did not approve this at the last story meeting!" he whines. "I'll just see about this!" And then he goes into the bathroom and closes the door behind him. Before he leaves, though, he slaps some pages onto the table. They turn out to be the last thing Brad ever wrote.

The next thing we hear is not a pretty thing.

Chapter Fourteen
Red LIGHT at the END OF YOUR nose

Back at the park, Ray's brother Farrell Jr. was having his own problems. His heart was breaking, too, but in a different way. He and his buddy, a Guy Named Brad, had been drinking for three straight days, and Farrell had noticed that instead of dulling the pain that was now shooting down his arms, the wine had intensified it. One more bottle should just about do it, he thought.

The two of them had been sitting under the trees at the darkened edge of the park. They were drinking Rock'em, Sock'em Red, a Cayuga Lake table wine, straight from the bottle, and laughing at the people in the lake who were catching the buzz of long life from the stuff that young Daniel dispensed.

"You manage your high, I'll manage mine," yelled Farrell Jr. at them, but nobody paid attention to him. Daniel didn't notice him. He was standing knee-deep in the water with his girlfriend Jodi, handing out swigs of something from a bottle to a line of people, and from the way the people opened their wallets and handed out cash, the kid was making out.

The conversation turned to Farrell's brother, Ray. "Poor fucker," said Farrell Jensen, Jr. "he still don't know what hit him." He told Brad about what had happened to his father, and how Ray had spent the rest of his life grieving since he'd left. He didn't mention that Ray had more grief coming to him soon, courtesy of the shooting pains in his, Farrell Jr.'s arms. Soon enough, soon enough. Everybody dies, and the trick, Farrell had figured out, was to beat the rest of them to it.

"That's what I'm talking about," said a Guy Named Brad. "If he just had a red light at the end of his nose, he could have gone on with his life and it would have stayed lit up the whole time until the grieving period was over. People would have showed him some respect because they'd-a saw the red light. This way, everybody just thinks he's crazy and pathetic."

Farrell frowned. "Lemme get this straight," he said. "Your kids die in a fiery blaze that used to be your house, and you walk away humming a happy tune, but the red light on your nose is shining like a damn spotlight. You don't feel a thing about it one way or the other?"

"Precisely. You're spared the pain of grief."

Farrell shook his head. "And you fall off a building when you're doing the roof and break your leg, but you don't feel nothing. A red light at the end of your nose just starts glowing."

"Yeah, something like that. You never have to feel pain. The key here is that it doesn't hurt. Nothing hurts when you have the red light at the end of your nose. Human suffering is just a design flaw."

"Sounds to me like you've got a red light up your ass," grumbled Farrell. "You just want to be happy all the time, and never feel sad?"

"Why not? I'm just saying," said Brad, his voice rising. "I'm just saying that there must be some other way. I'm just saying why does our heart have to break every time our old man or our old lady checks out? Fiery blaze, car wreck, die of cancer…those are just details, man. The bottom line never changes. Why should we feel such pain when everybody dies, and it was just his turn? Shit, my old man drank himself to death when I was twelve years old. TWELVE YEARS OLD, man. And I haven't had a day of peace ever since." He reached for the bottle of wine, found it empty, and threw it into the lake.

Farrell Jr. reached for his pocket and froze. The pain was like electric shocks when he moved, like daggers. "Hey buddy," he said, "light me a cigarette."

It is a quality of drunks and philosophers – you decide if it's good or bad – that universal suffering breaks their hearts but an individual's obvious pain barely fazes them. Brad reached for the pack, put one in Farrell's lips and lit it. "You know, you don't look so good," he said.

"Yeah," said Farrell Jr. "If I had a red lightbulb at the end of my nose, it would shatter. Naw, I'm okay. I'm exactly where I want to be." He was thinking that he had six kids and no way to pay the mortgage, and he was having a heart attack, and there was a $100,000 life insurance policy in his name from back when he had belonged to the union. And he was older than his old man had ever been, and he had no right to expect more life. If children can die, how dare anyone grown up complain when their number is up? "Just help me up," he said.

A Guy Named Brad struggled to his feet. He stood behind Farrell Jr. and wrapped his arms around his chest. Farrell cried out in pain as he was lifted to his feet. He slumped over double, but did not fall back to the ground. "It's okay, it's okay," he said through clenched teeth. "Do me another favor, buddy. Take me down to the college."

Brad was surprised. "You want to go to the college?"

"Yeah," he said. "I've got a lesson to teach. Come on, I know where there's one more bottle of wine." He took two steps forward, stopped and sucked in his breath sharply from the pain, and then let Brad half-drag him the rest of the way to the pick-up truck. He didn't have the strength to step up into the passenger seat, so he had Brad open the tailgate, position his butt on the edge of it, and then push him backwards into the bed, where he rode silently, the pain settling all around him like a spiky blanket, like finding yourself surrounded by vicious animals who will attack you if you move. They bumped and jostled out of the park, and then Farrell was rolled to one side as Brad turned left, and the tires made a humming sound on the newly paved road out to the college. Biting his lip, he held onto consciousness as they drove down the lake in the cool night air.

Chapter 15
RAY gets to THE POINT

The Point to which Daniel referred was a small spit of pebbly land at Morongo College that jutted into the lake and served as a community beach for the students and faculty. The college chapel was constructed on a high bank of land above the Point, and its presence seemed to sanctify the spot, or at least reassure it, since nobody had ever drowned in this particular part of the lake. Like most faculty children, Ray spent a good deal of his childhood summers at the Point, swimming under the supervision of a lifeguard while Farrell Sr. was at work in his office in Slater Hall, which overlooked the lake.

During Ray's youth there had been a swimming platform with a diving board a few yards offshore that had been erected and was maintained by the college. The platform had witnessed several epochal moments of Ray's development, at least as far as he was concerned, as he gradually advanced from being allowed to swim to the platform and touch its side, climb the ladder, dive off the board and, finally, by dint of adolescence, claim the right to lounge bare-chested on the platform amongst the white-skinned young coeds from Poughkeepsie who claimed it as their tanning spot.

(Historical footnote: The platform was gone now thanks to a lawsuit by a dickwalter family in Morongo whose son – who was definitely NOT college material -- had fallen from the platform awkwardly and broken his leg. We was wronged!, the family dimly gathered. The incident became the basis for a Morongo truism that a dickwalter with a lawyer is the most dangerous dickwalter of all.)

Driving down the lake to the college, Ray was surprised that Daniel even knew about the Point. It was not a place to which they had returned during Daniel's childhood. That's because Ray doesn't go to the college. Ever.

There's a good reason for this. Ray can live without the pain.

The last time he was there was ten years earlier, at Donna's graduation from nursing school, and Ray's departure from campus was accompanied by a solemn oath, signed in tears and snot and heaving gasps from a chest that had been re-infected by a re-broken heart. The oath was, "No más, never again."

No more higher education in the complexities of human sorrow, Morongo College-style. No more self-knowledge and insight. Thanks but no thanks to self-awareness; Ray's self was aware enough to know that the red light at the end of its selfish nose began to throb painfully at the college, and throb painfully it meant to avoid for the foreseeable future. The problem with pain, as a wise man once pointed out, is that stuff hurts.

Ray had powerful and quite unexpected memories during the weekend of Donna's graduation, and the memories all related to either his father or his marriage, neither one of which had turned out well. Ray could not get out of the memories' way. In no particular order, the revelations included...

...A sudden, intense memory of the day he met Janice, delivered by a library table with discarded books placed just so on the corner of the table and the chair so adroitly angled to suggest a slender, young woman with her legs stretched out and feet propped on another chair, poring over molecular biology notes while absently chewing on a lock of soft, brown hair. Ray stopped in the same spot where he had stood some eighteen years earlier and first laid eyes on her. He had the sense of watching himself. He recalled the feeling of forcing himself to approach her ("Don't do it, son!" the hindsight portion of his brain-pan might reasonably shout at the handsome young man in the memory. "It won't turn out well!"). She looked up, quizzical but interested, and had the good mating instinct to remove her hair from her mouth. A quiet exchange, a gathering of books and notes: Their footsteps on the carpet seemed to be retained as they walked out of the library and onto the long, green lawn for the first of many talks that led, in something of an unbroken line, to their marriage, mating and parting.

...Memory Number Two: Turning a corner in Slater Hall and finding himself at the open door of his father's former corner office, which was the repository of much family history. As he stopped to gather in the odd, disorienting sight of new books and shelves and furniture in the once-familiar space, Ray was visited by vivid recollections of Farrell the Elder. In one memory, Ray is ten and bursts in on his father during a student conference. There is quick motion in the vicinity of the desk as father and student become disengaged (graciously gathered by the child as having interrupted them while poring over notes together, but in retrospect, why so close? Were they sharing a pair of reading glasses?). They look up with pained smiles and Ray launches into a dramatic reenactment of his excitement at receiving a high grade on his fifth-grade essay ("Why Vegetables Matter," if you must know). Father and student emit polite noises of encouragement. Student hastily excuses herself. Ray never does get her name.

...In another memory, Ray and Farrell arrive at the office one Saturday morning and find it ransacked. Books on the floor, papers scattered everywhere. Father sighs and, wordlessly, begins to straighten things up. Ray just watches from the corner, nervous and fearing that he'd done something wrong. Farrell quietly, and with a patient quality in his voice that is reassuring to the boy, begins to explain how squirrels have been entering his office lately, looking for the bag of seed that Farrell keeps to feed the birds through the window -- that window in the corner that is pushed open wide, gapingly wide really. And Farrell must have left the window open the day before – foolishly; he should have known better – and look at what the squirrels have done. Ray leans over to pick up a pad of paper on the floor, and sees that someone has scrawled, "You BASTARD!" in an angry hand on the first page, but before he can read more, Farrell snaps, "Don't touch that," and takes the pad from him. So Ray sits the rest of clean-up out and just watches from the corner for a solid hour as Farrell, stooping and humming, restores the office to order.

...And finally, simply and sweetly, of Farrell behind his desk, smiling and attentive of Ray, for it was at the office that Jensen *pere* was the most comfortable. Ray notices the gray in his father's hair for the first time. The two are bantering and happy. "Will there be anything else, Sir?" asks Ray. "No, that will be all, Rodney," replies Farrell. Rodney is the name that he uses when Ray drives him anywhere these days. Ray recently got his driver's license, and dropping his father off at the office is still a delicious novelty. Ray bows and turns smartly on his heel, a chauffeur to the end.

...Janice again. A girl walking by wearing knee pads and a field hockey stick, looking as fresh and healthy as Janice had looked in the same outfit. The girl walked into the dormitory called Space Hall, where decades before, in Janice's dorm room, *amour* between her and Ray had first been suggested, rejected, reconsidered, hotly debated and then consummated, all during the course of a long Friday evening. Afterwards she had held his arm tightly at the bicep, stuck her nose into his shoulder and said, "Don't you ever leave me." And then cried, and then bit his ear so hard that it hurt, and then laughed.

...Janice's face of happiness – also red-faced and swollen, but with tears of relief – as she and Ray walked down the steps of the Chapel, a married couple.

...Janice's face of anger, still red, still swollen, this time with rage and hurt, when her master's thesis was rejected and her graduate program was permanently stalled.

Walking into the first house that they rented and throwing her notebook at Ray's chest hard and saying, "Well I guess it's back to working at the diner for me," and then crying in his arms. And then, over the course of a rollicking weekend, blaming him for not supporting her work, not helping her more in her studies, not making more money so she wouldn't have to work side jobs while pursuing her master's, and then shutting up long enough to conceive Daniel in the upstairs bedroom of the cottage on the lake that they rented until they couldn't afford it any longer.

The Point. We were getting to the Point. These memories and more came to Ray as he turned left off the highway and reluctantly drove towards the entrance to the college. It was spring break and the campus was nearly deserted as he turned past the simple, stone wall where he had once thrown rocks with Artie Griffiths in such an extraordinary way as to knife through the thin strips of metal that constituted welcoming lanterns and shattered the lightbulbs inside, and then ran like hell home. He drove around Slater Hall and past the broad, green lawn that surrounded the Chapel.

He stopped in the gravel drive above the stairs that led to the Point and took a deep breath. His heart was racing. Colleges, at least this one, made him nervous. And sad. He didn't know if Daniel would be there, and what he might say to him. You might think that Ray was just a big baby, a mush-ball who curled up tightly into a fetal position and mewed like a kitten at the memory of anything sweet and dear, such as his childhood, marriage and divorce. But then you haven't heard about Memory Number Seven, revisited to Ray so intensely during his last visit to Morongo College that it put him in bed with a sore heart for a week then, and was making a return engagement now.

...Number Seven isn't so lucky, but it is significant. It features father Farrell dead in the office, with Adolescent Ray an hour too late to save him. Oh, we know, Farrell died at home on the porch overlooking the lake. We told you that in the first chapter, and that is something that (for once) we can't change. But people can die more than once. The last time that Ray saw his father in his office at the college was the only time that his father presented himself feet first. Ray had arrived late to pick him up, a trifle disdainfully and annoyed that he had to be called away from his friends, just because he had the only working car in the house that week, and why couldn't his dithering, ineffectual parents get theirs fixed and JUST LEAVE HIM ALONE?

He opened the door of the office to see Farrell's stocking feet poking out from under the desk like the Wicked Witch of the East. The feet were connected to the father; the father was on the floor gagging and turning purple, his heart only recently failed. Ray's own panicking, racing heart told him what to do, and he called emergency services, campus security and anyone else within earshot to come quick, come now, HELP!, a professor and scholar and father were all at once down. They descended on the office all at once, too, pushing Ray out of the way and leaping upon the body like it was a rugby ball in a scrum.

"You did the right thing, son," said one volunteer firefighter as they wheeled Farrell out on a gurney and loaded him into an ambulance. Ray stood dumbly, holding his father's shoes, and it took him a half-hour to gather that he still had the keys to the car and could drive himself to the hospital.

Which gave him plenty of time to think: Arriving an hour late to pick up his father with a seriously indignant and resentful attitude was the right thing to do?

The textbook response to finding a father collapsed on the floor is to stand around screaming while said father gurgles mortal pain in his throat?

Smoking one more cigarette with Artie Griffiths and discussing how one's parents didn't know dick about squat, while the object of one's derision is writhing on a floor – in which textbook does one find that procedure?

Ray mulled that one over for the week that his father lay in the hospital in Rochester. If those were the right things to do, what might a wrong thing to do have possibly been?

Farrell's heart was revived, failed once more in the hospital, and then was revived again, but it was damaged in a way from which hearts of the '70s did not fully recover. "Another ten minutes and we would have lost him," the doctors told Ray, Caroline and Farrell Jr. They didn't add, at least not vocally, the rest of the thought, but Ray had no trouble filling it in for himself: "Of course, if you'd gotten there an hour sooner, and (this is asking a lot of a teenager) noticed him sweating profusely and acting disoriented, you might have rushed him to the hospital. And this might never have happened."

As it turned out, another month was all that Farrell Sr. had left. If it's any consolation, he died peacefully on his own porch, watching the light on his own lake. But he died nevertheless. Ray wasn't home for that one, either. Nobody told him that his father could go at any time. Bored and restless and unnerved by the somber mood of the household, he left the house that morning and looked for something to do, but the best he came up with was throwing rocks at the old incinerator can behind Knapp & Schlappi Hardware until he ran out of rocks and decided to go home and see if the heavy gloom that had descended on the lakefront cottage might have lifted. He was the first to find his father, which was when he heard Farrell Sr.'s dying words: "You're next."

Ray got out of the car and walked down the stairs to the Point. It was always odd to see the old retaining wall and rocky beach without the platform. The platform had been strangely satisfying and solid throughout his childhood, offering (as platforms do) a goal to reach, a bit of firmness underfoot, a level surface from which to dive and play. Without it the beach looked vaguely sinister and unprotected. He walked from one end to the other. Daniel wasn't there.

From the beach, Ray could look up the hill to see the college Chapel, a handsome building of white stone and thick, exposed beams. As a child, Ray had played on the lawns that surrounded the building, and as a teenager he had shoveled snow from the stone walkway that encircled the building, and attended services inside. His heart sank; his father's funeral had been held there, and Ray had never returned. But now he saw that someone was standing on the walkway of the Chapel, facing the lake, and watching him. It was Daniel. He waved to Ray, and Ray waved back, and began the long climb up the hill to find his son.

the NARRATORS EXPLAINING *the butter; A PLAUSIBLE explanation for the* TIGER *in* THE BATHROOM

There is a theory about enormous weight gain that the diet books prefer not to mention that goes something like this: The layers of flab that a person puts on are a kind of padding against the world, a protective shield achieved through a sumofication of the body that acts as a buffer against life's inevitable and more painful events. As I think about it in Penthouse Suite 1125 with my father furiously scribbling and horrific sounds emanating from the bathroom, that might explain a lot.

It might, for one thing, explain the butter. I keep finding it. Let me first tell you a little story. When I was in college, many years ago, I took my friend Diane to a New Years Eve party at a friend's house. The friend – nobly, I think – invited her parents and some of her parents' friends to the event in order to make it more civilized and less about draining the keg as quickly as possible and then puking in the bushes. As I made civilized conversation during the course of the evening with several people, poor Diane got buttonholed by a particularly bitter old lush who decided, after far too many martinis, to describe in detail her first husband's quite astounding ability to ejaculate prematurely. The woman gripped Diane's young and horrified arm tightly, brought her face close, and said the words that I've never been able to forget:

"Honey, it was on my hair, it was on my dress, it was on the wall, it was on the rug. It was everywhere except where it was supposed to be."

And that's how it is with the butter. It is in my socks in bright, aluminum foil wrappers. It is in my shoes in the back of the closet in little pats filched from the breakfast buffet, and it is in the pockets of my tuxedo jacket. Everywhere I look there is butter. I had no clue that I was accumulating it, and God only knows what I intended to do with it. Perhaps I am padding Penthouse Suite 1125, just as I have been padding myself, keeping the room fat and guarded against any insights or devastations that might be brought upon by life.

I try to explain this to my father. I also have something to tell him. I creep up to his chair and get down on my knees and say I am sorry.

Forgive me.

Excusez-moi.

[292]

My bad.

I'm really sorry. I really didn't mean to leave you dying in your office. I really shouldn't have been late. I really should have been there at your side when you eventually did die. Really, would you please accept my most profound apologies? Can I possibly make it up to you in any way? Is there any way that we could, maybe, shake hands and let bygones be bygones? Or is my only redemption to come from suffering the same fate as you, and buttering up my heart into its own state of cardiac surrender? Because frankly, I did just about everything I could do to not make it past Zero Day, but that little matter of bitter-orangey self-preservation preserved in a wine bottle thwarted my efforts. I couldn't help it. I kept living. My medicine was a little better than yours. And I kind of feel like all bets are off now that I'm older than you ever were.

He waves his hand at me impatiently. He is busy writing. His little note-making, achieved through extraordinary concentration and will, has, unfortunately, become something of a cottage industry. As with many people who take up the pen, he just can't stop. It takes him hours and hours to scratch out a single letter, and his missives have taken on a form that became quickly dreary and repetitive, but he keeps beckoning for more paper, and tries so hard to grip the substantial pen with his insubstantial fingers. After the uplifting note of B-O-K, he produced, many hours later, this message:

Spent, exhausted and slightly fearful, I imagine, at what might happen if he were caught delivering messages from the beyond, he sat back, dropped the pen and motioned for me to pick up the paper.

"Thanks, Dad," *I said.* "*I guess that's somewhat true. I'll cherish this always.*" *I put the note on top of the dresser. It quickly shone through in four places from butter seeping through its papery fibers.*

I thought he was done, but a few hours later his hands started to twitch and he motioned again for pen and paper. This note was an addendum to the previous one; I could tell from the happy way that he presented it that they were meant to be linked. This one said:

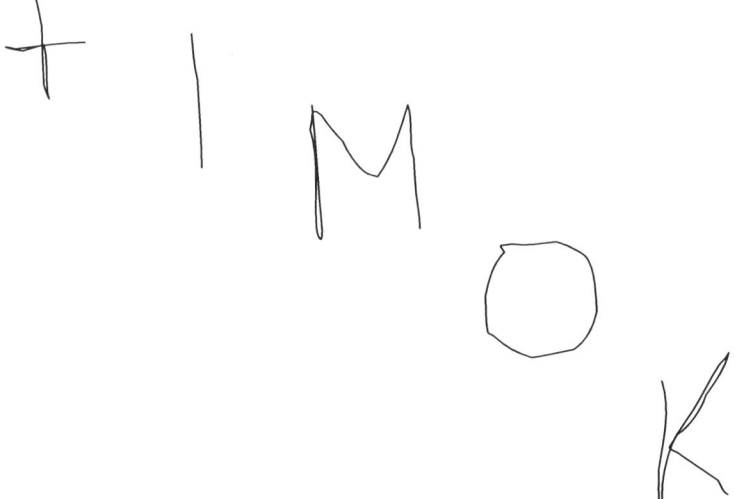

Which I took to mean, given the simple syllogism, that he meant to say that I am okay too.

I thanked him for that and made polite noises that he needn't exert himself any further. But he motioned for more paper, and then gingerly, with the most painstaking effort, as if he were trying to relearn all over again how fingers work, how things are grasped, how space can be manipulated, he took up the pen. It took him all night to scratch out this next bit of sage advice from beyond the pale (advice, I might add, which you can find in just about every dime-store magazine rack, frequently preceded by the headline, "10 Great Ways to Find Your Very Best You").

This time he wrote:

As I mentioned, during his lifetime Farrell Sr. had never been a particularly prolific writer, nor a thoughtful one. It's startling to learn that he didn't get much better in the afterlife. But then, I suppose we're all still waiting for the first great novel from beyond the grave. I gathered up the paper when he was finished and said, again, "Thanks, Dad. I will."

He nodded his head and smiled. I didn't dare to tell him how far pop psychology had come since he died.

I want to ask him more about forgiveness, but the noise from the bathroom has become intolerable. There is a perfectly plausible explanation, by the way, about the tiger in the bathroom. I wish I could relate it to A Guy Named Brad, but it sounds like he is in the fight of his life in there, and doesn't have much time for conversation. Just imagine, as I write these words and you read them, a high-pitched scream unlike anything you've ever heard or imagined pulsing in the room where you sit. The sound approaches you like an oncoming ambulance, filling all of the space before it, reaching a peak that attacks you in the forehead and makes you close your eyes in pain, and then recedes slightly, as if the ambulance has passed you in a rush and is looking for someone else's forehead to attack. But then it comes right back around and repeats the cycle. I and Poodle and Falubio sit quietly, clutching our ears to no avail, because this sound wells up from inside us as much as from outside, and it is only after a dozen or so cycles that we realize what is going on in there: The tiger is chasing A Guy Named Brad around and around the bathroom, and by the frequency of the screams and the piercing intensity of their crescendos, the tiger is gaining ground.

What I would tell A Guy Named Brad if I had the chance is that the tiger belonged to a crew member. A few months earlier – I lose track of time, so bear with me if the dates aren't entirely accurate – there was a knock on my door late at night. I thought it was Costas offering warm milk and cookies, but it was Sarang, one of the Malay deckhands. He was holding a bundle of towels tightly to his chest, and inside the towels, something small and cute was squirming. We were docked in Vladivostock (Mysteries of Siberia, Tour #1255) and he had been offered, and gratefully purchased, a tiger cub in the shady street market of the wharves. His intention was to get it back to his native island and begin to repopulate the tiger population. This had been his dream and the goal of his life for many years, he said in broken English. He had tried to leave the tiger cub in a lifeboat and sneak it scraps of food throughout the day, but the officers were getting suspicious. Could he leave it with me for a few days until we reached Sumatra?

"Sure," I said. "Put it in the bathroom."

God only knows what became of Sarang. I never saw him again. The tiger has been in there ever since, and God also knows it got big and hungry. As far as I can figure, it has grown up on nothing but a steady diet of butter, and it is probably dying for a little meat to go with it.

Now the mosquito-like ambulance screams are growing in intensity, and the durations between the times they recede and the times they return are growing much shorter. They finally merge into one prolonged, ear-splitting shriek. "EEEEEEE!" screams A Guy Named Brad as he runs around and around the bathroom. There is a deep, throaty growl of satisfaction and victory from the tiger, and then the oddest sound, like a ping-pong paddle hitting a hard-boiled egg, followed by the sound of the mirror crashing into shards of glass, followed by a deep and profound silence.

"Got him," says Falubio. Poodle nods in agreement.

I just think of A Guy Named Brad standing before his creator, whomever that may be, and asking in his whiny voice, "What good does it do you to have people killed by tigers? Why is that part of your divine plan?"

First Floyd, now this. I put my hands up to my eyes, rub them a long time and just shake my head. What more can life throw at me? How long do I keep cruising in this primordial soup? What are my options here?

Poodle stands up and yawns and stretches her arms. "Do you want to know what I think?" she asks.

Falubio and I don't answer, but she goes on anyway.

"I think that it's so sweet that we all have this longing for life, and even though we all know that we're going to die, it comes as such a huge surprise and shock when it happens to us or the people we love. I think it's neat [she really said neat] that we mourn each other and are so touched by stories. Our love is stronger than the simple fact of death. And the stories are what keep us all alive, and the memories are sometimes more real than the people we remember. And I think it's cool [ditto cool] that we can all make up our own stories."

Falubio and I just look at each other. Everyone's entitled to their own opinion.

There is a knock on the door and Poodle smoothes her hair and wets her lips. She is obviously planning something here, and hasn't run it past the remaining members of the story committee.

Lap dancers: Always winging it.

She reaches for our father's hand and raises it to her cheek and holds it there for a moment, kisses it and then *returns it gently to Farrell's lap.* "Goodbye, Daddy," *she says.* "Thank you so much for everything."

She walks to the door and opens it, and I'm damned if the actor George Clooney isn't standing there, grinning shyly and doing that thing where he pretends to look away at the floor but then turns his eyes back to look at yours. He is wearing a gorgeous tuxedo with an open-collared shirt, and is holding an unopened bottle of champagne. Poodle is so excited and thrilled that she jumps up and down twice, clapping her hands.

Another plausible explanation: He had been invited on board that week by the Royal Precious Platinum with a bunch of actors to sign autographs and give a seminar on Hollywood filmmaking, tell some old war stories. And he mistakenly thought my cabin was where Julia Roberts was staying.

Implausible explanation: Poodle willed him onto the ship, writing her own story and her life exactly as she wanted it to be.

Poodle sashays to the door and takes his arm. "Goodbye, everyone," *she says gaily,* "try to enjoy the rest of your lives." *And then George elegantly wheels with her still attached and whisks her down the hall, and they are gone.*

And then I do something stupid. I get up to go to the bathroom. Falubio, who is sitting so coolly in the chair in the corner that you might have thought he is either asleep or oblivious to the rather sudden departure of Poodle, suddenly becomes agitated.

"Boss, don't do that," he warns.

"Do what?" I say, reaching for the door handle. "I've just got to go in here for a minute."

"Boss," he shouts, "The tiger!"

"Oh, it won't hurt me," I say. As I open the door to go inside, Falubio leaps onto the desk, trying hard to find the highest point in the room. It is the fastest I've ever seen him move.

I am wrong. The tiger doesn't wait for me to come in. The tiger springs out of the bathroom. It leaps into the center of the room with a fearsome growl. I seize the opportunity to close the door quickly, locking myself into the bathroom. There is no sign of A Guy Named Brad or the struggle that he had, only a brown streak of butter that wraps around the four designer walls of the room.

I hear Falubio stage-whispering to the tiger. "Nice kitty, nice kitty," he says. I peek my head out the door and notice two things. The chair where my father sat is empty, and the tiger is fixing its gaze not on Falubio, who is trying hard to blend into the wall, but on the verandah. The sliding glass door is open and I can hear the gentle rush of ocean water far below.

I peek my head out the door even further, and then I see what the tiger sees. My dear, departed father, Farrell Sr., is standing on the railing of the verandah and doing a little dance. He tiptoes from one end of the verandah to the other, his eyes fixed on the tiger, beckoning it forward. He does a little pirouette, a balance-beam hop and turn, and then tiptoes to the other end.

I step out of the bathroom and scream, "Dad, don't do it!" The tiger doesn't turn its attention away from Farrell for even a second.

"Please, Dad, don't go!" I holler.

He is somehow holding a sheet of paper in his insubstantial hand, and as a gust of wind blows from the ocean, almost toppling him from the railing, he lets it go. It floats down, miraculously, past the tiger and to my feet. It says:

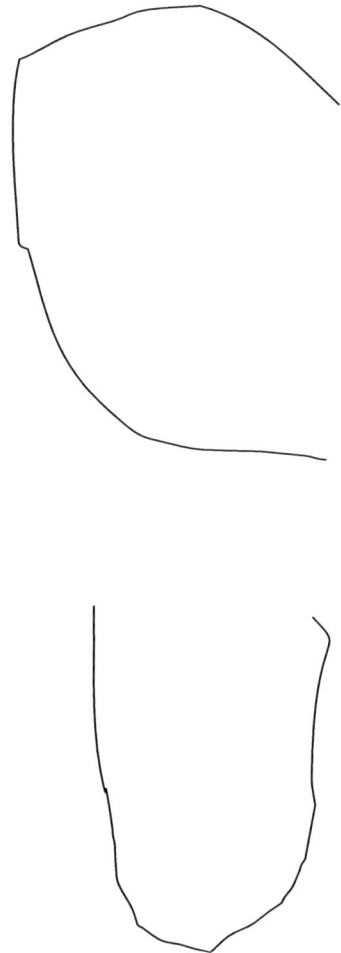

[304]

"Dad," I cry, "I still need you!"

He looks at me levelly and just shakes his finger.

"Yes, I do," I say, but much more quietly, almost to myself.

The tiger lowers itself, does a little, positioning shimmy on the carpet with its butt and haunches, and then leaps. My father allows himself to fall backwards off the railing just as the tiger reaches him. They hurtle through the air together, eleven stories down. I get to the railing just in time to see the splash. They disappear into the wake of the ship, but then emerge seconds later. Dad runs; the tiger swims.

As I look out over a gray-blue dusk that seems to extend in every direction, I can see a wisp of him running across the top of the water, with the tiger swimming fast behind him in hot pursuit. I watch them all the way to the horizon, and then for some time after that, as the stars come out and a full moon casts a yellow streak atop the waves, I watch some more.

Falubio has returned to the armchair and is carefully studying his nails. Our little penthouse suite on the Royal Precious Platinum is suddenly expanding, it seems. Everyone has left us and suddenly you can stretch out on the sofa without Poodle complaining, "Quit it," when your legs go over her lap, can see into the corner *without running smack into Floyd Little's stiff arm. My father isn't reading quietly in the chair, which seems looming and empty as a result, and there is no annoying buzzing sound from the part of me that is formerly A Guy Named Brad.*

And there is less of me. I am getting smaller. You could say that the butter is coming out of me, too. I seem to be deflating like a balloon, the way that the pounds are dropping off of me. I am losing weight as if I was being viewed in time-lapse photography (and to my knowledge, I am not). If I knew how or what was happening, I would write a weight-loss book and make a million bucks, but I have no idea what is going on.

"Falubio," I say, "I don't know how much longer I'm going to be around. Look at me, I'm shrinking."

I don't add that I am losing my grasp on the story. I don't dare to let Falubio know how little control I have left over what is happening in the book. I fear that he may have sensed that.

He shifts the toothpick in his mouth and just nods. "Don't worry, boss, I've got it covered," *he says.*

"What's happening to me?" *I ask him.*

Silence. He moodily looks out the window and shrugs, the same way that Robert Mitchum used to look out of windows and shrug. It is a shrug that suggests that his hands are tied, the world is what it is, he can't make life begin or end. He isn't, after all, God. He can only occupy his space as long as he is supposed to, and, classic careworn existentialist that he is, he doesn't find any reason to question things like why or how long or when. It isn't worth the energy. Falubio is all about conserving energy and not getting too worked up.

"If you're not God," I ask him, "who is?"

He looks at me knowingly. "You really need a God?" he asks.

"It wouldn't hurt."

"Maybe it's the butler," he says.

And then we both crack up.

I fear that Costas hears this, because his face is white and his manners are even more elaborate than usual when he arrives moments later with petits fours and a pot of the Sri Lankan tea that I enjoy. He leaves hurriedly and with something of a haughty turn of the shoulder, his back stiff as a ramrod as he exits the suite.

That is a dumb thing to do, to get Costas mad.

Chapter Sixteen
MORONGO COLLEGE
less KNAPP, more SCHLAPPI, no HARDWARE

There was a comedy routine that Ray liked to do with his brother Farrell Jr. when they were young men and driving around Morongo in Farrell's car. Whenever they passed by Knapp & Schlappi Hardware, Ray would assume the voice of a vaudeville comedian, elbow his brother and say, "Hey, Knapp."

Farrell got the routine right away. In the voice of the duo's straight man, he would say, "What is it, Schlappi?"

"Well Knapp, I was thinking. What do you call it when you cross a two-by-four with a bucket of galvanized nails?"

Farrell would pause a moment and then say, "I don't know, Schlappi. What DO you call it when you cross a two-by-four with a bucket of galvanized nails?"

And Ray would say, "I don't know either, Knapp, but I bet it's some kind of stud."

Farrell would conclude the routine by saying, "If you say so, Schlappi."

And that's what the brothers did when they passed Knapp & Schlappi Hardware, right up to the time that Ray turned thirty and married Janice. He wondered if Farrell would remember it, and if years could be peeled away from their lives just by pretending for a moment that they were young men again.

Daniel had left the walkway, and as Ray approached the Chapel's main entrance, he saw that the door was open. The interior of the chapel was dark and he could make out rows of empty pews. The space looked cool and peaceful and inviting; it had always been one of his favorite places, and he had missed it from his self-imposed exile from the college.

Inside he found Daniel, sitting alone in the middle of the space. Light filtering in through stained-glass windows tinted the air, and Ray ran his hands along the polished, pine wood of the pews, as he had as a child walking through the space. He sat down next to his son, and Daniel turned to him and attempted a rueful grin.

"Don't ask, Dad, it's a long story."

"Your mother has been worried about you," said Ray. "I have too, for that matter."

"I'll come home soon," said Daniel. "I like to come here sometimes, especially when it's empty. It's like…peaceful, or something."

"Something like that," said Ray.

"You and Mom got married here."

Ray nodded. "A long time ago."

Daniel waved a bottle that he was holding, a green wine bottle that he had boosted from the basement of John Piczak's cottage. "You know, this stuff doesn't work," he said. "It's just wine. People pay me a lot of money to drink it when I tell them the story of how it saves lives. And the better the story is, the more they pay. I feel really bad, Dad."

Ray reached for the bottle and took a swallow. "And really bad wine at that," he said. "You need to give them their money back."

"Oh, that's not why I feel bad," said Daniel. "They pay me for the story; they think they'll live forever when they drink it. They get their money's worth; the bad wine is just a bonus. I learned that from my marketing class. This is what I feel bad about." He reached into his pocket and produced an envelope that had been stamped and mailed to Ray. He recognized the handwriting as from Donna; the letter had been opened, and was creased from Daniel carrying it in his jeans pocket.

"You opened my mail?" Ray said.

Daniel nodded and looked straight ahead, at the altar. "Dad, I didn't want to read it. Donna called me and asked me to open it before I gave it to you. She wanted my advice."

Ray sighed and opened the letter, and read about Donna leaving him, and her regrets, and how she would always love him and Daniel. "But Ray," she wrote, "this sadness that you carry around with you, this place that you go every year at the time of the anniversary of your father's death...I can't help you, and I just can't be there for you anymore." He put his fingers to his brow and shook his head, not so much in grief but as in resignation. The grief and hurt would come later, he knew.

"So what did you tell her?" he said, rubbing his forehead.

"I told her that you would want her to be happy," said Daniel, "I had no idea what to say. I'm really sorry. Dad...what happened?"

Ray began to talk: to confess, really. He told Daniel about his marriage to Janice, and how things went bad, and the car accident that almost killed all three of them – Janice and baby Daniel driving one way on Water Street, Ray the other and the two cars colliding head-on – and sealed the divorce. He told him about his father and the heart attacks, and how he had kept things bottled up for years.

When he was finished, and the words seemed to hang in the sanctified air of the Chapel, Daniel shrugged and said, "Dad, it was just his time to go. It wasn't your fault."

Ray nodded. "I guess so," he said. "I know that in my head, but not in my heart. You still wish that there was something you could have done. You wish that you had been a little better in a crisis, so you wouldn't have to live with a lifetime of guilt." Ray looked around. The Chapel was old and worn, but still lovely. "The last time I was here was for his funeral," he said, "and I kind of decided that I wouldn't come back."

Daniel kissed him on the cheek. "I wish we could all live forever," he said. "But we can't. Come on, Dad, I have something to show you."

He led Ray down a staircase to the basement of the Chapel, where a large meeting room was dark and austere, its metal chairs folded up on racks, and round tables on their sides, their legs folded and rolled into a corner. Daniel obviously knew his way around the building. He walked through the meeting room and through the swinging doors of a kitchen, then opened a walk-in pantry closet in the back of the kitchen. Hanging on the wall was a portrait of Farrell

Sr. painted in oils by an amateur artist. He wore his doctoral robes, but there was a hoe in his hand and a garden in the background, and behind that was a slice of the lake.

"Remind you of anyone?" asked Daniel.

Ray blinked back tears. "I remember this from a long, long time ago," he said. "I saw it when I was a kid. It's a self-portrait that your grandpa painted."

"Look a little closer, Dad."

Ray stepped closer to the portrait, and Daniel flicked on the lights to the room. Ray carefully grasped the frame with two hands and lifted it off the wall and looked at the back. Written in a careful hand was the name of the artist, Farrell Jensen Sr., and the year, 1973. There was an inscription, too: To Farrell and Ray.

Ray replaced the frame on the wall and stepped back to admire it. "He painted this the year that he died," said Ray. "These are the things that your grandfather loved. His robes, because he was a teacher. His garden, and the lake. He really was funny guy sometimes."

Daniel reached for the painting. "Should we steal it and bring it home?"

Ray looked at his only son and just shook his head. So many things to teach a young man before he comes of age, so many lessons that a father should deliver before he dies. It was his turn to grab Daniel by the elbow, turn him towards the door and steer him from the pantry, turning off the light as he left.

"I'll take that as a no, Dad," said Daniel. Arm in arm in arm, the two of them left the Chapel. They opened a basement door and found themselves outside, on the far side of the building, opposite the Point. Ray could look up the hill to Slater Hall. He was surprised to see that he could just make out his father's former office from where they stood. The windows facing the lake were all closed, and their green tints made the lake's reflection seem black and still.

Except one, and from where Ray and Daniel stood, they could see a figure sitting inside one of the windows that faced the lake. The window had been pushed open as high as it could go. Ray craned his neck and walked closer to get a better look. It was his father sitting in the window, staring out at the lake. Ray's heart jumped into his mouth, and he moved closer and looked again. It wasn't his father; it was his brother, Farrell Jr., who was sitting in his father's former office at Slater Hall. As he watched, Farrell's head turned in his direction, and then it ducked out of sight below the window. A moment later, a curtain was drawn over the glass.

"Did you see that?" Ray said.
"See what?" said Daniel.

Ray began to run up the path towards Slater Hall, and Daniel broke into a jog to catch up.

He paused for a moment when they reached Slater Hall, waiting for its layout to come back to him. The doors to enter the building were closed and locked while the campus was on break. Ray walked around the corner of the building and remembered, when he saw the rusted staircase that served as a fire escape, that he had had a secret way to enter Slater Hall as a child. When the college was closed and he wanted to play basketball, he could scale the brick wall, using handholds that were hidden in the ivy, to climb the ten feet up to the fire escape, and then enter through the second floor fire door that was never locked. Even Harry van Buren, the head of campus security, didn't know how Ray snuck into the building. The ivy was slick and even slimy where it fastened itself to the building, but Ray found the old projections of brick where they had always been. He knew that he couldn't haul himself up the wall, but Daniel could. The boy boosted himself up onto the first bricks and then climbed to the landing, where he tried the door. He disappeared inside, and appeared a minute later inside the vestibule, where he opened the door for Ray.

"This is so cool," said Daniel who, as has been previously noted, enjoyed the sensation of breaking and entering.

The lights had been turned down by half for spring break and the halls of the floor were dark and hollow, the doors to the offices and classrooms shut as if they had been sealed. To Ray, Slater Hall looked like it had been closed off and preserved since the last time he had left it, in a dreamy haze of fear and heartbreak, three decades earlier. He smiled at his nervousness and the sudden, looming awareness of his heartbeat. He led Daniel past the former gym, still floored with the old basketball parquet whose lines had faded and grown dull. The baskets and backboards had been removed, and mirrors and a ballet bar had been installed across the longest wall.

On the way to his father's office, Ray passed the building directory. He instinctively looked for his father's name, but of course, it was not listed. Instead, Room 104 now belonged to a Thomas Fitzgibbons, Ph.D. Ray went to the door and tried it, but it was also locked. He rattled the door handle and wondered again what he was doing, and if his day might be better spent by not prowling around a college, looking for ghosts of his father. He began to move down the hall towards the exit, but then another memory visited him, of the conference room down the hall that connected to the English department's suite of offices. He had once watched his father conduct a senior seminar in that room, in the evening when education, at least to a grade-schooler, seemed somehow vital and delicious, and he had sat quietly and confidently in the corner and watched yet another version of his father deliver a lecture to a group of rapt young women who seemed to think that every word that he said was important. Or maybe they thought that every word might appear on the test. Ray went to the conference room door and tried it. It was also locked, but the latch had some give in it. Ray stood there, wondering what to do, and Daniel stepped forward. He pulled his student ID card from his wallet, slipped it between the door and its jamb and wiggled it. The old door, built in an era before credit cards and credit theft, opened with a click. Daniel winked at Ray and stepped back to let his father go first.

They moved through the conference room and found that the doors into the English suite were closed, but unlocked. Ray hesitated, unfamiliar with the layout of the suite from that direction, but then saw that there was a dim light in the corner office, and the door was stenciled with Professor Fitzgibbons' name. Ray went to the door and tried it, found it locked, and motioned to Daniel to use the card a second time.

The door pushed open, and Ray believed that he was indeed going quietly mad when the first thing he saw was a pair of stocking feet on the floor extending beyond the desk. Ray's heart jumped again and his blood roared in his ears. What are the odds, he wondered, of stepping into a professor's office twice in thirty years and finding him prone on the floor? Who has such luck? He calmed an urge to close the door and run, and stepped into the room. The feet twitched.

"Farrell," said Ray.

"Ray."

The word seemed to echo in the space. Farrell Jr. sat on the floor with his back pressed against the wall in a way that suggested wounding, the way that soldiers in movies sit after they've been shot but before they say a few poignant last words and then slump over for the final time. His legs were extended straight out before him and his head was propped against the wall as if he were paralyzed. Ray moved to his side and sat next to him. His brother's eyes were red, from either pain or crying or both, and when Ray instinctively reached out to touch the forehead, it was hot and sweaty. Farrell moved his head to evade Ray's touch, but his hands and arms did not move.

"Daniel, go get some water," Ray said calmly. Daniel, whose face had gone white from the sight of his uncle, turned and quickly left.

"We've got to get you to a doctor," Ray said.

"Oh, I've been to the doctor," said Farrell. "I've been to the fucking doctor more times than I can tell you. Didn't do a thing for me, neither."

Farrell had minutes, not days, to live. Snops or no snops, Ray gathered this acutely, in his bones and in his heart. He took his brother's hand gently, and Farrell did not resist.

"Why didn't you tell me?" he said.

Farrell smiled weakly. "You've got enough problems of your own, with that kid of yours. And, excuse the expression, your wife."

Ray smiled. "Ex-wife."

"Like you two don't act like you're still married, calling each other and fighting all the time. Worst goddamned divorce I've ever seen, if you can never get away from your ex."

Ray looked up. The desk and shelves and décor of the room were different, but the office still seemed familiar. It smelled of old wood and books and paper. The floor was chilly through his trousers. "What are you doing here?"

"Wanted to see the old man's place one more time," said Farrell. "And figured that nobody would be dumb enough to look for me here. Thought I'd come back to take a look and get away from everybody."

"You should be home. Well, you should be in the hospital, but if you won't go there, you should be home."

Farrell's eyes reddened. "Don't need to have my kids see me die," he said.

Ray watched him silently and squeezed his brother's hand. "What is it? Cancer?"

Farrell shook his head. "No. Heart's weak. Just like the old man, except I can't seem to keel over and die like he did. Just keep getting weaker and weaker, and can't hardly breathe."

"You really need to get to the hospital."

Farrell shook his head again. "No, I ain't going back there. At least not alive."

"Does it hurt?" asked Ray.

"Fuck yeah it hurts. I have to say that I'm not finding a lick of good in dying. Not real clear on why it has to hurt so damn much. Pain is supposed to remind you to not do something again, but where I'm going, I don't need no reminders."

"Maybe it makes you appreciate the living part more," said Ray. It was actually something of a rote answer. Ray didn't know why it had to hurt, either.

"I always did appreciate the living part," said Farrell. "I didn't jump up and down and hug every goddamn person that I met on the street, but I appreciated it all the same. And now I'd appreciate it if my body just worked a little better. It's like my muscles and organs have already died, but my pain receptors are just getting warmed up. This dying suddenly of a heart attack on the porch is looking pretty good from where I sit."

"Yeah, but look at what it does to your family," said Ray. "You check out suddenly on the porch and they spend a lifetime wondering why they never got a chance to say goodbye. Stuff like that."

"That's too bad for them," said Farrell. "That's none of their business, how you die."

"We need to get Bump here. She should be with you."

"I am, Ray," said a woman's voice from the doorway. Bump stood there holding a cup of water that she had retrieved from the staff lounge. She was still wearing her pale-blue waitress outfit from the diner. Daniel was standing beside her. "I told him the same thing, about the hospital, but he won't leave here. Says this is where he wants to die." Her eyes misted and she steadied herself with a hand against the doorframe. She took a sip of the water and then brought it to Farrell, tipped it to his lips and wetted them. He grimaced and turned his head away. She knelt down beside him and took his hand and held it in both of hers.

"Bump," said Ray. "I thought you said you couldn't find him."

She looked at him and her face was calm, practically angelic. "Didn't say I didn't know where he was, Ray. I said that you should find him. There's a difference. And you did." She rubbed her hand quickly down Farrell's arm and then was silent. She looked at the room. "Guess this is where the Jensen men come to die," she said.

A small smile passed across Farrell's face. His eyes were closed and his head rested against Bump's shoulder. "Guess so," he said softly.

Ray beckoned to Daniel, who knew instantly what his father wanted. He slung the backpack from his shoulder, unzipped it and pulled out the bottle with the last of the Piczak snops. He quickly brought it to Ray, who carefully pulled out the cork. He knelt down beside his brother.

Farrell smiled weakly and his eyes opened. "That your miracle wine, Ray? Stuff that cured my little girl of her fever?"

Bump smiled too. "She spit it all up an hour later. But it broke her fever, I'll say that. We thank you for that, Ray."

Ray and Daniel exchanged a look of understanding, and then Ray moved closer to his brother. "Farrell, listen to me. This stuff is special. I don't really know what it is, but I'll tell you that I got it off one of those chemistry professors from the college. And I think it's the real thing. If you drink it, it can keep you alive. I don't know how, I don't know why, but I'm pretty sure that it works."

"Is that right?" Farrell slowly raised a hand and beckoned for the bottle. He gripped it and passed it in front of his eyes and took a sniff. "Doctors pump me full of drugs and they don't do a damned thing for what I've got, but your bad wine here is more powerful than all the drugs in the world, huh?"

"It might be. It might be a miracle. You need a miracle, don't you? Why don't you just take the chance that it might work?"

Farrell held the bottle in his hand and looked at it. He sniffed it again, and then waved the bottle at Ray and Daniel. "You two can no more control how long people are going to live as you can control the weather. Shit, Ray, you want to have the power of God? You can barely balance your checkbook. Answer me this: What good is the power of God if the person with the power is a dumb-ass, Ray? If he's got no more wisdom than a squirrel's got brains? What good is it, Ray?"

"I don't know," said Ray. "I just know that I don't want you to die."

"Well, I appreciate that, but I gotta go sometime. Gave me six months to live a year ago, and miracles have kept me alive this long. Don't need no more goddamn medicines or cures. What I need to do now is to die. You aren't gonna keep me from dying, are you Ray?"

"No, I don't suppose that I can do that," he said.

"No reason you should. You couldn't keep the old man from dying, and neither could I. It wasn't your fault that he went when he did. I'll go when I'm supposed to go, too, and I bet it ain't long."

"God, I wish it was that easy for me," said Ray.

"Here, I'll make it easy for you," said his brother. With surprising strength, he snapped his arm forward and hurled the bottle of snops across the room. It smashed against the side of a file cabinet and left a slick of fluid dripping down the smooth, metal surface to the wood floor.

"God damn it, Farrell," shouted Ray. He sat staring at the broken glass and the puddle of snops. Daniel stood still and gaped, but Bump acted. She slid across the room on her knees, frantically tearing off her apron. She pushed aside the fragments of glass with one hand and tried to collect the liquid in the apron with the other.

"There, now you can be at peace when your time comes," said Farrell. "No more miracles." He looked exhausted, and his eyes began to close. He was still for a moment, but with his eyes still closed, he said, "Just wanted to grow up to be like the old man. But that never happened."

A tremor passed through him, and then he grew silent and still in a different way. Bump screamed, "Farrell!" and put his head in her arms and held it and kissed it. Ray's eyes spasmed and he began to cry. He looked up, and Daniel was crying too, so he put his arm around his son's bare shoulder.

"We can't just leave him here like this," said Daniel between sobs, and it gave Ray an idea. He took the apron from Daniel's hands and crawled on his hands and knees to his brother's lifeless body. He touched the wet part of the cloth to Farrell's lips and squeezed out a drop of the snops. The body stirred and Farrell moaned something soft and unintelligible, from far away.

"Oh Holy shit," said Daniel. "Look what it's doing."

Farrell's breath was faint, but steady. Wringing the apron hard, Ray squeezed another drop of the precious fluid into his brother's mouth, and then stood up. "Come on," he said to Daniel and Bump. "Help me. We've got to get him to my house. Daniel, run and get my car and bring it as close to the door as you can."

They left Slater Hall by the front door. It was quite a procession. Bump and Ray carried Farrell in their arms, straining and stumbling from the dead weight of him, and Bump held the damp apron to her husband's lips. She slipped into the backseat of Ray's car and they laid Farrell's head on her lap and folded his legs to fit into the seat. Daniel slid over to let Ray drive. Every few minutes they could hear a faint sigh escape from Farrell Jr. as Ray drove as fast as he could back to his cottage.

[fewer] NARRATORS
you call that an ending?

    With a small, some might say rueful smile lingering on my thin lips, I give Falubio a good, long look. He pretends to ignore me, but I keep it up.
    "What?" he says.
    "Did the snops revive my brother or didn't it?" I say.
    He pretends to study his manicure. Coughs a little breath-polish on his nails, rubs them on his shirt. "You were there. You know what happened."
    "Yes, I was. But couldn't we just have some clarity for a change? And for that matter, since we're making all of this up, couldn't we give the story a little happier ending, and let him live?" I waved my hand to take in the cruise ship cabin, the butter, the mess I'd made of my life. "If this is real life, who needs it? Couldn't we make up something better?"
    He pretends to be intent on his nails, but I catch him peeking a glance at me. "Stories need action," he says simply. "Movies need gunshots. Lives need deaths, or they

don't amount to anything, do they? Your brother was going to die one way or another. Does it really matter how or when? Wouldn't we all rather die in a blaze of glory in the final reel of the movie of our lives?"

"Are you quite done?" I ask.

He stands up and yawns. "Actually, I'm completely done, Boss. That's the best that I've got for you. And if you'll excuse me, I've got a dinner party to attend." He unzips his wet suit – did I ever mention that Falubio has been wearing a tight, black wetsuit this entire time? – and peels it off to reveal that he has been wearing a perfectly pressed white dinner jacket, black tuxedo trousers and a hand-tied white bow over a pleated shirt with diamond studs and cufflinks.

The door opens then and Costas is standing there. But he isn't holding any mints for me; likewise no canapés, after-dinner drink, or Portuguese remedy for a broken heart. Costas in fact has nothing for me. Falubio shakes himself once and the dinner jacket snaps to attention as if it has just been pressed. He walks to the door, and as he passes Costas, Falubio pauses for a moment and then leans his face forward, almost accidentally, it is so subtle, until his lips barely brush Costas' freshly shaved cheek.

"Which room is yours?" Falubio asks.

"*Last door on the left,*" Costas says. "*I'll be there in a minute.*"

Without so much as a wave in my direction, my leading man strides off down the hallway and is gone.

"*Oh, for fuck sakes,*" I say. "*You two…?*" *I actually punch Costas on the arm lightly, like buddies punch. I didn't know he was gay! To my recollection, it is the only time on my tenure on the Royal Precious Platinum that I've ever touched him. When I do so, I see that there is someone else in the hallway. It is Tennis de Jong, ship's purser extraordinaire, who is waving a fistful of papers and grinning like he has just won the Dutch lottery.*

"*You're krispbrot, Jensen,*" *he cackles. (He pronounces it Yensen.)* "*You know what I have here, ja?*"

"*I wouldn't even venture a guess, dick-less,*" I say. *My manners are failing me. Spending one's life in the cabin of a cruise ship makes one coarse; vulgar, even.*

"*Repeal of the Maritime Incumbency Act. For two years we lobby for dis, and now we got it. Passed last night in the Nederlander legislature. In Amsterdam, you know*"

"*Yeah, I know where the Netherlands are.*"

"*You're off of this ship in the morning, Mister. I will escort you personally to the gangway. Seven a.m. sharp.*"

He throws the papers into my cabin, and they scatter on the floor.

"Do I still get dinner?" I ask.

He makes a sound in his throat like he's coughing up a hairball, turns on his heel and strides off without another word.

I come back in and sit down heavily on the chair where my father used to sit. "I guess this is it," I say. "Now what am I supposed to do?"

Costas clears his throat. "There is a saying in my native Portugal," he begins, "that a man's story is never truly told."

"Great saying," I say.

"Yes, I repeat it often."

"Costas," I say, "I have no narrators and I have no ending. And there is no story if there is no ending. And there will be no ending if I have no narrators to tell it."

He clears his throat again. He obviously has been thinking about this. "I think I can help, Sir," he says. He reaches inside his handsome jacket with tails and produces a sheaf of papers that are secured by ribbons. "I've taken the liberty to write you an ending."

I take them. My hands are shaking. "Costas," I say, "I can't thank you enough. But honestly, I can't accept this. I mean, it's my story that we've all been writing."

"I don't think you'll be displeased, Sir."

I look at the first sentence. And then the next. I read three paragraphs and suddenly I am turning the page. It isn't bad. Except for a few obvious grammatical and spelling errors, it is actually pretty good.

"Costas," I say, "I think you have done your duty very well. You are one fine butler, Sir. And if I had a dime to my name, I would give it to you as a tip with my most heartfelt thanks."

He bows. And then cocks his head in the direction of the last door on the left. "Oh, you've repaid me handsomely for my service, Sir. But I've kind of got to go," he says. "My shift is almost over. If you need anything else, I'm sure that the night butler can help you."

"Go ahead, Costas. And here's a saying from my native Morongo: Vaya con Dios."

He smiles. "In Portugal we say that Dios is in the details. And on any given day, he might be inside any one of us. The trick of life is to find out where he is and stop him for a few moments. Ask him to pay you some attention and shine his light on you, soothe your life for a moment. It's something like your American game of freeze tag. When he moves on to someone else, you wait until it's your turn again." He bows again. He turns on his heel and is gone.

I read more. It really isn't bad at all. At any rate, it will have to do. It's all I have.

Chapter Seventeen
A cottage on MORONGO LAKE
A FLOYD LITTLE cut-out, leaving it UP TO THE LAKE

The wind picked up as they drove back towards town and the air grew chill, a reminder that winter was not so long passed, and a cold front could sweep across Lake Ontario from Canada at any moment, rush down the glacial valleys of the Finger Lakes and bring with it a late snow. By the time they reached Ray's cottage, the wind was blowing hard, and the screen door on his porch had unhooked itself and was flapping against the storm door. Ray drove the car over the lawn and got as close to the porch as he could, and he and Daniel and Bump carefully lifted Farrell Jr. from the backseat and carried him into the house. His eyes were closed and his skin was as white as marble and cold to the touch. Ray could not get a pulse from his neck or his wrist, but Farrell was still summoning short, infrequent breaths. They laid him on the living-room couch and covered him with a blanket.

"We should have taken him to the hospital," Daniel said. "We still can."

Ray hesitated, but Bump spoke up. "Leave him be," she said. "He's where he wants to be now. It won't be long." She knelt down on the floor and took her husband's arm from under the blanket, and stroked the skin from his elbow to his wrist. Into his ear, she whispered the names of their children, over and over. Daniel's face went white and he stepped back and supported himself with one arm against a counter.

Bump looked at Daniel. "There any of that stuff left?" she asked. Daniel was still clutching the apron with the last of the Piczak Snops.

"I don't think there is," he said, but handed her the rag anyway. She put it to her own mouth, bit it to try to find the last of the moisture inside, and then threw it aside. Her kids needed her to live forever now, and that's what she intended to do.

Daniel was shivering, so Ray found a jacket hanging on a hook in the hallway, got it down and brought it to his son. He had to drape it around the boy's shoulders and guide his arms into the sleeves. He put his arm around Daniel and held him. Daniel was watching his uncle and looked scared and fascinated at the same time. "Stay with them," Ray said.

"I will, Dad." Bump led Daniel to the other side of the couch, where they sat on their knees, and gingerly reached over the back of the couch and put their hands on Farrell's shoulder. Ray was going to do the same, but he heard a banging noise upstairs in the bedroom and ran up to check on it.

Upstairs, he found the windows open and the outside shutters banging against the side of the house from the wind. The lake was dark and made ominous splashing sounds at the dock and the beach. His life-sized cutout of Floyd Little, the former star running back of the Denver Broncos, which Ray had had since childhood and had occupied one bedroom or another of his since he was eight years old, was standing in his customary spot with his knee raised, his stiff-arm resolutely forward and the ball tucked into the crook of his elbow.

Ray reached for the shutters, but before he could close them, he heard a rumbling sound that Ray first thought was thunder, but then realized was coming from inside the house. He looked back to the door of the room and saw his brother Farrell Jr. bound into the room from the staircase. But it wasn't the same Farrell Jr. whom Ray had brought home from the college. This one was much younger and leaner. His hair was jet black and his face was smooth. He wore the confident grin that Ray remembered from a young man, thirty years earlier, a man who could whip every living soul in Morongo, and knew it. He looked at Ray and nodded; Ray fell to his knees, and his hands instinctively clasped in front of him in a gesture of supplication.

Farrell Jr. gently took Ray's chin in his hand and raised it so the brothers' eyes met. He tapped his heart and pointed to Ray. It could have either meant that he loved his brother or "you're next." He touched his finger to his lips in a kiss and then used the finger to draw two letters in the air: C U.

He walked towards the wall facing the lake. The window was still open and the shutter was banging. Without a glance back, Farrell Jr. leaped out the window. Ray stood up and walked quickly to the window, and he saw his brother running, as fast as the wind, off the end of the dock, onto the lake and across it, in the direction of Bath. He watched until Farrell disappeared from sight.

Ray heard steps on the staircase, and then Bump appeared in the bedroom. She said, "Ray, you need to come down here. He's gone." Then she walked to him and took his hand and sat him down on the edge of the bed. "Honey, are you alright?" she said. "You're as white as a sheet."

Ray nodded. "I'm just going to miss him. I feel so bad."

She sat down next to him and held him.

When they returned downstairs, Daniel was still kneeling alongside the prone body of Farrell Jr. The body was still, and they covered it with a sheet.

"He's gone, Daddy," said Daniel.

"I know," said Ray. He moved to Bump and gently took her by the shoulders, turned her and hugged her. "He loved you his whole life," Ray said. "I remember the look on his face the day that you met. He never lost it. You made him happy for a long time."

She nodded in his shirt and cried. As he held her, Ray caught Daniel's eye and motioned for him to get the phone. Daniel knew what to do, and called 911, and reported that somebody had died and an ambulance was needed. They came ten minutes later, tried to revive Farrell Jr. and couldn't, and loaded his body onto a stretcher. Bump went with them.

"Oh, jeez, you've got to call your mother," Ray said, remembering that Janice hadn't yet heard that Daniel was all right, and knowing he'd catch hell for it.

"It's okay, Dad. I need some air, so I'm going to walk back to Mom's." He kissed Ray on the cheek, hugged him, and then he left and Ray was alone.

Ray walked out to the porch facing the lake. The wind had died down but the water still slapped at the dock and showed whitecaps in the middle of the lake. He sat on the porch for several minutes, but the morning air was chilly, and he realized that he was uncomfortable. He went inside and sat down heavily in his chair. Something bumped him from underneath it, and he reached down and found the bundle that contained John Piczak's notes and volumes. He idly flipped through the pages, and read again the experiments that produced The Piczak Snops. He asked himself, What good has the Fountain of Youth done me?

He answered himself: None.

Can't save his brother. Can't keep his girl. Can't stop his son from running rampant with good intentions. Can't make his father come back. What good is it to have the power of God if you're insensitive, uncomprehending, unloved and a dumb ass? Ray wished to know. No answers were forthcoming from his quiet house, the lake or the Piczak tome.

Ray left the volumes of notes on the chair. He walked back outside, and then stepped off the porch and walked down the narrow, gravel path to the lake. His old dock was in need of repair, and he walked carefully to the end of it, avoiding the broken slats. As he did so, he began to remove all of his clothes, and he was naked when he got to the end. He squatted for a moment and gazed at the water. The lake looked cold and uninviting. Ray thought for a few moments. And then he allowed himself to fall headfirst into the water.

He did not swim, he did not sink. He left it up to the lake. Cold and numb, he began to float, first towards the center of the lake as a cool breeze whipped across its surface, and then in the direction of Hammondsport, thirty miles away. He went under several times that night, but something kept him alive and returned him to the surface each time. Every time he surfaced Ray felt something bitter and orange pass over his tongue. He passed the college and the Point at three a.m. At dawn, he was blown to shore near his mother's house, far down the lake. Disgusted, but still alive, he went inside, quietly so as not to wake her, dried himself and found some of his old clothes in the spare bedroom closet.

He walked all the way home, arriving at nine a.m. He climbed into the big chair in the living room and fell asleep with John Piczak's volumes on his lap. He slept twenty-four hours and woke up ravenous, starving.

After an enormous breakfast at the Morongo Diner, he booked himself on a cruise to Alaska. Among the things he packed were another half-bottle of snops that he found under Daniel's bed, a tuxedo for formal night, a Wolfman mask for masquerade night, and his life-sized cardboard cut-out of Floyd Little, Ray's childhood football hero. He left no notes as to his whereabouts, and he didn't lock the doors. In Morongo, nobody ever locks the doors. It is one of the little benefits of living in a small town.

THE (final) NARRATOR
every BLARNEY STONE in lower manhattan; a child named CHUBBY

Is there a finer sight to be seen than the one a cruise ship enjoys early on a fine, summer morning when she crosses under the Verrazano Bridge and enters New York harbor? Your faithful correspondent, Mr. Raymond Jensen, a first-time cruiser from Morongo, New York, would agree that little compares to it, particularly when one is sprung from his self-imposed exile in a penthouse suite and experiences passing under the bridge from the Sports Deck of the Royal Precious Platinum, the luxurious and well-appointed sailing ship that boasts five-star service and an award-winning staff of hospitality experts.

That last paragraph was the last thing that Costas wrote. I'm on my own from here on out. I'll tell you something else that I enjoyed, and that was the view of the farewell breakfast buffet on the Lido Deck. One's butler can, and dutifully has tried very hard to provide a *sumptuous array of breakfast choices for the cabin-bound passenger, but a Lido breakfast buffet in its full glory can scarcely be comprehended. Especially when said passenger has not stepped out of his penthouse suite in over a year and a half and is seeing the buffet through hungry eyes, as one might say in Portugal, a seaside country with a long and rich maritime history.*

Word of my sudden expulsion from the ship had gotten around, and the chefs knew that I would be making my farewell appearance at the buffet. They lined up at the door of the Lido in their starched whites and gleaming toques to greet me. I paused to shake the hand of each one and offer a kind word, for the food during my rather extended voyage had been nothing short of spectacular, not to mention offered without question or with a concern over quantity. For my part, I had consumed more of it than any passenger in the history of Royal Precious Platinum cruises.

For my final meal, the chefs outdid themselves. Eschewing the usual trays and steam tables laden with breakfast delicacies, they had instead paid tribute to me by producing literally thousands of single, plated servings of my favorite dishes from the menus of the ship's six kitchens. Every available surface in the Lido Lounge was covered with a dish or bowl, and passengers were given a knife, fork and spoon at the door and welcomed to graze at will, moving from table to table, banquette to bar and piano top to dance floor to eat to their heart's content. There were dollops of coconut rice pudding artfully sculpted and plated to represent the Hawaiian islands; breaded and fried shrimp struggling to escape from gossamer, vermicelli nets; tender slices of halibut, cod, lobster and a dozen other fish swimming against the stream in rivers of a dozen sauces; tiny, nine-layer chocolate cakes no bigger than your thumb; prime rib roasts the size of silver dollars attached to rib bones that had been painstakingly filed down to the size of finishing nails; and butter sculptures assembled from butters that were collected in each of the three-hundred-forty-five ports in which the ship had stopped with me on board. I ate with great relish, like a man who does not know where his next meal is coming from, which in my case was unerringly accurate.

    Costas laid out my disembarkation outfit, all of which had been provided free of charge by the ship's stores and made me look like a wealthy Chief Executive Officer who had just stepped off a golf course. After we passed under the Verrazano Bridge, I stood on deck as the ship passed Ellis Island and the Statue of Liberty, and even a morbid dickwalter like myself felt something akin to a chill down my spine over the experience. My bags were packed *by Costas as I ate, and were transported to the gangway by a gang of coolies. At seven a.m. sharp, Mr. Tennis de Jong promptly arrived at the Lido Lounge to greet me and personally oversee my disembarkation. I gather that such personal service from an officer is reserved only for passengers with special needs.*

"What do I owe you, Chief Purser?" I asked. I was kidding; at that point, I couldn't have paid for a breath mint.

Through clenched Dutch teeth, or perhaps they were dentures, he replied, "It has been taken care of, Sir. An anonymous benefactor has paid your bill."

I nearly fainted over that one. "You've got to be kidding me. How much was it, anyway?"

DeJong smiled again. "Six hundred forty-three thousand dollars and eighty-nine cents, including interest. And the Royal Precious Platinum appreciates your business."

"How much is that in guilders?" I asked, but he only turned on his heel, and with a firm hand on my elbow to steady me and avoid any wrong turns, tripping or mishaps that might mar this customer's cruise experience, Mr. de Jong led me to the gangway and offered some kindly parting words to the effect that the ship might be considered a second home to Mr. Jensen, but only if the first home

burned down and all relatives came down with a communicable disease. I laughed heartily and offered to salute Mr. de Jong with a customary five-toe fusillade to the rear of his trousers. He politely declined. My bags and myself were delivered to the dock, and I must admit that I almost fell over when I stood on terra firma for the first time in years.

Sea legs.

I just stood there, unsure of what to do next. The ship would sail that evening with an entirely new group of passengers, nearly all of whom would not even think about stowing away in their cabins for a couple of years and leaving their fates to the good graces of the butler staff. I, on the other hand, would have to produce my own turn-down chocolate on my pillow that night. I felt like I might cry. With a long, last look at my ship, I turned my back and vanished into the interior of the terminal, bound for U.S. Customs. A half-hour later I was standing in midtown Manhattan with my suitcases on a cart and my manuscript in my arms. Unlike nearly everyone who rushed past me with a purposeful stride, I did not have the slightest idea of what to do next. Having been released by my ship, my past, my father and my narrators, I was suddenly lousy with opportunity, yet utterly lacking in ideas.

I had a few random thoughts of how to spend the day, but none of them particularly gelled. I considered finding my way to lower Manhattan and visiting every bar with the word Blarney in its name and begging drinks from friendly businessmen and other drunks. I considered finding a cozy corner on the Staten Island ferry and making it my domicile. I even, I admit, considered jumping into the Hudson River and swimming as far as I could upstream until I could swim no more. But as I have pointed out, I am not a suicide. I'm the opposite. I'm an embracer of life.

Just as I began to turn circles in confusion on that Manhattan street corner, a very large and very black limousine pulled up to the curb beside me. A window was rolled down. For a moment I thought that Tom Cruise had come to rescue me, but it wasn't Tom Cruise at all. It was my son, Daniel, who, since my lengthy absence, had changed his hair to a short, spiky cut and begun to favor accessorizing with sunglasses, gold chains and open-collared shirts that were hand-woven by Cuban virgins. "Get in, Dad," he said happily.

"Daniel," I said, and never before or since has a name sounded so sweet. "Where are we going, Son?"

"We're going home, Dad." He sounded rather triumphant, and his grin told me that he had even more surprises in store for me. I didn't care; not only was I thrilled to see him, but if he had said that we were heading to a forced-labor camp in the Adirondacks, I would not have complained.

"How is this happening?" I asked as I settled, suspiciously, into the plush blue leather of the car's enormous interior. "How can we afford this?"

"We can't, Pop," he said. "I can. Guess what I did while you were away?"

I splayed my hands out. The last I'd seen of him, he was selling snops on the beach for fifty bucks a pop, and I'm pretty sure that he ran out. "I can't guess," I said.

"I wrote a screenplay," he gushed. "And it sold, Pop. It sold for two million bucks."

My hands flew to my mouth. I was astonished, and thrilled. A screenwriter in the family! I wish I could have told Falubio. "And let me guess," I said. "It was about discovering a secret formula that would keep people alive forever, but had a few fairly severe side effects."

He threw back his head and laughed at my feeble, advanced middle-aged attempt at imagination. He had become quite an animated character since he turned eighteen. "That stuff never sells in Hollywood, Dad," he said. "My screenplay was a love story about Iraqi warlords who find weapons of mass destruction in a Syrian cave and blow up just about everybody before they in turn are obliterated. But it's a love story. Reno McTavish is all signed to direct it."

"Fabulous," I muttered.

We had a lot to talk about as the limousine drove north through Westchester County and then hung a left at the Catskills. I told him what I had been doing for the last two-plus years, of my companions on the ship and about my father. Lots and lots about my father. And I showed him the notes that my dad, his grandfather, had written from beyond the grave. "It was you who paid my bill, wasn't it?"

He grinned and shook his head. "Not telling, Dad. That's a secret that won't be broken."

And then he pulled out some papers and a familiar set of singed, bound, leather volumes. They were the Piczak notes, along with the four missing pages which he had retrieved from an incinerator can that was only warm to the touch to myself and my closest relations, and had a special way of looking after us. "Get a load of these," he said. I took them and carefully placed them inside the bound volume of the Piczak notes. Volume five, where they belonged. I haven't looked at them since, nor will I.

It was dusk when we arrived in Morongo. The lake looked beautiful, a blue jewel in a valley bracketed by rolling hillsides. When we pulled up to my cottage, I almost didn't recognize it. The exterior had been professionally scraped and painted, and there were flowers growing in bright blue windowboxes outside all of the windows. The deck that had once been so treacherous on which to walk had been torn out and replaced with a shiny, new, wraparound porch with a sunroom. There was somebody inside the sunroom, a woman. Her back was to me.

"Go inside, Dad," said Daniel from the car. "You have a future, and it's waiting for you in there. Call me when you need me. No, call my agent." He laughed again, the carefree laugh of a wealthy youth who has no doubt that he will live forever. "That's something we Hollywood people say. Also this: Gotta dash." And he got back into the limousine, and it dashed out of my driveway.

I walked with some trepidation to my old cottage. I walked onto the porch, and then around to the sunroom. When I got to the door, I saw that it was a woman in the room, and at first she did not seem familiar. When I opened the door, she stood up. It was Irmi, my wife and former chambermaid. She was holding a baby. She had not been familiar because I'd never seen her outside of her uniform.

Perhaps I should amend that last sentence, the same way that Brad, Floyd and Poodle had amended so much of my story. I had seen her out of her uniform once, come to think of it, when the doors of Penthouse Suite #1125 were closed and the drapes were drawn. On the night of our wedding.

"Hallo," she said in her charming Austrian accent. "Vee vait for you all the day. And now you are home."

She handed me a perfect little bundle wrapped in a snug blanket. "You hold him," she instructed me. To the bundle she said, "This is your Daddy. You vill call him Papa. When you are able to make the talk."

She looked at me with something akin to adoration. I did not then, and still do not believe that I deserved it. I held that little bundle tightly; I didn't want to drop it. "Vee call him Chubby," she said. "He is our son. And now we live here and stay alive until he grows up, ja?"

What else could I say? "Ja," I answered. Here's to your health and long life.

CODA

  Ray Jensen is having a dream. It is a dream about God.
  Says God, "Hey, it's Ray Jensen, and I see that the red light at the end of his nose has finally stopped shining."
  Ray blushes and says, "Oh God, I had forgotten about that."
  God laughs and then begins to pitch batting practice to Ray in the most beautiful, celestial ballpark. The infield grass is emerald green, the basepaths are manicured dirt and the whole thing is surrounded by 45,000 empty seats. It is a perfect day for ball.
  God is dressed like Al Schact, the Clown Prince of Baseball, a big goof in floppy, old-style baseball pants, a pin-striped jersey two sizes too big and spilling out over the belt, and an oversized cap placed sideways on God's skinny head. God sticks his tongue out and mugs as he throws pitches to Ray with a big, exaggerated pitching motion.
  He begins by throwing beach balls that billow up to the plate as perfect strikes, right in Ray's wheelhouse. Ray

smashes them with a beautifully turned wooden bat and watches, astonished and delighted, as the beachballs fly high up into the air on impact, as high as the third deck of the stadium, and then waft slowly over the centerfield wall. The balls get smaller and harder as God continues to hurl his best stuff at Ray. They go from the size of basketballs to softballs to baseballs to golf balls to aspirin, all delivered with high heat, right down the middle of the plate. Ray launches shot after shot over the left and centerfield walls.

"So this is what it's like to be Hank Aaron," thinks Ray.

"So this is what it's like to be Al Schact," thinks God.

Ray finally has enough. He steps out of the batter's box, removes his cap and makes a respectful bow to God.

"God, I can't thank you enough," says Ray Jensen. "Thanks for everything." With a sweep of his cap, he takes it all in: The field, the ballpark, the balls, the grass, the clouds, the atmosphere, people, PEOPLE magazine, the Village People.

"Hey, don't mention it," says God. "It's really nothing."

A NOTE FROM THE AUTHOR:

There really was a Costas; he was a terrific butler (and by no means an idiot or a bore) on board the Crystal Symphony cruise ship when I had a travel-writing assignment and took my family on a wonderful cruise to Alaska several years ago. We really did stay in Penthouse Suite #1125 (but we left it willingly at the end of the cruise).

And I did lose my dad, Dr. Joseph F. Gullo, to heart disease at a painfully young age. I still can't quite believe that happened, or that I drove him to the hospital as he was having the second heart attack, which would kill him. It was a week before I turned twenty.

And as I approached the age of his death, I began to wonder how to synthesize these experiences that I've had and try to answer some questions that have lingered with me my whole life.

I hope you enjoyed Fountain of Youth; it has been a long labor of love writing it. Several years of piecing together the story, revising it, pondering it, and now, finally, sending it off into the world to live on its own, as we would our children.

And now I have to ask of you, the ever-patient reader and audience, to do one thing for me:

Drop me a line and tell me what you thought of Fountain of Youth. If you hated it, tell me so. If you loved it, I don't mind hearing that either. If you got 100 pages into it, or 10 pages, and couldn't bear to continue, I'd like to know that, too. Send me a message on my e-mail or my blog. If you remind me, and if you'd like to linger with these characters a bit longer, I'll send you the story of how Ray and Janice crashed into each other and wrecked their marriage along with their cars.

And, of course, if you really, really like Fountain of Youth, I hope you'll tell your friends about it, and buy them a copy or lend them yours.

I know…that's two things.

Cheers, and thanks again for sitting down with me and my story. And from my heart to yours: B-O-K.

Jim Gullo
McMinnville, Oregon
www.jimgullo.com
jim@jimgullo.com

Made in the USA
Charleston, SC
15 February 2012